THE EXTRA ORDINARY
LIFE OF FRANK DERRICK,
AGE 81

Born in London ages ago to his two parents, Frank and Jenny, J. B. Morrison is a musician and already the author of two novels – *Storage Stories* and *Driving Jarvis Ham*. *Goodnight Jim Bob* is an autobiographical account of his ten years as singer with punk-pop band *Carter The Unstoppable Sex Machine*. That was when he was called Jim Bob. Like in *The Waltons*.

With *Carter USM* Jim Bob had 14 Top 40 singles and a Number 1 album. He played all over the world, headlined Glastonbury and was sued by *The Rolling Stones*. He's also made a ton of solo albums and written the screenplay for a film. Plus he was in a musical, in 2010 at the Edinburgh Fringe.

Is there no end to his talents?

Yes. Everything not mentioned here. Don't ask him to put up a shelf or cook you dinner. The shelf will fall off the wall and you won't like the food.

To find out more about J. B. Morrison visit **http://www. jim-bob.co.uk/** or say hello on Twitter @mrjimBob.

THE EXTRA ORDINARY LIFE OF FRANK DERRICK, AGE 81

J. B. Morrison

PAN BOOKS

First published 2014 by Pan Books
an imprint of Pan Macmillan, a division of Macmillan Publishers Limited
Pan Macmillan, 20 New Wharf Road, London N1 9RR
Basingstoke and Oxford
Associated companies throughout the world
www.panmacmillan.com

ISBN 978-1-4472-5274-0

3 5 7 9 8 6 4

A CIP catalogue record for this book is available from the British Library.

Typeset by Ellipsis Digital Limited, Glasgow
Printed and bound by CPI Group (UK) Ltd, Croydon, CR0 4YY

Visit **www.panmacmillan.com** to read more about all our books
and to buy them. You will also find features, author interviews and
news of any author events, and you can sign up for e-newsletters
so that you're always first to hear about our new releases.

For my mum –
even if those are the only
three words she reads

THE EXTRA ORDINARY LIFE OF FRANK DERRICK, AGE 81

PROLOGUE

I'm eighty-one.

I'm probably supposed to be saying that a lot now.

Ooh, look at you. And how old are you?

I'm eighty-one. That sort of thing.

Sometimes not even waiting to be asked.

I'm eighty-one.

Proudly offering the information at every opportunity, like when I was five years old.

Perhaps I should wear a badge. Like the ones you get stuck on the front of a birthday card. An eighty-first birthday card – if such a thing exists. Do they even make those? Eighty, maybe, but eighty-one? Maybe I could hang some balloons with '81' printed on them above my front door. But there's probably no market for eighty-first birthday balloons either. I'll just have to keep saying it.

I'm eighty-one.

Come inside. Have a seat. Why don't you talk down to me like you did when I was a child? See how my faculties are. Talk to me in a loud baby voice. Get me to fill in a form. Better still, you fill it in for me. Just get me to sign it. I'm probably too blind to read any small print. Sell me things I don't want. Look around for antiques. Case the joint.

I'm eighty-one.

Come and have a go, if you think you're hard enough.

1

1

On Frank Derrick's eighty-first birthday he was run over by a milk float. He would have preferred a book token or some cufflinks, but it's the thought that counts.

The milk float was travelling at about five miles an hour when the milkman somehow lost control of the slow-moving vehicle, mounting the narrow pavement and coming to a stop, with the wheels of the milk float in the air, on the low stone wall at the front of someone's garden, sending crates of milk, empty bottles, cartons of cream and a few dozen eggs sliding off the back and onto the pavement.

Aside from making a mess of the garden of one of the expected big hitters in the upcoming Villages in Bloom competition, the milkman hadn't done Frank any favours either. He was underneath the vehicle. The only part of his body visible to the outside world was his right arm, sticking out from underneath the milk float, his palm facing upwards, still holding on to the pint of milk he'd just been to Fullwind Food & Wine to buy. It was exactly what the scene really needed – more milk. The upended milk float, protruding pensioner's arm and the steady stream of dairy produce floating down the gutter at the side of the road was like a spoof news story waiting for a punch line at the end of an episode of *The Two Ronnies*.

Frank was in hospital for three days. He had concussion, a broken arm and an acute fracture of one of the metatarsal bones in his left foot.

'Like the footballers get,' the doctor said. 'Do you play football?'

'Not any more. Not with this metatarsal injury.'

'Well, anyhow. It should respond well to some fairly simple self-care techniques. RICE therapy.'

'Ice therapy?'

'No, rice.'

'I don't like rice. Never have.'

'No. RICE. It's an acronym. Rest, ice, compression and elevation.'

'An acronym?'

'That's right.'

'Like the stroke one?'

'Like the stroke one,' the doctor said. 'I'll find you a leaflet.'

Frank also had a broken toe – the one next to his big toe, the little piggy that stayed at home, which was also his prognosis: to stay at home. He had a few cuts, some tyre marks and bruising, and a face like squashed fruit. He looked like one of those horrific newspaper photographs of a mugged pensioner.

'One or two of these cuts on your face may scar,' the doctor said.

'When you get to my age every cut is a scar.'

Frank's right arm was in plaster from the wrist to just past his elbow. They'd set his arm at an angle. Like in a cartoon. His arm would be stuck in a curve for at least six weeks. He looked like he was permanently trying to shake hands with everyone. If you'd sawed his arm off at the shoulder and thrown it, it would have come back.

Before he left hospital Frank had to take the Mini Mental State Examination to check his cognitive state. A young and exhausted-looking doctor in a striped shirt with a plain collar and sweat patches under just the left armpit pulled up a plastic chair next to Frank's hospital bed and flipped open an A4 pad of paper.

'Right, Frank,' he said. 'This test is a standard test. Some of the questions are probably going to seem a bit easy and some of them less so. Are you ready?'

The doctor asked Frank what year it was, what season, what month and the date and day of the week. Frank got them all right – although the doctor didn't say so. He just wrote stuff down and asked another question.

'What country are we in?'

'England.'

'What city?'

'Technically, it's a town.'

'You seem quite angry, Mr Derrick.'

'I was run over by a milkman. How's your day been?'

'Yes. I see,' the doctor said.

'I just want to go home before I catch MMSE.'

'That stands for Mini Mental State Examination, Mr Derrick. That's what we're doing now. I think you mean MRSA.'

'What does that stand for?'

'Deep breath,' the doctor said and he took a deep breath. 'Methicillin-resistant Staphylococcus aureus.' He smiled,

pleased with himself as though he'd successfully pronounced the name of that famous Welsh railway station.
'Now, shall we get to the end of the test?'

The doctor asked if Frank knew where he was and the
name of the hospital and what ward they were on. Frank
only passed on the name of the ward. The Mastermind
trophy was as good as in the bag; he was picturing a place
for it on the mantelpiece next to three porcelain penguins
he'd never really liked that much. He was convinced the
middle one was plotting a coup.

'Now, Frank, I'm going to name three objects and I want
you to repeat them back to me and try to remember them,
okay?'

Frank nodded. It hurt his head.

'Apple, pen, table,' the doctor said.

'Apple, pen, table.'

The doctor asked Frank to spell WORLD backwards
and Frank said something about how it certainly was a
backwards world. The doctor asked him to subtract seven
from a hundred and then seven from the answer and to
carry on doing so till he told him to stop. Frank made it as
far as fifty-one and was a bit disappointed when the doctor
said that was enough. He'd never been great at maths and
thought that maybe the bang on the head had actually done
him some good.

'Can you tell me who the Prime Minister is?'

Frank told the doctor who the Prime Minister was and
that he thought he was an idiot and that he, for one, had
definitely not voted for him. The doctor said that wasn't
important.

'Oh, but it's very important.'

'Great,' the doctor said, but he didn't mean that it was great at all and he skipped a couple of questions to make the test end sooner. He wanted Frank to go home as well. The doctor wanted to go home. Everyone in the hospital wanted to go home. Who wants to be in a hospital?

'Can you remember the three objects I asked you to name earlier?' the doctor said.

'You mean the apple, the pen and the table?'

The doctor pointed at his wristwatch and asked Frank what it was.

'It looks like quite a cheap wristwatch.'

The doctor wanted to punch Frank. If it wasn't so frowned upon in his profession, perhaps he would have done.

There were a few more questions and a couple of physical tests, including folding a piece of paper and then unfolding it again and writing a sentence on the piece of paper. Frank wrote, 'Can I go home now please?'

Later that day he was discharged from hospital. As the porter wheeled him to the lifts a nurse handed him a walking stick that he'd tried to leave behind when she'd given it to him earlier and a carrier bag containing his carton of milk. The milk had been out of the fridge for three days now and it was warm and probably turned into cottage cheese or clotted cream. Frank thanked the nurse and planned on leaving the bag in the ambulance on the way home.

After the accident Frank's daughter offered to immediately drop everything and fly back from America to look after him but Frank said there was no need, she had far more important things to do, she had her own life to live, her own family to look after, he'd be fine, it didn't even hurt that much, it was too far, don't be silly, it would cost too much, all that kind of bollocks. What he really wanted her to do was hang up the phone and get a cab to the airport.

'Let me at least arrange for somebody to come in and look after you,' she said.

'I can look after myself.'

'Let me do some research online. Make a couple of phone calls. Just to see what the options are.'

'Really, there is no need. It will cost a fortune. I'm fine. I've had worse hangovers.'

'Dad.'

'Don't you have crime reconstruction shows in America? They'll tie me to a chair and steal my pension.'

'Dad.'

'They'll use my water tank as a toilet. Actually, that might be plumbers.'

'Let me at least look into it. For my peace of mind, Dad. I don't want to worry about whether you've got enough food or if you've set fire to the house making toast.'

'Do you realise how much work I've put into keeping people out of my home? Word will get out. If I let Robin Williams in a dress come inside to strap me to a chair and steal my antiques, I'll have a queue of boiler insurance salesmen and equity release people halfway up the road.'

'Dad.'

'I'll have to get a revolving door fitted. I'm sure there'll be somebody in the queue willing to sell me one. And once I've let in all the people who want to get inside my flat, what about all the people who want to get on top of it? That queue will stretch for miles. You'll be able to join the back of it without leaving California.'

8

It was true. People were keen to get on Frank's roof. His flat had something that there weren't a lot of in Fullwind-on-Sea: stairs. Fourteen of them. Making him the go-to guy for stair-lift companies, window cleaners, gutter clearers, chimney sweeps and roofers. Hardly a week went by without him having to make his way down those fourteen stairs to answer the door to a man sucking his teeth and shaking his head.

'You do realise your roof is about to fall off?' Teeth-suck.

'Your chimney is listing to the left.' Head-shake.

'Have you seen how bunged up your guttering is?' Teeth-suck. Head-shake.

Maybe his roof *was* about to collapse, but if he did let somebody up there, he wouldn't be able to see what they were doing without walking fifty yards up the road with a pair of strong binoculars. He'd have no idea if they were actually fixing anything. They could be reading the newspaper or having a nap, or simply counting to fifteen thousand and then climbing back down to suck their teeth a bit more before presenting him with a bill for a million pounds.

Frank carried on telling Beth why he didn't need any help and about not wanting strangers in his home and she didn't interrupt. She let her dad complain because she knew it would make him feel better about the inevitable outcome – which was giving his daughter what she wanted. In this case, she wanted her dad to be safe and well.

He ranted a bit more and then he said, 'I'm not going to tidy up. I'm not lighting candles and brewing fresh coffee.'

'Of course not.'

The following day a man with an annoying whistle from the care company screwed a key safe to the outside wall of

Frank's flat. He put a front-door key inside the safe and programmed Frank's birthday into the combination lock. Three days after that, in the middle of one of the hottest springs since records began, less than a month after Frank had finally got round to putting the fairy lights and tinsel back in the loft, Christmas came to Fullwind-on-Sea.

2

When Kelly Christmas parked her little blue car opposite Frank's flat for the first time, with two wheels up on the grass verge, bumping into one of the white concrete bollards that were there to prevent people from parking on the grass verge, she did so in front of one of the largest captive audiences in the South of England.

A lot of people were at home on Sea Lane that day. A lot of nosy neighbours and bored pensioners, housebound by agoraphobia or because it was too hot to go outside or because they were waiting for hip replacements or for their mobility scooters to fully charge or because the free bus to the big Sainsbury's doesn't always run on Mondays. The crunching of the gears as Kelly tried to find reverse was a reveille for everyone to abandon their word searches and daytime auction shows and get to their windows.

As the only stair-rich person on the street, Frank had the best view. Every other building on Sea Lane was a bungalow. People were cricking their necks down in the cheap seats – which were actually more expensive – looking for something to stand on so that they could see who was making all the noise, furrowing tyre tracks into the grass and threatening Fullwind's chances of a rosette if a judge

11

from the Villages in Bloom competition turned up unannounced.

Frank watched the little blue car shift backwards and forwards on the verge opposite until it finally hit a concrete bollard. And then whoever was behind the wheel grew bored with parking, or perhaps they decided that it was the best they were going to be able to manage, or maybe they simply ran out of petrol.

He couldn't see the driver's face yet. He could just about make out that they had a face. Frank was 90 per cent certain that it was a woman. Maybe 95. She was nodding her head up and down and singing along with whatever music was playing on the car stereo. She checked her hair in the rearview mirror until she seemed happy enough with the way it looked to stop checking it.

At a quarter past eleven, the car door opened and the driver stepped out onto the grass verge and all the curtain twitchers and Venetian blind twiddlers tripped over their furniture and popped their new hips trying to see who it was. From up on the first floor Frank watched her put a 'Nurse on Call' sign in the windscreen of the car, lock the doors and walk across the road.

By the time she reached his front gate he could see the hair that she'd been checking in the mirror. Her fringe was cut perfectly straight. It underlined the top of her head, drawing attention to her face. She didn't look as much like Robin Williams as he was expecting. And less like Margaret Thatcher or that woman from the James Bond film with the knives in her shoes, who also fitted Frank's expected image of a home help nurse. He immediately regretted the dirty protest he'd been carrying out for the past five days.

Although Frank had agreed that Beth would pay some-one to come round once a week for three months to tidy up, check he was taking his painkillers and stick a thermometer in his mouth (he hoped it was his mouth), he hadn't said he wouldn't do his best to make sure they didn't get too comfortable and feel like hanging around long enough to steal his wallet or do a poo in the kettle.

For the next five days Frank slept in his clothes. He didn't shave and his long white hair had started to dread-lock. He left his teeth in a glass in the bathroom and dirty dishes piled up in the sink. He deliberately dropped cake and biscuit crumbs on the living-room carpet. There were DVDs out of their boxes on the floor and – his pièce de résistance – he hadn't flushed the toilet for two days.

The first time Kelly saw Frank he was in the hallway where he'd collapsed like Bambi while trying to make it to the toilet to flush it before she managed to force the front door over the hill of free newspapers and junk mail that had accumulated behind it. When Kelly appeared in the hall at the top of the stairs Frank had just made it back up onto his feet. He was out of breath and sweating, wearing slept-in clothes, all wild-haired and hairy-faced, looking like a black-and-white photograph on one of the many charity begging letters that came through his letterbox every week.

'Mr Derrick?' Kelly said. 'I'm Kelly.' She pulled her thin blue anorak to one side and lifted the badge on the front of her blue uniform to show him. She gave him enough time to read her name. 'You look a bit flustered. Shall we go and sit down?' She placed a hand on his good arm. Her touch was gentle and reassuring, firm but caring, calm but in control; all these things. She was like a hostage negotiator at a bank siege or a cowboy calming an angry horse. Kelly the pensioner whisperer. She led Frank quietly into the living room.

'Armchair or sofa?' she said.

'Armchair please. You'll have to excuse the mess,' he said, referring to himself as much as he was to the living-room carpet.

'You should see my flat,' Kelly said. 'You'd call the police to report a burglary.'

Frank sat down. He was breathing deeply.

'You sit there for a bit,' Kelly said, 'and I'll make some tea. Or coffee? Which do you prefer?'

'Yes,' Frank said. 'Thank you. Tea please.' He offered to show her where everything was kept but Kelly said not to worry.

'People tend to keep things in the same place in their kitchens,' she said.

While Kelly was in the kitchen, Frank sat back in his armchair and continued to make excuses for the mess.

'I was in a traffic accident,' he called out. Without his false teeth in, his speech was slurred. She probably thought he sounded as drunk as he looked.

'I know,' Kelly called out from the kitchen. 'Do you have milk and sugar?'

Frank wondered if she was making a comical reference to his accident.

'Just milk, thank you.'

While the kettle boiled Kelly came into the living room and picked up all the dirty plates and cups.

'I haven't had the chance to tidy up,' Frank said.

'That's all right,' Kelly said. She took the dirty dishes out

14

to the kitchen. Frank wanted to get his teeth from the bathroom and flush the toilet but he was still feeling lightheaded and thought he might fall over again. She came back in and picked up the DVD cases from the carpet and put them on the table.

'I'll leave these for you to put away,' she said. 'In case you have a system.'

He had a system.

Frank's alphabetised DVD collection was the only properly organised part of his life. It had taken him quite a while to do. Mainly because he'd spent so much of the time doing impressions of the actors in the films as he rearranged them – from cockney Michael Caine in *Alfie* to posh Michael Caine in *Zulu*.

Kelly brought Frank a cup of tea and put it on the table next to his armchair. She sat down on the sofa and took a wad of A4 notes out of her bag.

'Let's have a look at your care plan.'

While she read through her notes she asked Frank how he'd been feeling since he'd come home from the hospital, if he felt he was managing and if there was anything in particular he needed help with that hadn't already been arranged with his daughter.

Frank said he couldn't think of anything.

'I'll have a bit of a tidy and make your bed and you see if you can think of anything else in the meantime,' Kelly said.

While she was out of the room, Frank sat and looked at his reflection on the blank TV screen. He looked like Howard Hughes. It had taken ten years and millions of dollars for Howard Hughes to end up looking like that,

Frank thought. And he had managed it without trying, in less than a week for no money whatsoever.

He could hear Kelly in his bedroom, singing quietly to herself. He heard her shutting the wardrobe door and drawing the curtains and then what sounded like her fluffing the pillows, and although it was obviously unlikely because there were two walls between them, Frank thought he felt a waft of air as she flapped the quilt into place on his bed. She sneezed three times, there was a ten-second pause when Frank imagined she was trying to stifle a fourth sneeze and then she sneezed again. On her way back to the living room she flushed the toilet.

'I think the pollen count is high today,' Kelly said when she came back into the living room.

After she'd checked again that Frank was definitely all right and safe to be left alone, she started to collect her things together to leave.

'I can go to the shops for you on the way here next time, if there's anything you need,' she said, while Frank signed a time sheet to prove that she'd been there. His broken-armed signature looking like an unconvincing forgery, the ink lines wavering up and down the page like the polygraph of somebody telling an enormous lie. She put the time sheet back in her bag.

'I'll see you at the same time next week, Mr Derrick.'

'Yes, thank you. It will be you again, will it?'

'Yes,' Kelly said. 'Me, I'm afraid. Every week for the next –' she took a diary out of her bag and flipped a few pages over – 'twelve weeks.'

She told him to ring the care company if he had any questions or if there was something in particular he'd like her to do on her next visit. She put her diary and the rest of her paperwork back in her bag, said goodbye and left.

Frank was surprised how sorry he was to see her go. The flat felt emptier than it had before she'd arrived. Was it always this quiet? He switched the TV on to fill the silence and to get rid of his reflection.

While he watched a mother and daughter on television in matching fleece tops lose money selling their family heirlooms at an auction, Frank wished he'd had his teeth in so that he could have talked more freely while Kelly was there. He wanted to tell her that he was usually a lot funnier than this. He wanted to apologise about the mess again. And he wanted to say that if she was going to be coming here every week from now on, she was going to have to start calling him Frank because he hated it when people called him Mr Derrick. It made him feel like he should be working with Basil Brush.

3

It was pitch-black when Frank woke up on Tuesday. He had no real idea how long he'd been asleep or what time it was. His watch was over on the bedside table, which seemed like a hundred miles away. He decided to wait until he heard the first aircraft taking off from Gatwick and flying over his flat. That would be around 5 a.m., which felt like an acceptable time to get out of bed. He didn't want to give himself any extra empty daytime hours to fill. It was hard enough as it was.

By the time the day reached about 6.30 p.m., other than waiting for his dinner to digest, there was very little reason for Frank to stay up. He'd started going to bed so early that it was often still light outside. He had to buy thicker curtains from the charity shop to stop the sunlight keeping him awake.

Frank lay in bed waiting for the aeroplanes and thought about the extraordinarily dull dream he'd woken up from. In the dream he was in the queue at a supermarket checkout. There were no aliens or supermodels in the dream. The shopping in his basket didn't talk to him or chase him down the road. It was hardly a dream at all.

The only real clue to it being a dream was that he was

young in it. His shopping basket didn't feel so heavy that he had to put it on the supermarket floor and gradually nudge it along with his foot every time the queue moved nearer the tills. He wasn't wearing slippers. In the basket there were four cans of lager. No tinned spaghetti or soft and easy to digest meals-for-one. There was perhaps one other clue that it was a dream: it was the sense that there was somebody waiting for him at home to help put the shopping away. Frank placed the basket on the counter and the cashier looked at the cans of lager, then looked back at Frank and said, 'Party?'

And then Frank woke up. The dream had ended.

But he still felt young.

There was nobody to help unpack his shopping.

But he still felt young.

Frank had discovered the secret of eternal life.

He just had to stay in bed.

Providing he didn't get out of bed to creak and crick and groan and limp and fart and cough and wheeze and splutter and wobble his way to the bathroom he could stay young. As long as he didn't see his face in the bathroom mirror or his teeth in a glass by the sink he could stay young.

Providing he didn't get out of bed, or simply move too quickly, or go to the bathroom, or breathe in too deeply, or bite into a hard toffee or listen to music radio or watch television after 7 p.m. on a Saturday. He could stay in bed and be young forever.

He counted six planes pass overhead and wondered where they might be going to or coming from. He wondered if he'd ever fly in an aeroplane again. And where would he go? He didn't have a valid passport any more. Weren't they

19

free for people of his age? He made a mental note to find out. He already had his free TV licence and bus pass. Even though there was nothing on television and nowhere to take the bus to. The older he got the more free access he had to things that he was too old to take full advantage of. A seventh aeroplane flew over. He closed his eyes and tried to get back to his dream. He was almost asleep again when the doorbell rang.

It would be a slow and difficult walk down the stairs to answer the door. And so, seeing as he wasn't (ever) expecting anybody, he decided not to bother answering it. He closed his eyes. The doorbell rang again. He sighed and decided that he might as well at least get out of bed. He started to move and noticed a numb feeling in his legs. Like a cat had slept on them. Was this it? Is this how the end begins? Numbness in the legs? Spreading up the body. Paralysis and then death? Then he remembered that he did have a cat and it was sleeping on his legs. He shook the cat onto the floor and stood for a moment with his good hand resting against the wall, until he got his balance. When had feeling dizzy all the time started? Before or after the milk float accident?

He followed the cat into the kitchen, creaking and cricking and groaning and limping and farting and coughing and wheezing and spluttering and wobbling behind him.

In the kitchen he took a tin of cat food out from the cupboard under the sink and struggled to get it open. Even with the electric opener it wasn't easy to open the can with one arm in plaster. He looked down at the cat.

'I'm not very good at being retired, am I, Bill?' Bill hadn't seemed such a stupid name for a cat when Ben was still alive. 'I should be playing golf or gardening.' The tin of cat food slipped from the magnet of the opener and it dropped on the floor. Frank bent down to pick it up, groaning on the way down and again on the way back up. 'I could be on a round-the-world cruise now, or brewing my own beer. I should have at least put my name on the waiting list for an allotment. Although, from what I hear, if I joined one now I doubt I'd make it to the top of the list in time to grow anything. Eh, Bill?'

Bill looked up at Frank, pulling the only face he had available. Bill's expression was exactly the same when he was waiting to be fed as it was when he was filling his litter tray. It was like a paper mask, cut out from a magazine and attached by two rubber bands hooked over his ears. It was the same unfathomable blankness when Frank let him out into the garden in the morning as when he came back in again in the evening. Bill's face gave nothing away of what he'd been up to all day. There were no clues as to whether he'd been chasing mice or birds or what territory he'd marked or which other cats he might be dating. Frank had seen both versions of *Doctor Dolittle* a number of times, he knew the words to some of the songs, he could probably even speak rhinoceros or chat to a chimp in Chimpanzee, but he still had no idea what it was that Bill was trying to say. Which, on this occasion, was:

To be honest, Frank, I couldn't really give a shit about the quality of your retirement. Just make my fucking breakfast.

Frank opened the cat food and scooped the foul-smelling meat onto a saucer. He took a cup out of the cupboard, put a teabag in it, poured in the milk, flicked the kettle switch on and made his way slowly downstairs to get the newspaper.

The stairs had always creaked but now he wasn't sure how much of the creaking was the stairs and how much was him.

There were two silhouetted shapes on the other side of the frosted glass of the front door. Not fully awake yet he opened the door to two young men wearing suits and smiling broadly. The same two men who had rung his doorbell ten minutes earlier and had either come back or not yet left.

'Good morning,' the young man on the left said. 'Could we ask you one very quick question?'

Without waiting for an answer, the one on the right said, 'How do you feel about all the death in the world?'

Frank was ill prepared. He hadn't made notes. He wasn't dressed. He hadn't even had a piss yet. What time was it? At least seven aeroplanes.

He stood on the doorstep not listening, nodding every once in a while and alternating his short responses between 'Yes', 'Of course' and 'I see', and looking anxiously up the stairs behind him as though he might be burning his breakfast or be in the middle of something important he needed to get back to. He wished he had his watch on so that he could look at it because the two men on his doorstep really weren't getting the message.

They showed him their little fan club magazine. On the cover there was a drawing of a tiger in a garden or a forest with trees and flowers that didn't exist in the real world. The tiger was playing with some children. Everyone in the picture looked so fantastically happy. The two young men carried on talking and Frank nodded and looked anxiously back up the stairs some more. He really needed to get back to his important meeting.

Frank wondered if he had enough strength in his body to

make a fist and punch both men until they went away. Would that prevent him from spending his afterlife in paradise? Would it stop him from playing with all the smiling tigers and the happy children in the garden? He didn't even know whether that was part of what they believed in. Would they turn the other cheek if he punched them? Was that one of theirs? He'd been given a ton of their little magazines over the years but had never actually read one. He made a mental note to look them up on the Internet next time he was in the library. Yes, Frank knew how to use the Internet. He could send emails, too, and he knew how to use a mobile phone. He could send you a text message with a smiley face at the end of it if he wanted to. Not that there was anybody for him to send a text message with a smiley face to, and there wasn't really anyone other than his daughter to email. His inbox on the library's computer was just another way in for the stair and bath lift people.

While the two men continued to talk he wondered, if he *could* make a fist, would he actually use it to punch anybody ever again? It wasn't that he particularly wanted to punch anyone – not even present company excepted – it was just that he wondered whether punching someone was one of the things he would never do again. Like running or going on a bouncy castle, or chewing gum or eating corn on the cob. He needed to make a bucket list. He'd seen a film about it.

Eventually, the men stopped talking and Frank took their fanzine and closed the door. He was almost halfway up the stairs when he heard, 'Vehicle reversing, vehicle reversing.' He hadn't put the bins out. He could still see the two men through the frosted glass. He didn't want to open the door and give them a second go. Why did they always move so slowly? He waited until they eventually turned and dawdled down the path. But by the time they were finally gone, the dustmen were gone too and he would now have four weeks' worth of uncollected rubbish at the end of the garden. The editor of the village newsletter would be writing him another letter to follow on from the one he'd sent last year suggesting that the village might have fared better in the Villages in Bloom competition if certain people, mentioning no names (Frank), had slightly greener fingers and slightly fewer old fridges in their front garden.

There was only ever the one fridge.

It was gone now.

4

For Kelly's second visit it was like the Queen was coming.

Frank had increased the square footage of the flat just by removing the dust from around the charity shop ornaments and nontiques on the mantelpiece and the sideboard in the living room. He'd put all the DVDs back in the right boxes and into alphabetical order without stopping to impersonate Michael Caine, and in the bathroom he cleaned the bath and sink and straightened the towels. He moved the pile of old newspapers and magazines from the floor next to the toilet into the cupboard in the hall and put one of those blue things in the toilet bowl. In the kitchen he wiped the outside of the fridge and polished the sink so that it was shiny enough for Kelly to be able to check the geometry of her fringe when she was filling the kettle. He polished the kettle. Frank vacuumed every room in the flat, even the kitchen and bathroom lino and then, before putting it away, Frank hoovered the Hoover.

After cleaning the flat Frank began work on himself. He shaved for the first time since before the accident, starting with his old battery shaver until the battery ran out, catching the tip of his chin between the blunt foils, which was when he switched to the only other razor he had – a bright pink disposable women's razor he'd bought in a packet of four from the charity shop to remove the bobbles from his jumpers.

Frank combed the knots from his long, silky white hair that often made it hard for people to determine his age. Hair that people had described as being Kenny Rogers hair.

Richard Harris hair.

Gandalf hair.

Emmylou Harris hair.

Rapunzel, Rapunzel, let down your hair.

Apart from its white colour, Frank's hair was the kind of soft, long hair you might expect to see on the head of a much younger man – or, more accurately, a girl.

Sometimes he wore it tied up in a ponytail.

Once, Frank was in the charity shop and some school-children were sniggering about something. Frank looked over and they turned away quickly. He went back to browsing the second-hand books and the school kids started laughing again. Frank saw their reflection in an old mirror. They were pointing at him and then at a shelf of toys and, in particular, at a pink My Little Pony with a rainbow on its arse and a long silver white mane.

At least he wasn't bald. Science would suggest that he should be. According to research a person with a balding father was two and a half times more likely to experience hair loss themselves. And Frank's father had been very bald.

Kojak bald.

Yul Brynner bald.

Sinéad O'Connor bald.

Frank had once shown his friend Smelly John a photo-graph of himself standing next to his father and Smelly John had said, 'Were you and your dad related?' He followed up with a hundred old jokes about whether the milkman used to make a lot of home visits while Frank's father was out at work. And how hairy was the milkman? And did Frank have a photograph of himself standing next to the milkman? Frank wasn't looking forward to telling Smelly John the circumstances of his accident when he was fit enough to go and visit him.

On Monday morning, Frank sat at the window waiting for Kelly. He'd combed his hair again. He'd dipped the comb in Brylcreem and parted his hair on the side. He looked like he was waiting to be picked up for church.

At 11.15, when Kelly climbed out of her car, Frank limped across the living room and sat in his armchair and tried to look casual. He took a deep breath and felt a sharp pain in his ribs. He gripped the arm of his chair and clenched his jaw, sucking in air between his teeth like a roofer pricing up a job. His dentures moved. He'd run out of fixative powder and he needed to go to the chemist. He could have asked Kelly to get some for him but his vanity had prevented him from doing so. Maybe he would ask her today. He heard the front door open.

'Hello?' Kelly called out from the bottom of the stairs. 'Mr Derrick?'

She came upstairs and into the living room.

'Good morning,' she said. 'How are we feeling today?'

'I can't speak for you but I feel like I've been run over by a milk float.' It wasn't a rehearsed line but he had planned on saying something witty. He was pleased that Kelly had set the gag up for him.

'You seem a lot livelier today,' she said. She took her anorak off and hung it over the back of the chair by the window. The nosy neighbours on the other side of the road would already have started talking about how they'd just seen 'that young woman at the window of Frank Derrick's flat again'. 'She's taken her coat off.' 'And it isn't his daughter. I think she's got her own key.' Hilary, the head of the Neighbourhood Watch who lived directly opposite, would have made a note in her 'incidents' book.

Kelly put a small paper bag on the table next to Frank's armchair.

'Your painkillers,' she said. 'How does the foot feel?'

'It still hurts quite a bit.'

'Hmm.'

She took a cushion from the sofa and put it on the carpet in front of Frank's armchair and told him to rest his foot on it.

'How are the headaches?' she said. 'Is the high-pitched ringing still there?'

'It's more of a beeping now. It sounds like a lorry reversing inside my head. *This vehicle is reversing. This vehicle is reversing.* I keep getting the urge to put the bins out.' This was a line Frank *had* rehearsed. He'd tried it out on Bill a few times earlier in the morning, in a voice that was supposed to be Groucho Marx or Woody Allen but sounded more like Kermit the Frog. The reaction on Kelly's face was a more satisfactory one than Bill's deadpan stare.

'I'll go and get something for that toe,' she said. 'Have you got an ice pack? Shall I put the kettle on?'

She didn't wait for him to answer either question and

went out through the hall and into the kitchen and filled the kettle.

'Some of the food in your fridge is a long way past its sell-by date,' she called out from the kitchen, possibly with her head actually inside the fridge.

'Those dates are more of a guide,' Frank called back.

The kettle started to boil. Kelly raised the volume of her voice. 'These sausages are so old they'll be back in date again in a couple of months. Can I throw them away?'

'I suppose so. They are only of sentimental value. They aren't worth anything without their original packet.'

Kelly came into the living room with a bag of frozen peas wrapped in a tea towel. She crouched down in front of Frank and put the towel-wrapped pea parcel on his toe.

'How does that feel?' she said. 'Not too cold?'

'No, it's fine. Thank you.'

She went back to the kitchen. 'Have you been spring cleaning?' she said. The kettle was making a lot of noise now and she raised her voice with it.

Frank looked around the living room. His dust and cobweb collection was definitely ruined. He was going to need a new hobby.

'Not particularly,' he said.

'It's very tidy,' Kelly called out. 'You've left me hardly anything to do.' She was now practically shouting to be heard above the sound of the kettle. 'I can see my face in the sink.' It was like she was talking from inside a wind tunnel. 'And the kettle. Are you after my job?'

Of course he wasn't. He was years past retirement age, he had one arm in plaster and he'd look ridiculous in her shiny blue uniform.

Kelly brought a cup of tea in and put it on the table next to Frank. She took half a packet of custard cream biscuits out of her bag and put them next to the tea and then she went off in search of any housework that Frank might have left her. She wiped the draining board in the kitchen and remade Frank's bed, sneezing a few times as she flapped the quilt into place. She ran water from the rubber shower attachment around the already spotless bath and turned the soap round in the soap dish so what remained of the logo was the right way up. Kelly came back into the living room and rearranged the cushions on the sofa, picked up the crumbs from the custard cream Frank had just eaten, and washed up his empty cup.

Before she left she put the frozen peas back in the freezer and hung the tea towel on a hook on the kitchen door. She made Frank another cup of tea while they shouted at each other between rooms, then she gathered her things together and Frank signed her time sheet while she put her anorak on in front of the window – as though just for the neighbours' benefit. Frank gave her the signed time sheet. His signature still looked like a lie detector printout but he was getting used to his cast and it was now the polygraph of somebody telling just a small fib. Kelly put the time sheet in her bag, said goodbye and left.

When the front door closed Frank went over to the window. He sat back from the glass so that she couldn't see him if she looked up. He watched her climb into the car and remove the On Call sign. She started the engine and Frank heard the sound of pop music and then the bump and grind of the car's gears as he watched her drive away, almost taking another bollard with her.

The flat seemed empty and quiet again. But somehow not as empty as before. It was as though she had left something behind this time. Not just the custard creams and the paper bag with Frank's pills in it. Something else.

5

Frank had fifteen telephone cold-calls in the next three days. He thought it might be a record. He dealt with them in different ways. Politely saying no thank you, hanging up without saying anything, pretending he didn't speak ze Eengleesh, and, on the fifteenth call, saying, 'You'll have to talk to my wife', and then putting the phone on the sofa next to his sleeping cat, who purred into it for five minutes while Frank went to the toilet.

On Friday, Frank busted out of Alcatraz.

It took forever to get ready. Trying to thread his boomer-arm into the sleeve of his jacket was a reverse Houdini act that deserved a bigger audience than just one vague-faced cat. Frank cricked his neck putting his arm into the sleeve of the jacket. Then he got his fingers stuck in a hole in the lining. When the jacket was finally on, he got the zip stuck halfway up. And then he had to go and sit down in the living room until he got his breath back. Somebody should have been filming it all in black and white accompanied by a man on a piano. Next week he would swing from a broken clock hanging on the front of a tall building and let a wooden house fall on top of him while accompanied by a live pianist.

He realised that he would probably have to wear the jacket and the plaster cast underneath for the rest of his life now. It was an ugly blue jacket with a broken zip, torn lining and a missing detachable hood, and he'd never liked it. At least the blue canvas matched his navy deck shoes. You never knew when *Tatler* magazine might take your photograph.

Frank hadn't worn anything on his feet other than his red slippers since the accident. He started with the right foot first, which was difficult because of his dodgy arm but at least the right shoe fitted comfortably over his foot. The left one was more complicated, as though it was from a different-sized pair. He untied the shoelace and opened the shoe out as wide as possible and even then it was still a tight and painful squeeze. The laces were so stretched out that they were too short to tie. Frank stood up.

'We *shall* go to the ball,' he said to Bill, who had at no point raised a paw to help. He hooked his bag for life over his boomer-arm. *Bag for life*. It was hardly a bold guarantee for the charity shop to have printed on its canvas shopping bags, considering the average age of its customers. Frank took a look at himself in the hall mirror and after deciding, yes, he looked awful, he picked up the walking stick the hospital had given him, bribed the guards, let Bill out and limped off down the path. He stepped around the bollard that somebody had tipped over on the grass outside his flat, promising himself he'd pick the heavy lump of concrete up as soon as the plaster cast was off.

It was the first time he'd been outside with the walking stick and he hadn't worked out how to walk with it yet. Did he lean on it? Or sweep it in front of him like a blind man?

Frank had walked up and down the hall with the stick, he'd tried out a few different limps, and he'd swung the stick around the living room like Charlie Chaplin. A broken table lamp and beheaded china swan would both testify to that. Using it as it was intended, however, was another matter. Perhaps he could dance his way down Sea Lane, throwing the stick in the air and catching it at the end of a pirouette like Fred Astaire. He hoped a couple of cheeky kids would run past blowing raspberries and calling him a wanker, so that he could wave the stick at them and shout, 'Why, I *oughta.*'

It wasn't even a great stick. Frank would have preferred one with a dog's head or a crystal ball for a handle, a jewel-encrusted cane or a stick with a mosquito preserved in amber for a handle like the one that Richard Attenborough had in *Jurassic Park*. He would have liked a stick with a hidden sword inside or at least one that doubled up as a seat in case he got tired on the way to the shops. Frank's walking stick was a boring functional rubber-tipped aluminium thing with a right-angled plastic handle and a PROPERTY OF WEST SUSSEX HEALTHCARE TRUST sticker.

As he walked along Sea Lane, Radios Three and Four wafted through the open windows of pretty bungalows. He could smell seaweed used as fertiliser on gardens in preparation for the upcoming Villages in Bloom competition. A single prop aeroplane flew overhead, birds whistled and wood pigeons were doing that 'poo poo poof' thing they do.

It all reminded Frank of the Monkees' song 'Pleasant Valley Sunday'. He found himself humming it. Yes, Frank had heard of The Monkees. It wasn't all Vera Lynn and Max Bygraves. Frank had also heard of the Arctic Monkeys, although he probably didn't know any of their music.

At the end of Sea Lane a couple of half-sized bungalow FOR SALE signs were uprooted and lying on the ground. Another white stone bollard was tipped over on its side. When Frank went into the charity shop everybody was talking about the crime spree that had swept through the village the night before. Three short-arsed FOR SALE boards had been uprooted and almost a dozen concrete bollards, including the one outside Frank's flat, had been tipped over – causing havoc among the village's woodlice community – and the road sign on the corner of Renis Crescent had been altered. It was worse than South Central LA out there.

All the old dears in the charity shop were doing their Miss Marple impressions.

'It's kids,' one old dear deduced as she priced up some cardigans.

'Definitely kids,' another Miss Marple, restocking the Dan Brown shelf, agreed.

'Kids,' a customer at the counter paying for a knitting pattern said.

Everyone agreed. It had been the same in the queue for stamps at the post office next door.

'Kids,' a man queuing for a stamp said.

'It was kids,' the woman working behind the security glass said.

Only the lone voice of an old dear trying a nightie on behind a curtain in the corner of the charity shop was keeping an open mind until there was at least a little more evidence. 'It's probably kids,' she said from behind the curtain.

Why was it always kids? Frank thought. Why do the young have the monopoly on mindless vandalism? Why can't the rest of us smash up a phone box or graffiti a park bench once in a while? Why did it always have to be kids?

The woman paying for the knitting pattern read his mind and had the answer.

'They're bored,' she said.

Bored. Ha. Really. Bored. They didn't know the meaning of the word. Frank could teach them something about boredom. What did the young have to be so bored about? They had slides and swings, they had computer games, football and kiss chase. They could run and jump, skip, hop, somersault and cartwheel. They could make fists and punch each other. They could chew gum. They had their own television channels and virtually all the radio stations. They had the Internet and bicycles, mobile phones and skateboards. If kids were so bored they should try and spend a couple of hundred afternoons in a row sitting on their own watching repeats of *Murder She Wrote*. Then we'd see what they've got to be so bored about. It was the elderly who should be smashing things up.

If Frank pushed the charity shop's greetings card carousel over right now, nobody could really blame him. He could dropkick the tall glass cabinet at the centre of the charity shop to the floor and jump up and down on the supposedly valuable oriental vase the shop kept locked up inside it like it was the Pink Panther diamond. Not a judge in the land would say that he hadn't been provoked. He'd show them what boredom does to you.

The next time he went to see Smelly John he was going to bang on all the doors of the sheltered housing block where he lived and run away. He was going to get in the lift and push all the buttons – ground and first. He was going to jump up and down in the lift until it got stuck between floors and the warden had to call the engineer out.

As soon as everyone stopped nattering about the crime spree and let Frank pay for his ornaments and DVDs he was going to push over some bollards. He'd wait until the estate agent had been round the village replanting the FOR SALE signs and then he was going to pull them all up again.

Hilary was going to need a bigger incidents book.

Frank paid for his mantelpiece ornaments and DVDs. He'd bought an egg cup, a fish and two small china giraffes. He now had twelve giraffes. If he bought enough of one thing, he thought, it became a collection and somebody in Japan or America would buy it. He'd bought two DVDs – *The Great Escape* and *Gattaca*, both of which he already owned copies of.

Frank left the charity shop and went next door to Fullwind Food & Wine. He bought a small loaf of sliced bread, three tins of spaghetti and a pint of milk.

'You're not going to win *Ready Steady Cook* with this lot,' the man on the till said. It was just like Frank's dream. A dull trip to the shops with a sarcastic smartarse at the checkout counter. He should be waking up any second now.

Unlike in his dream, though, he definitely didn't feel young. If anything he felt slightly older than usual. Frank left the shop and headed back home, where no one was waiting to help unpack his bag for life.

Back at the flat he stepped around the fallen bollard on the verge.

'Kids,' he said to himself and walked through the gate into the front garden where a man was standing looking up at the roof, sucking his teeth and shaking his head.

Frank imagined drawing his sword from the inside of his hospital walking stick, shouting '*en garde!*', and running the roofer through. Then he realised that he'd left the stick in the charity shop. He'd also forgotten to get cat litter for Bill.

6

A year ago, for Frank's eightieth birthday, his daughter had sent him a birthday card from America. In the envelope with the card there was a leaflet about preventing dementia. Again, he would have preferred a book token but, well, you know.

There was a cartoon drawing of an old man on the front of the leaflet. He was doing a crossword in a newspaper. In the cartoon the old man had the end of his pen between his teeth and he was deep in thought about something – presumably one of the clues in his crossword. Above the picture it said: *Use Them or Lose Them*. Americans, eh. They were talking about the old man's marbles. He needed to use them or lose them.

The leaflet talked about the importance of a healthy diet and regular exercise, of keeping physically and mentally active. Play a musical instrument, the leaflet said. Learn a foreign language. The next time he was in the charity shop Frank had bought a Spanish language cassette. When he got back home he realised that he didn't have anything to play it on. He had no idea whether forgetting he didn't have a cassette player was a sign that he was losing his marbles. There was nothing in the leaflet about it. He decided not to let it worry him too much. If a cassette player came up for sale in the charity shop Frank would buy it. And if a saxophone or a banjo or a drum set appeared in the shop, he'd buy that too.

Inside the leaflet there was another cartoon drawing of the American marbles man. Let's call him Ron. That sounds a bit American, doesn't it? Ron was sitting in his house now. His apartment. Ron was sitting in his apartment. There was an apple on the arm of his chair (healthy diet) and a tennis racket leaning against the side of a table next to the chair (regular exercise). He was keeping mentally active by reading a book.

On Ron's wall there were two clocks and a calendar. He was wearing a big wristwatch. Being aware of the date and the time would help keep dementia at bay, the leaflet said.

On Frank's kitchen wall there's a free calendar from a stair-lift company and hanging in the living room there's one for a stray dog charity. He also has one of those tear-off block calendars on the living-room desk. Every morning he tears off the previous day's date and says the new date out loud. He walks downstairs and picks up the newspaper, buried amongst all the charity begging letters and offers for walk-in baths and stair lifts – Frank can still get up and down the stairs, a lot slower now, since the accident, but he can still do it. Every morning he picks up the newspaper from the bottom of the stairs, looks at the top of the front page next to the lottery numbers and the little picture of a shining sun or a fluffy rain cloud, and he reads the date out loud. Occasionally he reads it out in a Glaswegian, Liverpudlian or cockney accent. Or a comic American one, like the one Ron the dementia marbles man might have.

But now and again Frank wonders whether he's already

torn yesterday's date off the calendar and it's now showing tomorrow's date? Or what if he thought he'd torn yesterday's date off but hadn't actually done so, and the calendar was still showing yesterday's date? Which he now thought was today's? Or what if the paperboy hadn't actually been today and Frank had picked up and was now reading the date from yesterday's paper? There were no answers to any of these questions in the leaflet. He decided to not worry too much about it.

The dog of the month on the stray dog calendar in the living room was an arrogant-looking poodle. It looked like the stick it was chasing had somehow got stuck up its arse. No wonder it was abandoned. It had probably been yapping all day long and annoying the neighbours. Frank would be glad to turn the page on it next month – perhaps for an Irish wolfhound or a miniature schnauzer. In the meantime he'd drawn a pair of glasses and a Hitler moustache on it.

Frank gets a lot of free calendars in the post. They come with begging letters and direct-debit forms that just need his signature. The older he gets the more junk mail he receives. Charity biros. Pictures of starving kids. Donkeys in distress. Beneath the Hitler poodle's picture Frank had marked today's date with a red cross.

He looked at the clock above the fireplace. It was 10.30 a.m. It was four minutes later on the clock in the kitchen, two minutes earlier on Frank's wristwatch. And flashing a row of eights on and off on the DVD player. Kelly would be here soon.

He should probably put his teeth in.

*

41

At 11.15, Kelly arrived, parked the car, put the Nurse on Call sign in the windscreen, locked the doors and crossed the road.

Frank limped across to the other side of the living room, sat in his armchair, switched on the TV, picked up the newspaper and tried to look nonchalant, ready to sound surprised that she was here, as though it had completely slipped his mind that she was coming, because it wasn't the highlight of his week, the only red letter day on his Nazi poodle calendar.

He waited while Kelly typed his birthday into the key safe and removed the key. He heard the front door open.

'Mr Derrick?'

She came into the living room. There was a bunch of flowers sticking out of the top of her bag.

'Do you have a vase?' she said.

Frank started to get up.

'Don't get up. I'm sure I'll find one.' She went into the kitchen and found a vase in the cupboard, filled it with water and put the flowers in. She brought the vase into the living room and put it on the sideboard. She rearranged the flowers slightly and stood back to look at them.

'There,' she said, before rearranging them once more. 'I've brought your clothes back from the launderette, Mr Derrick,' she said. 'They're in the hall. I'll put them away for you.'

She went into his bedroom. Frank heard her opening and closing drawers. He tried to remember what he kept in the drawers, hoping it was nothing more embarrassing than an old man's Y-fronts and socks. After tidying up, Kelly asked Frank what else needed doing.

'This itches,' he said. He held his plaster cast up. 'It's driving me mad, actually.'

'Hmmm,' Kelly said. She started rooting around in her bag. 'They prefer us just to tap on it or hold a hairdryer against the cast.' She stopped looking in her bag. 'You don't have a hairdryer, do you?' She looked at Frank's long hair.

'No,' he said.

'Oh well,' Kelly said and continued to search through her bag, taking out things she wasn't looking for and putting them on the sofa next to her. It was a cream-coloured cloth bag. Packed tightly with things. Bag for life was a more suitable boast for Kelly's bag. She took out two purses and a thick diary, a sandwich and a pair of scissors.

'It's like Mary Poppins's bag,' Frank said. 'Is there a hat stand in there too? Or a ladder? You could fix my roof.' Frank thought he would probably trust Kelly to go up on his roof. She wouldn't disappear from view to read the paper and have a nap. Kelly would fix any loose tiles and give him a very reasonable bill for the work carried out. Kelly wouldn't suck her teeth or steal the lead from around his chimney.

'Ah,' Kelly said. She took out a ball of wool with two knitting needles poked through the centre. She pulled out one of the needles; it was a foot long with the number '3' printed on its head. 'We aren't really supposed to do this, but.'

Kelly carefully stuck the knitting needle inside Frank's plaster – which had started to smell a bit – and she began to scratch the itch on his arm. It was the greatest feeling in the world; he was probably going to be disappointed when it stopped.

'So, what's been happening since last week?' Kelly said.

And in spite of everything that had happened in the past few days – the village crime wave, going out for the first time since the accident, using his walking stick, losing his walking stick, all the cold-calls he'd dealt with so cleverly and hilariously and all the television shows and DVD films that he'd watched – he couldn't think of a single thing.

7

On Thursday or Friday, maybe even Saturday, it made no real difference to Frank, he was sitting at the living-room window pretending that he was James Stewart in *Rear Window*. Confined to his flat following an accident he spied on his neighbours, hoping to catch the man in the bungalow opposite dragging a heavy crate containing his dismembered wife's body down the hall. Or perhaps he might see Anne, three doors further down the road, dancing around her bedroom in just her bra and pants, although he hoped not. Anne was ninety-four with a thicker moustache than the Hitler poodle. The postman cycled past. He was a large man with little hair left. There goes Alfred Hitchcock, Frank thought, making his cameo appearance.

Frank can do Jimmy Stewart's voice.

In the nineteen seventies it would have been a good enough impression to get him his own Saturday-night TV series. He could have just turned his face away, ruffled his hair and then turned back to face the audience, and as long as he began with 'Hi, I'm Jameshh Shhstewart', the audience would have loved it.

Nowadays he would have to get the face right as well as the voice. He'd need a wig and historically correct costume.

He'd have to spend five and a half hours in the prosthetic make-up chair. Frank would need to hire a wheelchair and an actress to play the part of Grace Kelly. He'd need people to say that his James Stewart was a better James Stewart than James Stewart's James Stewart.

It hardly matters really.

There wasn't much of an audience in Frank's living room. Just a few disinterested-looking ornamental china animals on the mantelpiece, his own distorted reflection in the window and a Nazi poodle.

That's show business.

Just as Jimmy Stewart's plaster cast does in *Rear Window*, Frank's was really making him itch. He picked up the knitting needle Kelly had left behind and carefully threaded it into the top of the cast and started to scratch his arm. It wasn't quite the same.

'It's like trying to tickle yourself,' he said to Bill, who seemed even more disinterested than usual, sprawled on his back on the sofa like Cleopatra waiting for a grape. Frank tapped the outside of the cast. His arm still itched, possibly slightly more. He scratched it with the needle again. The doorbell rang. Frank looked at Bill, waiting for him to move. 'I'll get it, shall I?' Frank said.

He opened the front door to a comically short man wearing a green sweatshirt with the picture of a tree on the front.

'Hello, mate. Sorry to bother you. Do you see that tree?' The man pointed to the tall tree at the corner of Frank's garden. 'The roots of a tree like that could be as deep as the height of the tree itself.'

'I'm sorry,' Frank said. 'What do you want?'

'It doesn't belong there. The roots of that tree.' The man

turned and pointed at the tree again in case Frank had forgotten what a tree was since he'd last pointed at it less than ten seconds ago. 'Those roots are going to get into your pipes, they're going to muck up your sewage, your drainage, they'll cause cracks in your foundations. That tree,' the man said, turning and pointing one more time, 'is going to knock your bloody house over.'

'Really?' Frank said.

'As sure as eggs.'

'As sure as eggs?'

The man nodded. 'Do you want me to cut it down for you?'

'It's all right, thank you,' Frank said.

'It will knock your house down, mate.'

'I doubt it.'

'You doubt it?'

'Well, I'm not as sure as eggs, but I'm willing to take a risk.'

'Are you a tree surgeon?'

'Me? No.'

The man seemed to become suddenly bored with trees and stopped talking. He was looking at Frank's plaster cast.

'You've got something. The top of your . . . out of your arm there,' he said.

Frank looked at Kelly's knitting needle sticking out from the top of his cast.

'God, it itches, doesn't it?' the man said. 'I broke my leg last year. Plaster right up to my thigh. Itched like nobody's business. I used a coat hanger. Opened it out. One of them wire ones. Is it stuck?' the man said. 'The – what is it? Is that a knitting needle?'

'No,' Frank said. 'It's not stuck. I hadn't finished. I had to answer the door.'

'Right. Yes,' the man said. 'You should get your missus to do it for you. I used to get my missus to itch my leg. It's not the same doing it yourself.'

'I was just saying that to my cat,' Frank said. 'It's a bit like trying to—'

The man interrupted him. 'Like trying to strangle yourself, I know, I know.'

'I was going to say tickle, but yes,' Frank said.

Neither man said anything for a few seconds, as though they'd forgotten what it was that had brought them together on the doorstep in the first place, the catalyst that had led to this inaugural meeting of Cast Scratchers' Anonymous. Then Frank said, 'It's not my tree. I only rent the upstairs flat. And I have to go now. I'm quite busy.'

'Yes. Of course,' the man said. He talked about and pointed at the tree for a bit more anyway and then he gave Frank a business card and left. Frank closed the door and went back upstairs to unravel a coat hanger.

8

Kelly was earlier than usual. Half the neighbourhood had been watching her for almost ten minutes and she still wasn't due for another five. Frank thought about going downstairs to invite her in but he thought she might not want to come in to spend extra time with him when she wasn't being paid for it – as though she was some sort of care prostitute. And if he went outside to invite her in, Kelly would realise that he was more active and capable of walking downstairs than he'd implied on the questionnaire he'd filled in on her first visit – when he had answered D instead of B to the question: 'How is your mobility?' She might stop coming. He wasn't ready for that yet.

While he was waiting Frank gave some of his neighbours Sioux names. At the far end of the road he saw Trims His Lawn With Nail Scissors was hard at work in preparation for the Villages in Bloom competition and Washes His Car Too Much was hosing the soap off his car for the fifth time that week. At the bungalow next door, Picks Up Litter held a spiked stick with a crisp wrapper impaled on the tip. Frank's Sioux name would be either Watches Television or Buys Things From the Charity Shop.

Kelly climbed out of the car, which was parked so badly

that a large removals lorry had to drive onto the wrong side of the road to pass by. She shut the car door and started to cross the road. Frank took his seat and waited. A few minutes later he heard the front door open.

'Mr Derrick.'

Kelly came into the living room carrying two 99 ice cream cornets. They had started to melt and she licked ice cream from the edge of her hand. She gave one of the ice creams to Frank.

'Where did you get these?' he said, thinking she must have carried them all the way here in her car. Which would explain her atrocious parking.

'The ice cream man,' Kelly said. 'I had to wave to get him to stop.'

Frank held his ice cream, looking at it as though he'd never seen one before and didn't know what to do next. Ice cream trickled down the cornet.

'Don't let it melt,' Kelly said.

Frank licked the ice cream.

'I didn't hear "Popeye the sailor man",' he said.

'"Greensleeves",' Kelly said. She leaned across and wiped a bit of ice cream from Frank's cheek with a tissue that seemed to magically appear in her hand.

'Thank you,' he said. 'We don't get a lot of ice cream men here. There are no children. This bit of the village is like Vulgaria for ice cream men.'

'What's that?' Kelly said.

'It's from *Chitty Chitty Bang Bang*. It's where the Child Catcher lives.'

'Oh, he terrified me when I was young,' Kelly said. 'He still does.'

'Me too,' Frank said. 'You know you're doing that wrong.'

'What?' Kelly said.

'When you've finished the ice cream at the top of the cornet, you have to push the chocolate down into the cone, then bite the end off and suck the rest of the ice cream out. Like it's a straw.' He demonstrated with his ice cream. Kelly copied him.

'Ice creams aren't just for children,' she said.

'In a cornet with a flake, bought from an ice cream van playing "Popeye the sailor man", they are.'

'"Greensleeves",' she corrected him again. 'And there's no age limit on ice cream.'

'By my age we should be sucking mints,' Frank said. 'Wearing cardigans and drinking cups of tea. Now, eat the rest of the cornet with the chocolate inside.' Kelly did as he instructed. 'We should have chosen a television channel,' Frank continued. 'Preferably one showing repeats of old programmes and we should never turn over again. We will have forgotten how to use the remote control anyway. Life begins at forty. And ends around sixty or sixty-five.' He rubbed his forehead. 'I think I've given myself a headache.'

'Well, I don't think that's true,' Kelly said. She stood up. 'The world is still your oyster. I'll get you a glass of water and you can take some painkillers. You need to take them for your foot anyway.' She went into the kitchen. 'Maybe I should make you a cup of tea too,' she called out. 'Just to be on the safe side. I'll get you a cardigan. There are some mints in my bag.'

Frank heard the sound of the kettle being filled.

'I wonder if the ice cream man still sells those,' he said.

'What's that?'

'Oysters. It was an ice cream. It came in a sort of round-shaped shell that opened up into a sort of –' he demonstrated the shell for himself with the cupped palms of his hands – 'like an oyster, I suppose. Do you know, I'm not sure I ever made that connection until just now.'

Kelly came back into the living room.

'Was there a correct way to eat one of those too?' she said.

'I'm sure there was.'

'I was thinking,' Kelly said, 'we should clear some of your cupboards out.'

'My what?' Frank thought it might be a medical euphemism. He wondered whether a knitting needle would be used.

'And your fridge. Before something in there kills you. Next Tuesday maybe.'

'Tuesday?'

'Monday's a bank holiday.'

Kelly went out into the kitchen. The kettle had started to boil.

'A bank holiday? What for?' Frank called out.

'I'm not sure. Spring?'

'Bank holidays don't really mean anything to me.'

'Pardon?' Kelly said. The noise of the boiling kettle increased in volume and Kelly raised her voice. 'Even these peas are out of date.'

'I don't notice the difference. It's just another day.'

'Pardon?'

'Bank holidays.'

'Right.'

'All the shops are open.'

'Uh huh.' She couldn't hear what he was saying over the noise of the kettle.

'Even the banks. Does frozen food go out of date?'

'Pardon?'

'I thought if things were frozen the date was frozen too.'

'Pardon?'

The kettle boiled louder still and Kelly raised her voice again so that he could hear her, even though it made no difference as she was the one standing next to the loud kettle and he could hear her perfectly well all along. She was just a woman standing next to a boiling kettle, shouting. Like she'd forgotten she had earphones in. It was she who couldn't hear what Frank was saying. He took advantage of that.

'I like it when you come,' he said.

'Sorry?'

'I wish you could stay longer.'

'I don't think they even make this breakfast cereal any more,' Kelly said. She brought a cup of tea in and put it on the table next to the armchair. She put a bag of frozen peas and a tea towel next to the tea and piled some cushions on the carpet in front of the armchair.

'I'm not sure your toe should still be so swollen,' she said. 'Put your foot up on the cushions.'

She took a marker pen out of her bag, pulled the lid off with her teeth and wrote 'For external use only' on the packet of peas before wrapping them in the tea towel and putting them on Frank's foot.

9

On the first day of May, Frank said *auf Wiedersehen* to the Hitler poodle and hello to a bulldog that looked like Winston Churchill.

'We shall fight them on the beaches.' Frank's Churchill impression needed some work.

Because of spring, or the Equinox or the Queen's birthday or something, Frank wouldn't see Kelly until next Tuesday. He would have to have to wait an extra day for his finest hour. There was something else on the calendar this month though. A VE Day party at Greyflick House – the sheltered housing block where Smelly John lived – and Frank was John's plus one. Which meant he was going to have to go on the bus.

The free bus to the big Sainsbury's terrified Frank. It would only be him and the driver – who was protected by an inch of safety glass – preventing the bus from being entirely full of old women. As soon as the doors opened the giggling and high-pitched whooping would start. Making his way to the relative sanctuary of the seats at the back of the bus provided Frank with an insight into what it must be like to be a male stripper at a hen party for the over seventies. As he stepped around wheelie shopping baskets and support stockings he felt like Daniel Day-Lewis in that bit in *The Last of the Mohicans* that isn't the waterfall scene.

Once he was in his seat, the bus would start moving and the whispering would begin. It scared him more than the high-pitched screaming and laughter. He could never hear what it was they were whispering but it was obviously about him. The laughing and whooping would take over again as he re-walked the gauntlet to the front of the bus to get off. This was why Tom Jones always travels to his concerts by limo. Frank knew that whatever happened he mustn't let them catch his eye, otherwise he would never escape. They had a cave in Worthing.

It was 1945 in West Sussex's premier armchair museum – the communal lounge of Greyflick House – Union Jack bunting hanging from the ceiling, *Keep Calm and Carry On* posters pinned to the walls, spam fritters and jam sandwiches for lunch and a man called Ryan in a khaki army uniform with a keyboard and a drum machine singing songs from the 1940s. Everyone had newspaper hats on and they were waving little paper Union Jack flags along to the beat of Ryan's drum machine.

Smelly John was like a wristwatch on a *Ben Hur* chariot driver. At just sixty-four he was at least thirteen years younger than all the other Greyflick residents. He was wearing a bright red trilby, a yellow shirt with a butterfly collar and a crème suit with wide-lapelled jacket and huge-flared trousers. He was sitting in his wheelchair, in the same corner of the lounge that he always sat in, setting up a game of Buckaroo! in anticipation of Frank's arrival.

Smelly John didn't smell in the same way that Kevin

Costner danced with wolves and Washes His Car Too Much washes his car too much. That's not how he got his name. And if he did smell at all it was never unpleasant. John didn't smell of wee, or mothballs or TCP. On most days you could have boiled him up to make soap or an advent candle. But it's not how he got his name.

Smelly John is his punk rock name. He's had it since 1976. He was at the first ever Sex Pistols concert. He used to loiter on the King's Road. Tourists would take his picture for a pound. There are postcards with him on. His best friend was called Steve Piss and he had a girlfriend named Blobb. They all lived in a squat in Chelsea with John's pet rats Snot, Bogie and Prince Albert – which was also the name of the only piece of jewellery John claimed to wear, although Frank declined his frequent offers to prove it to him.

'I thought you'd died!' John shouted when Frank came into the lounge, causing Ryan to go out of time with his drum machine. 'Where have you been, Francis?'

Frank sat down opposite John and told him about his accident and Smelly John offered his sympathy and concern in the only way he knew how, by laughing hysterically and, as Frank had expected, making jokes about it.

'And you're sure it wasn't your father driving the milk float?'

'Yes, I'm sure it wasn't my father.'

'Your biological father?'

'Yes. It definitely wasn't my father.'

'Hmm,' John said and pretended that that was the end of it before adding, 'I suppose it's no use crying over spilt milk.' And he laughed like a tickled baby, slapping the arms of his wheelchair, uncontrollably breaking wind and blowing bubbles of snot from his nose.

And then, when he'd run out of jokes and laughter, in the middle of the celebration of the victory over fascism and the Third Reich, the two men attempted to place things on the back of a plastic mule without the mule kicking them all straight off again.

'Buckaroo!' John shouted as the mule bucked and Ryan lost his timing again and forgot what the three things everyone was supposed to do after packing up their troubles in their old kit bags were.

Most of Smelly John's favourite games ended with him shouting out the game's name. Buckaroo! Jenga! Mouse trap! Ker plunk! Frank wondered whether it was the shouting John enjoyed rather than the actual games. The destination rather than the journey. John's favourite games also tended to require a steady hand. With the spasms from his MS and Frank currently playing left-handed, this was something neither of them had.

John gathered together the Buckaroo! objects and reset the mule in place on the table. Ryan had started a new song about how brilliant the war was.

'Do you like this music, Francis?' John said.

'Not really.' Frank looked around at the other residents, who didn't seem to be enjoying it enormously either. A few were singing along, some just mumbling or mouthing the words or tapping their fingers. Their flag-waving looked like it was being orchestrated at gunpoint to massage an evil dictator's ego. Mostly everyone just seemed bored.

The Greyflick residents were the same as the kids who'd pulled up the FOR SALE signs and tipped over the bollards in Fullwind. They had keep-fit on Tuesday afternoons, salsa dancing every third Friday and sherry and a quiz on Thursdays. They had whist drives, bridge clubs, Bingo and tea dances. There was half-price swimming a mile up the road and every weekday afternoon it was 25 per cent off OAP tickets at the cinema. The buses were free and the trains were half price but they were all too bored to take advantage of any of it. Greyflick House was a riot waiting to happen. Teenagers would be talking about the vandalism and the damage.

'It's pensioners,' the boy on the Nintendo would say.

'Definitely pensioners,' his friend throwing chips at a swan would agree.

'They're bored,' a girl texting votes to a TV talent show would add.

'I bet most of the people in this room', John said, 'have more in common with the music of the Beatles or Elvis Presley or even the Sex Pistols than these old war songs. This is their parents' music.'

The warden who sat in the small office in the reception at the front of Greyflick House, the man who answered the residents' panic calls and carried their shopping up the stairs when the lift was broken – as it frequently was – came into the lounge. He had a slight limp. He slipped on a slice of spam and dropped a tray of teacups and saucers. Smelly John cheered.

The warden looked over. He straightened his tin hat. It had a W painted on the front like the man who shouts at everyone in *Dad's Army*. He picked up the dropped crockery.

'See the way he's looking at me?' John said. He placed the plastic saddle on the back of the mule.

'Who?'

'Graham,' John said. 'The warden. He's a racist. You go first.'

'I just went. It's your turn. He's not a racist.'

John picked up the plastic guitar. 'How would you know?' He hooked the guitar onto the saddle. Ryan started a new song as part of a medley. It had the same plinky plonky drum machine intro as the song before. Frank and John listened, both playing their own private game of Guess the Intro.

'What did you do in the war, Francis?' John said.

'The war?' Frank said.

'Did you fight? Which was your favourite. War one or two?'

'My favourite? How old do you think I am?'

'I don't know,' John said. 'You all look the same to me.'

Frank picked up the plastic lamp and hung it on the mule. 'I don't like talking about it.'

'Because you'd have to kill me?'

'Because it makes me feel old. Although I can kill you if you want.'

'No, you're all right, thanks, Francis.'

John picked up the frying pan. His arm jolted slightly. He waited a second for the spasm to pass and then carefully placed the frying pan on the mule.

'You *are* old,' John said.

'I don't need reminding all the time.'

Frank put the rope on the mule. This was a long game for them. Smelly John picked up the plastic Stetson. He took his red trilby off and put it on the table and he put the tiny toy cowboy hat on his head.

'Does it suit me?' he said.

'It makes you look slightly bigger headed than usual.'

'Ha ha.' Smelly John took the plastic Stetson off and put it on the mule and the mule kicked it straight back off again.

'Buckaroo!' John shouted, causing Ryan to lose his place again.

'Everybody. Sing along,' Ryan said, trying to rescue his composure. 'Let's show Jerry what we're made of.'

'Who's Jerry?' Smelly John called out.

'Come on, lads,' Ryan said. He probably hadn't expected to be heckled at this gig. The drum machine beat plip plopped to a finish.

'*Lads*?' John shouted into the now silent room. 'He's eighty-three.' He pointed at Frank.

'Eighty-one,' Frank said.

'Oh, I get it,' John said. 'You mean geriatric.' He looked at Frank. 'He's calling you old, Francis. You'd better be careful, mate,' he shouted across the room at Ryan. 'Francis is a trained assassin. He fought in two wars.'

'Has anybody got any requests?' Ryan said, doing his best to ignore the hecklers, keeping calm and carrying on.

'Play something we know,' John said.

'What would you all like to hear?' Ryan said, to anyone else in the room other than John.

'Do you know any Bob Marley?' John said.

'Come on, lads,' Ryan said. 'Play fair.'

'Lads again? I told you. He's eighty-two.'

60

'Three. I mean one.'

Ryan decided to ignore the heckling again and started singing 'We'll Meet Again' without accompaniment.

'Some Sex Pistols, then,' John said.

It wasn't the first time Smelly John had disrupted a special event at Greyflick House. He'd almost started a food fight at the Diamond Jubilee garden party the year before and ruined Mick's Marvellous Magic Show at Christmas by insisting the Ace of Hearts he'd chosen from Mick's pack of cards had been the seven of clubs. He frequently spoiled a quiet game of dominoes by dramatically slamming the tiles down on the table, and who would ever forget the time he played Hungry Hippos noisily on his own during the two minutes' silence on Remembrance Day.

Smelly John put the Buckaroo! pieces back in their box.

'The war's over, Francis,' he said. 'Let's go home. Give me a push.'

'I'll give it a try,' Frank said, showing John his plaster cast. He stood up and took hold of the handles of John's wheelchair, leaning on them like they were the handles of a Zimmer frame. He pushed Smelly John's wheelchair towards the exit of the lounge.

'She must be enjoying this,' John said as they passed a sleeping woman. Her make-up bag was open on her lap and it looked as though somebody had used the lipstick to draw on her face. Bored pensioners.

'Why's that?' Frank said.

Smelly John put the index finger of his left hand between his nose and top lip and with his right hand he did a Nazi salute. It wasn't the best Adolf Hitler impression Frank had ever seen. Somewhere between Freddie Starr's, Frank's

61

calendar poodle's and Charlie Chaplin's. Definitely not enough to get him his own Saturday night TV show.

'What are you saying?' Frank said.

'She's German,' John whispered, so loudly that even the deafer Greyflick residents could hear. Frank pushed the wheelchair faster to get John away before he caused any more trouble. Before the door had fully closed behind them John shouted *Yahtzee!* Although it sounded very much like Nazi! At least he was finally entering into the spirit of the day.

Frank pushed John along the sticky carpet of the poorly lit ground-floor corridor of Greyflick House, trying not to crash the wheelchair into the wall as his plastered arm wanted him to do. The wall on one side of the corridor was bare brick, more like an outside wall. With the sticky carpet and bad lighting it was more like the corridor of a neglected city-centre budget hotel than the 'luxury retirement apartment complex' the brochures in the reception area described Greyflick House as.

They stopped in front of the lift at the end of the corridor, John pressed the button to call the lift, and the doors scraped and screeched almost completely open. Frank wheeled John inside. After a long and shaky ride they juddered to a stop on the first floor, and the doors opened just wide enough for them both to squeeze through.

As he wheeled John along another sticky carpeted, poorly lit brick corridor, Frank thought that soon a lot more of the residents would be retired Sex Pistols fans like John. There'd be nobody left alive who remembered the war. Even less people would be singing along or mouthing the words to songs they'd never heard or had any connection to. Mods and rockers in their seventies and eighties would be chasing each other along the corridor on mobility scooters covered in headlights and wing mirrors.

They stopped outside the door to John's apartment – a word that always suggested to Frank that Audrey Hepburn might be inside smoking a long cigarette and drinking a Martini. John pushed the unlocked door open and Frank wheeled him inside.

Even the most verbose estate agent would have his work cut out describing Smelly John's 'apartment' for very long. A small, rectangular lounge with adjoining kitchen and bathroom and a bedroom that wasn't big enough to swing Bill around in. Other than the front door and the toilet door there were no other doors. Each room was reached through a poorly carved arch. It was more sheltered caving than housing. Along the walls and by the side of the bath there were grab rails and hoists and various fixtures to help Smelly John get around and in and out of things. John's apartment was like a showroom for one of the many home-mobility gadget catalogues that came through Frank's letterbox every month.

Through a small window Frank could see the top of a tree. There was a carrier bag full of dog shit hanging from one of the branches. It had been there as long as Frank had been coming here. Possibly before Greyflick House was built. Audrey Hepburn must have been downstairs in the lounge.

As Frank wheeled him inside John reached down and picked up a padded envelope.

'My medicine has arrived,' John said. He started opening the envelope, releasing a sweet but sickly smell into the air.

'Oh balls,' he said. He felt the top of his head, 'I've left my hat downstairs.'

Frank offered to go back down and get it for him.

'No need,' John said. He wheeled himself into the centre of the room and pushed the red panic-alarm button on the wall causing the pager to vibrate in Graham the warden's pocket downstairs in the lounge. 'I might as well get my money's worth.'

The gang of grannies were still on the big Sainsbury's charabanc for the return journey to Fullwind. Still giggling. Frank wondered whether they had even got off at the supermarket. Was there anything in their wheelie shopping baskets? Perhaps this was what they did all day. Riding the bus route to the big Sainsbury's and back, laughing and woo-hooing every time a man got on, like an all-female cast of *Cocoon*.

Frank got off the bus and went to the chemist. He bought some denture fixative powder and then went next door to the charity shop to get his walking stick back.

'It's got a price on it,' the woman behind the counter said.

'Yes, but I left it in here the other day.'

The woman turned the stick over in her hand. She checked the price label again. 'One pound fifty,' she said.

'Yes, but—'

'That does seem ever so cheap,' the woman said. 'June?' she called out. 'This walking stick – one pound fifty, is that right?'

Frank waited while the woman behind the counter and another unseen woman – presumably June – had a conversation about the pricing of his walking stick. A small queue formed behind him.

'One pound fifty, then,' the woman behind the counter said. 'A bargain.'

'But it's my stick.'

The woman looked at the stick.

'It says property of West Sussex Healthcare Trust.'

'I know, but—'

'Is everything all right?' June called out from behind the curtain.

'Yes, thank you, June. Do you want the stick?' the woman behind the counter said. 'It is for charity.'

Someone in the queue looked at their watch and tutted.

Frank bought his own walking stick back. He handed the woman the money.

'How much is that?' he said. He pointed at the shelf behind the counter. The woman took down a shirt with a colourful flowery pattern as loud as heavy metal. The shirt was still in its original wrapper. It was a few sizes too large but allowing for the plaster on his arm it should be a snug fit on one side of his body at least. Frank bought it. He also bought a bottle of aftershave that smelled like wallpaper paste.

10

Frank got out of bed before the aeroplanes to remove all the pins and strips of cardboard and plastic from his new shirt. He hadn't opened a new shirt for a long time. He'd forgotten what a simple thrill it was.

Putting the shirt on was less of a joyride. It seemed like he'd only just finished freeing himself from the blue canvas jacket and now he was forcing his arm into another difficult sleeve. After he'd squeezed his plastered arm into the shirt he put his good arm into the other sleeve and discovered he'd left a pin in the shirt. It stabbed his arm and a spot of blood started to bloom and grow at the centre of one of the shirt's many flowers.

Frank fastened the buttons and looked in the bathroom mirror. One sleeve was loose-fitting while the other was skin-tight, as though it was made from two different shirts sewn together – a cut-and-shut shirt. He put on some of the second-hand aftershave, and, looking and smelling like wallpaper, took his place by the window.

'Is that a new shirt?' Kelly said when she arrived. She was carrying black bin bags and two pairs of rubber gloves.

'This?' Frank shrugged. 'I've had it for years.'

'It's very flowery. Shall we start?'

Ten minutes later, Kelly was sitting on the linoleum kitchen floor. She'd taken her shoes off and her legs were tucked beneath her. She had her head halfway inside the fridge.

'I think this might be ham,' she said. 'Can you remember buying ham?'

'Not recently.'

'Pardon?'

'Not recently.'

Kelly came out from inside the fridge. She handed Frank an open packet of what was probably ham. 'I'm sorry. What did you say?'

Today's game of Chinese Whispers would be played with one contestant inside a fridge and the other contestant sitting on one of those stools that has a pointlessly short fold-out ladder beneath it. He would be dressed in a loud shirt with one tight-fitting sleeve and one loose. Like a man who has been working out, one arm at a time, and the gym has gone out of business at the halfway point.

'It's ham, I think,' Kelly said. 'Do you think it's ham?'

Frank had no idea. He dropped the ham-not-ham-maybe-ham in a black bin liner with the blue Scotch eggs and furry cheese triangles, with the grey potatoes and the rusty corned beef tin with the broken key.

'I may be saving your life today,' Kelly said and went back into the fridge. Without coming back out she passed Frank a fish finger and a soggy cucumber. He dropped them both in the rubbish bag. 'How was your bank holiday?' she said from inside the fridge.

'It may possibly have been my most eventful bank holiday ever.'

'Should these even be in the fridge?' Kelly came out holding a box of Oreos.

'It's my daughter. She keeps the tomato sauce in the fridge as well. And the jam – or the jelly. She's sort of American. I can never find things after she's been to visit. She puts everything in the fridge.'

Kelly looked at the sell-by date on the box of biscuits and worked out that Beth's last visit must have been quite a while ago. She didn't want to offend or upset Frank by drawing attention to it.

'Maybe I should put them back in the fridge,' she said.

'No, throw them away,' Frank said. 'She'll probably bring some more with her next time she's over. I might accidentally have told her they were my favourite biscuits. I don't actually like them that much.' Frank held his hands out to signal to Kelly that she should throw the biscuits across the small kitchen for him to catch. With one arm folded at an angle and the other held out straight in front of him it was more Tai Chi than baseball. Kelly leaned over and dropped the box of soft biscuits into the rubbish bag instead.

She sat up on the kitchen floor, pulled the yellow rubber gloves off, rolled them together in a ball, and threw them up and over, into the kitchen sink. As she started to get up from the floor, Frank wanted to jump off his stool ladder and offer his hand to help her up. He wanted to take his flowery shirt off and Sir Walter Raleigh it onto the puddle of melted freezer ice on the kitchen floor so that she could step on it and not get her feet wet.

But even if he could have got the shirt off in time he

probably would have felt dizzy and dropped on top of her like the sack of potatoes she'd thrown away at the start of the food clear-out. The potatoes were so old, grey and wrinkly that when Kelly tipped them into the rubbish bag the symbolism had almost been too much for Frank.

Kelly unfolded herself from the kitchen floor, standing up gracefully like a ballet dancer. Frank got up from his stool ladder, steadying himself against the cupboard door. He wondered how far past his sell-by date he was.

'Why was your bank holiday so eventful?' Kelly said, answering something he thought she hadn't heard because her head had been in the fridge when he'd said it.

'I meant compared to normal. Bank holidays don't feel like holidays any more. They're just Mondays with ever so slightly different television and a less frequent bus service.'

'That's a shame,' Kelly said. She shut the fridge door and tied the rubbish bag in a knot and when she left she threw it in the dustbin. The only food in the flat now were the seven tins of cat food in the cupboard under the sink.

But Kelly had never looked in the cupboard under the sink. She had also never looked in the room next to Frank's bedroom, where she would have found a wicker basket with a red tartan blanket inside and an orange plastic tray filled with torn pieces of newspaper, Sunday supplements and a picture of a poodle with a Hitler moustache. Kelly would have seen the beginning of an unravelled ball of wool that, if she followed it under the bed, would have led her to half a dead mouse and a fur ball.

Kelly hadn't seen the cat food, the wicker basket, the blanket, the orange tray, the wool, the fur ball or the dead mouse. If she had, she would have started to put two and

69

two together. And even though she didn't know that Frank had a cat and had never actually seen Bill in person, her throat would itch, her eyes would start streaming and she'd sneeze uncontrollably, because Kelly was allergic to cats.

11

Weekends were almost as pointless for Frank as bank holidays. It seemed like a very long time ago that he'd last thanked God it was Friday or felt sick when he heard the theme music to *Last of the Summer Wine* because it reminded him he had to get up early in the morning for the start of a new week of work. It was a feeling he still had for a long time after he'd retired, but now it was just music.

When Frank's daughter was a lot younger she would experience the same sick dread in her stomach when she heard the theme tune at the start of *The Antiques Roadshow*, telling her it was time for bed because she had to be up early for school. Frank wondered whether she still felt the same when she heard the tune now that she lived in America. Was *The Antiques Roadshow* even on the television in America? Frank thought about ringing Beth to find out. They hadn't spoken for a while. It would be a good excuse. Or at least *an* excuse. He'd been thinking about her ever since the fridge clear-out. He felt bad about throwing the biscuits away and had even contemplated fishing them back out of the dustbin. He wondered how much more American she would sound now. He probably wouldn't recognise her voice at all soon. She'd call him on the phone and he'd think it was another recorded-voice robot trying to sell him incontinence products and he'd hang up.

What was the time difference in Los Angeles anyway? Frank could never remember. Was it eight hours earlier there or eight hours later? She'd probably be out at a drive-in movie or eating a popsicle in a mall or something. He'd either be waking her up or interrupting her dinner or her breakfast just to ask her an unnecessary and expensive long-distance question about a TV show she probably wouldn't remember.

Last of the Summer Wine and *The Antiques Roadshow* were just part of the never-ending loop of repeats for Frank now. Nauseating Sunday-evening dread was available at any time and on any day of the week. Both shows were probably on now. He switched the TV on to see. Yes, there they were.

On Saturday morning a boiler insurance robot rang. Frank sussed it was a recorded voice straight away and immediately hung the phone up. An hour or so later he was so bored that he tried calling the robot back.

In the afternoon he fell asleep watching a war film. As he dozed off he tried to recall which accent he'd spoken with during the war – the posh one or the cockney one. When he woke up, the war was over. He presumed the Germans had lost again. He looked at the clock, wiped the dribble from his chin and swore to himself. This unscheduled siesta would probably mean he was going to wake up an hour early tomorrow morning and have to find even more meaningless activities to fill the extra daytime with.

He watched the football results even though he'd never really liked football. He listened to the man reading the results and tried to guess what the score was by the tone of his voice. He hoped that Forfar were playing East Fife and that they'd beaten them 5-4, but they were playing Cowdenbeath and it was nil-nil.

12

On Sunday the first plane of the day took off later than during the week, giving Frank a lie-in he had no use of. He fed Bill and went downstairs to pick up the newspaper. The thickness of his Sunday newspaper was the only thing that marked Sunday out as different to any other day of the week. Today's newspaper was thicker than ever. He thought he might have to make three trips to carry it all up the stairs. He would have left the supplements and brochures behind but he needed it all to use for substitute cat litter. Today Bill would be shitting on actresses and fashion models, pissing on opera reviews, gadget catalogues and '28 Colour Pages of Sport'.

In the afternoon Frank opened some of the junk mail he'd accumulated that week. He picked up the first envelope from a pile on the kitchen table. In the envelope there was a glossy A4 brochure. Seventeen pages of customer testimonies and photographs of smiling old people riding stair lifts like they were in Disneyland. Weee! On the front cover of the brochure a television presenter attempted to smile his face in half. Losing the use of your legs looked like such incredible fun.

'I wonder if they do stair lifts for cats,' Frank said to Bill and put the envelope and the stair-lift brochure onto the cat litter pile. He picked up the next envelope. *Don't let a child die*, it said on the front. Frank felt the shape of the free biro inside the envelope. He was already feeling guilty about what he was about to do. How many children's deaths had he been responsible for because he hadn't used the free pen to tick the £10 donation box? How many people had remained homeless, or died from heart disease because Frank hadn't unfolded and filled the plastic bags that came through his letterbox with his old clothes and shoes? He either threw the bags away or used them as bin liners. He was a monster. Frank opened the envelope, trying to avoid any of the starving children's staring eyes on the photographs inside. He took the biro out and put it in a mug with his other free charity pens, each one a further reminder of his lack of humanity. As was the charity mug he put them into.

Frank opened more junk mail for arthritis chairs and ocean cruises, for hearing aids that were so small he'd need new glasses to be able to see them. There were letters warning him the wiring in his home was out of date and about to burst into flames. Win a car! Adopt a monkey. Scratch these three numbers off and ring the telephone number. £2.50 a minute for your free gift. He put it all on Bill's poo pile.

The penultimate piece of junk mail was from a funeral-plan company offering Frank four different ways to be buried – Simple, Classique, Superb and Royale, next to a picture of an elderly woman on the phone, presumably arranging her own funeral. She looked even happier about dying than the people who couldn't climb stairs did about not being able to climb stairs.

The final piece of junk mail was from an optician offering free in-home eye tests for the over seventy-fives. Frank didn't believe anything could be actually genuinely free. There was always a catch. He knew the small print would be full of terms and conditions about him needing to buy an expensive pair of glasses at the end of his free in-home eye test. He didn't read the small print. There was too much of it and it was too small.

The left side of Frank's glasses – what did you call those bits? Arms? The left arm of Frank's glasses had been held together with yellow insulation tape since the accident and there was a scratch across the lens that he had grown so used to seeing that when he took his glasses off he thought there was something wrong with his eyes because he couldn't see the scratch any more.

'*Carpe diem*, Bill,' he said, but Bill didn't understand Latin. He took the optician's letter into the living room and rang up to arrange a home appointment. It was the first time he'd ever made use of a piece of his unsolicited mail, other than tearing it into strips for cat litter or to carry a flame from the cooker in the kitchen to light the gas fire in the living room when he'd run out of matches. The woman who answered the phone at the optician's sounded genuinely surprised that somebody was calling them rather than the other way around. Frank had cold-called the cold-caller.

'So it's just a free eye test,' Frank said.

'Yes.'

'I won't be made to feel obliged to buy anything?'

'No.'

'Or to sign anything or give my bank details?'

'No.'

'I won't need to buy expensive glasses after my free eye test?'

'No.'

'So, to clarify. I will have the advertised free eye test and then I'll ask for a copy of the prescription so I can order some glasses from the Internet for less than half the price?'

'Yes.'

'How much is this phone call costing me?'

'Ten pence a minute.'

'Thank you. Can I book an appointment then, please?'

'Are you at home next week?'

'Yes.'

'Morning or afternoon?'

'Yes.'

13

Kelly was singing to herself in the kitchen. 'Kelly put the kettle on, Kelly put the kettle on.' Even with two walls and a boiling kettle between them it was clear she had a lovely singing voice. If only Frank was in charge of television scheduling. Every week, she'd be the special guest halfway through his Saturday-night impressions show. Kelly would be his Elaine Page or Barbara Dickson. A pretty woman in a big dress with a lovely voice, in between the gags and sketches. Like on *The Two Ronnies*. Smelly John could be the other Ronnie. Corbett or Barker – Frank wasn't that fussed.

'We'll all have tea.' She came into the living room and put a cup of the tea she'd been singing about on the table and sat down on the arm of the sofa and asked Frank the usual questions – Was he feeling well? Was he eating enough? Had he been taking his medication? Frank just kept saying yes. It was an easy test. Even easier than the hospital Mini Mental State Examination. He would have to find more space on the mantelpiece for another cut-glass trophy.

'Not having too much trouble washing?'

Frank wondered why she'd asked that all of a sudden. It wasn't one of her regular questions. Did he smell? Piss and mothballs. TCP? Was it time to form a new double act with Smelly John? The Two Smellies?

'Not really,' he said.

Frank had been having trouble washing. His injuries and the need to keep his plaster cast dry made climbing in and out of the bath more trouble than it was worth. But he didn't want to admit to it. 'Although washing my hair has been a challenge,' he said as a compromise. He held his plastered arm up. 'Sometimes I'm sure I can still smell sour milk.'

'Would you like me to wash it for you?'

'My hair?'

'Your hair. I could wash it for you.'

'Oh. I –' Frank was surprised how awkwardly teenage the idea made him feel. He felt his face reddening.

'I could brush it for you at least?' Kelly said, noticing he felt uncomfortable. Without waiting for an answer she brought the chair over from the window and motioned for him to sit down. She took a hairbrush from her bag and pulled a few strands of hair from its bristles. She rolled them into a small ball and put them in the wastepaper bin next to Frank's armchair.

Kelly stood behind Frank. She smelled like the first rainfall on the pavement after a month of sunshine.

'You have lovely hair, you know, Mr Derrick. Most of the other old gentlemen I see don't have a lot left up top.'

It wasn't the first time somebody had told him he had lovely hair. Women in particular would often stop him in the street or tap on his shoulder in Post Office queues and at bus stops to comment on it, to tell him how envious they were of his hair. A woman in Fullwind Food & Wine had once asked if she could touch it. It was one of the reasons Frank kept his hair long. The ladies loved it. And now Kelly thought his hair was lovely too.

He was less happy that she thought of him as old, even if he was a gentleman. In fact, he found he didn't really like to think that there were other old gentlemen besides him. He wanted her to be his care worker exclusively. At least Kelly's other old gentlemen were all bald. In the land of the bald the long-haired man is king, Frank told himself.

Kelly took hold of Frank's long white hair as though it was the tail of a horse and started to brush it.

'So, Mr Derrick,' she said, in her best hairdresser small-talk voice. 'Is there a Mrs Derrick?'

'She passed away,' Frank said.

'I'm so sorry,' Kelly said. She stopped brushing Frank's hair. 'I wasn't thinking.'

If there was a Mrs Derrick, she was obviously either dead or estranged. The need for Kelly's weekly visits should have been enough to tell her that. If there was a Mrs Derrick, she was either long gone or busy on Mondays. Unless Frank was Britain's oldest-living bachelor or gay or Cliff Richard.

'It was a long time ago,' Frank reassured her. 'That's her.' He nodded towards a framed photograph at the centre of the menagerie of china dogs, cats, giraffes and pigs on the mantelpiece.

'Do you mind?' she said.

'No, of course not.'

Kelly picked up the photograph. She wiped the dusty glass with the end of her sleeve. It was a picture of a woman sitting on a blanket, sheltering from the sea wind behind a wooden breakwater on the stones near a sandy beach.

'There was more sand back then,' Frank said. 'It's practically all stones now. And they're piled so high it's an effort to get down to the sea. I sometimes forget how close by it is. I can smell the sea but I haven't seen it for years.'

Kelly put the photograph back on the mantelpiece, re-arranging the porcelain pigs standing guard on either side of it.

'What was her name?' Kelly said, and apologised once more for bringing the subject up and again for not dropping it.

'Sheila,' Frank replied, and again he said that it was a long time ago and she needn't apologise. 'She used to swim every day. It didn't matter how cold it was. She was a very good swimmer. She had medals. Sheila taught me how to swim. I mean, I could already swim. But not properly. She showed me how to breathe. How to use my feet as well as my arms. I was never as good as her though. She could swim for miles. I tended to wade around in the shallow end for a while and then get bored.'

Frank couldn't stop himself from talking now. Maybe it was the hair-brushing. He told Kelly how his wife would swim further and further away from the shore until he completely lost sight of her. Time would pass. He'd come out of the water, walk back up the stones, wrap himself in a towel and sit on the blanket by the breakwater until he stopped shivering. 'Or groyne,' he said to Kelly. 'I think those wooden breakwaters are actually called groynes.'

'Groyne.' Kelly tried the new word out. 'How do you spell that?'

'I'm not really sure.'

Frank said that after a while of not being able to see

Sheila he'd start to panic. Even though she'd swum out of sight many times before he'd think about shouting for help or going to the phone box by the café to call the coastguard. He'd get up from the blanket and shield his eyes from the sun with his hand to try and see her rubber-hatted head bobbing up and down with the waves.

'The tide would come back in sideways though. I always forgot that. I'd be looking out towards France when I should have been looking at the Isle of Wight. Sheila would turn up about a hundred yards along the beach. Waving as she came back over, taking her swimming hat off and shaking her hair. I'd hold her towel out to her and she'd wrap herself in it and sit and shiver for a while, her teeth chattering, letting the sun dry her off before taking her costume off and putting her clothes back on. She could do it all under the towel and appear fully clothed when she removed it. It was her party trick.'

Kelly looked at the picture on the mantelpiece.

'I used to love looking at old family photographs,' she said. 'My mum and dad would always get their photo albums out when people came to visit. Not *all* the ones of me are embarrassing. All my photos are in my phone now. I never get round to printing them or even putting them on the computer, and I can never find the little lead that connects the phone to the computer anyway.'

Frank told Kelly how his wife's illness eventually stopped her from swimming.

'I watched her disappear a little more each day. Like when she swam out to sea.'

He told Kelly how guilty he'd felt for sometimes wishing

it would all be over. That that day would be the last day he'd have to watch his wife change.

'Towards the end I realised that she wasn't mine any more. She belonged to the hospital now. On the night she died I told her that it was all right, she could go now, as though I was giving her my permission. Not like God exactly. More like Alan Sugar or Anne Robinson. I felt so selfish.'

Frank had never told anybody this before. Not his daughter, not Smelly John, not even Bill. He'd known Kelly for less than a total of six hours. He'd had longer relationships with some of the old women who worked in the charity shop.

Kelly hadn't spoken for a while. She was still holding Frank's hair but she wasn't brushing it. He turned his head. Her eyes were watering. He'd made her cry. She'd never come again after this. He'd have to brush his own hair, scratch his own itch. Go back to hoarding old food. He wished he could take it all back.

'Is there a Mr Christmas?' he said, hoping to lighten the mood.

Kelly sniffed and wiped the corner of her eye with the end of the sleeve she'd dusted Sheila's picture with.

'Only my dad.' She seemed to read Frank's mind and said, 'Yes, Father Christmas.' She sniffed again and put her hand on the top of Frank's head and turned it back round like she was screwing the lid shut on a jar. After she'd finished brushing his hair, Frank turned to face her, his hair was softer than ever and he was going to need to keep away from balloons for a while.

'Something for the weekend, sir?' Kelly said, revisiting her hairdresser impression.

That would make a nice change, he thought.

Kelly got her stuff together. She took her anorak off the back of the chair that Frank was still sitting on.

'I could wash it for you next week,' she said. She picked up her bag. 'Perhaps I could help you have a bath too,' she said. 'See you next week. Bye.'

And she walked out of the living room, down the stairs and out the front door. She put the key back in the key safe, walked down the path and out through the front gate. She got in her car, removed the Nurse on Call sign, wound the window down, started the engine and the stereo came on, playing what Frank thought was either Madonna or Kylie Minogue. She checked her wing mirrors, took the hand-brake off, and, watched by a dozen Jimmy Stewart impersonators, she drove away along Sea Lane.

As Frank, now standing at the window with his hair all brushed and static, looking like Miss Havisham, watched her disappear into the distance, all he could think about was her helping him have a bath and what that might involve, and how it might change the dynamics of their relationship. Dynamics that he was just getting used to. He was too old and broken-armed to start moving goalposts around.

Perhaps it would just be a bed bath, whatever a bed bath was. But Frank wasn't bedridden, she obviously meant an actual bath. Him, naked in a tub full of water. When was the last time anyone had seen him naked? He didn't even undress in front of Bill, and when Sheila was alive they were hardly ever a naturist couple. Sheila's beach towel trick wasn't just something she did for all the other strangers on the beach. They'd both always undressed for bed either in the dark or in separate rooms.

He was overreacting. Kelly was probably just going to turn the taps on, check the temperature of the water with her elbow and leave Frank to it before reaching her arm around the bathroom door to pass him a towel when he was finished. That was what she meant by helping him have a bath.

But he couldn't stop thinking, what if she planned on being more hands on? Was she going to scrub his back and rinse his naked old body with a sponge or a loofah? It was probably on her list of jobs that she was expected to carry out – he hadn't really read it. She'd probably seen hundreds of wrinkly old men in the nude before. She was a sort of nurse, wasn't she? It said so on a sign in the windscreen of her car. She had a uniform. There was a logo on the side of her car.

As Kelly's car disappeared from view Frank was confused and panicky about the whole thing and then it just got worse as he started to feel like Michael Gambon in *The Singing Detective* – trying to think of boring things to stop himself getting an erection when Joanne Whalley puts grease on his flaky body – only there was a twist. Frank couldn't stop thinking. Not: What if he got an erection? But: What if he didn't?

14

The day after Kelly had dropped her bath bombshell Frank went to the library. He showed his library card to the librarian and took a seat in front of one of the computers next to two other pensioners.

People who find it weird seeing their parents and grand-parents using new technology and who think it's just wrong when Granny makes a mobile phone call, should probably start getting used to it. The pensioners holding up the queue for the cashpoint because they can't remember their pin numbers or because they can't see the screen, the ones paying for their shopping by cheque – they're on the way out. The OAPs on the library computers, the ones in trainers and jeans drinking skinny mocha lattes in the coffee shops, texting each other on their mobiles, playing Tetris and Snake while they listen to their iPods – they're the future. This is your *Planet of the Apes*. Pull their earphones out: they're listening to the Arctic Monkeys.

Frank signed in to his library computer account and checked his email. There were seventy-six spam emails and one from his daughter:

Hi Dad,

How is everything? Is the cast off yet? I guess it must be itching like crazy now. Did I tell you Jimmy's company got the contract he's been working so hard for? It's a huge deal for him and for us, and once Jimmy is settled in with it all we should be able to come over and see you. We all miss you (of course!!).

Laura is doing so well at college. She misses you greatly. She's so grown-up now you would hardly recognize her. Her hair seems to change color every week!

I hope the care visitor is still working out OK for you. I know you weren't keen. I prayed they wouldn't send round some dreadful matron to try and boss you about and tell you off. Thank the Lord those days are long gone (except on TV, I guess). Everybody here seems to adore the old *Carry On* movies. And Benny Hill! Maybe you should think about moving here, you always loved Benny Hill.

I will call soon. Hopefully when you are not asleep! I sometimes forget about the time difference.

All our love

Beth xx

'Color' instead of 'colour', 'recognise' spelled with a z, or possibly even a zee. America had taken another part of his daughter away. And he'd always hated Benny Hill.

He stared at the computer screen thinking about his reply. What exciting things could he tell Beth about? A man had stood in his garden and told him his roof was dangerous. Two men had caught him unawares on the doorstep and he'd contemplated punching one of them. Some

87

bollards had been knocked over in the village. Woodlice had been disturbed. Bored kids were once again the prime suspects. Smelly John had tried to start a fight with a man singing Vera Lynn songs. Perhaps he should begin by answering his daughter's questions. He could answer them in red on the computer. He knew how to do that.

Was the cast off? *No.*

I guess it must be itching like crazy now? *Yes.*

Did I tell you Jimmy's company got the contract? *Yes, but I wasn't really paying attention. Something to do with wine?*

Should he tell her 'yes, the care visitor *is* working out for me. She isn't a bossy matron at all, she's actually very friendly and nice to talk to. In fact, I've found myself telling her things I haven't told anyone else before. About how your mother died, for example. That sort of thing. Oh, and she's very pretty, this care worker, she smells like rain on a hot pavement (sidewalk) after a drought. She has a geometrically perfect fringe, oh, and talking of hair, she brushed mine yesterday and next week she's giving me a bath. Yes that's right, a bath. And by the way, she's not just young enough to be my daughter, she's young enough to be your daughter, and PS: I've bought a loud shirt and some aftershave, probably because of her. PPS: She's thrown your American biscuits away. Byee. Dad x.'

Frank had always looked forward to spending his old age with his daughter. When he was in his sixties and she was in her twenties, he'd often tease her with horror stories of how she'd soon have to look after him, wheeling him about in a bath chair, feeding him and changing his underpants, apologising to people all the time because he'd become so politically incorrect and outspoken, which, he told her, were the last bits of your mind to go. He teased his daughter that she would have to deal with him constantly swearing at vicars and policemen, talking about 'foreign people' and coming on to the women in the library and the charity shop. Maybe that was why Beth had escaped to America. Before it was too late, just in case he wasn't joking.

To avoid replying to the email for a while Frank surfed the Internet. He looked on eBay for the china ornaments he'd found in the 50p box at the charity shop that were going to make him his fortune. He found a similar pair on the computer that had a current highest bid of 99p.

He clicked on other eBay links. They sucked him into a modern form of paper chase – a paperless chase – that led him from one worthless ornament to another. Every time he clicked a new link his browsing history would update and become more elaborate as the Internet tried to predict what it was he might be interested in. He clicked on a link for an ornamental bell that led him to another link for a teapot and another for something described as a 'pottery Italian donkey jam pot'. Frank then accidentally clicked on an ad for cheaper phone calls at the side of the page and a new web page opened. When he closed it and returned to his eBay page it was full of china and porcelain telephones and a painting of a donkey.

He couldn't concentrate on what he'd come into the library to do – sending an email to his daughter. His attention span seemed to be getting shorter the older he got. When was the last time he'd actually taken a book off the shelf of the library and taken it home with him, or bought and then actually read one of the second-hand books from the charity shop? He hardly read the newspaper properly any more. He just read the headlines, looked at the pictures and made the rest up based on what he got from that. It gave him a jumbled-up version of current events. Victims were murderers, murderers were victims, winners were losers, famous people celebrating birthdays had just died.

He stared at the computer screen, moving the mouse around on the mat, trying to hypnotise himself with the cursor. It was incredible how there was apparently so much stuff on the Internet and yet he couldn't think of a single website or thing to look at.

He wondered if the home care company Kelly worked for had a website. He did a quick search for Lemons Care – which hadn't seemed such a stupid name for a care company before Stuart and Linda Orange had pulled out of the business – and he found their website. All the old people in the photographs on the front page of the site looked so happy. Like the TV presenters or the crippled and dying in his junk mail. He clicked on 'Frequently Asked Questions' and on 'What Tasks Will My Care Worker Carry Out?' Number three on the list was 'Help With Washing'. Frank clicked on 'Meet the Team' and scrolled down the list of names.

> Kelly Christmas joined us in August 2012. She brought with her a wealth of experience having worked within domiciliary care for two years. Kelly has also undertaken a number of training courses to keep herself up to date with changes in home care. Kelly is a welcome and valuable asset to our growing business. Click for picture.

Frank looked at the picture of Kelly. She was pretending to check the temperature on a thermometer. She was smiling for the camera. She was dressed in the same blue shiny uniform that she wore when she visited him. Her hair was in a side parting, it was amazing how such a simple reframing of her face could change it so much. But not in any kind of a negative or bad way. Just different. It answered the question that Frank had asked himself – her horizontal fringe wasn't there to conceal a third eye, a BNP tattoo or a really ugly forehead.

Frank looked at the profiles of some of the other care workers. In his head he did his impression of Michael Aspel presenting Miss World.

'Angela has worked as a care supervisor for six years and has trained as a Registered General Nurse. She has a wealth of experience, speaks English and French and would like to see world peace and an end to poverty.'

'Anne-Marie has vast experience in the care of the elderly and has worked within domiciliary care for more than ten years. Her vital statistics are 36-28-36.'

Michael Aspel announced Kelly Christmas as the winner, he placed the crown on her head, draped the Miss Care Worker sash across her body, kissed her on both cheeks and gave her enough flowers for her to also be the winner of this year's Villages in Bloom competition.

Frank closed the Internet browser and went back to his emails. He wrote a simple reply to Beth. He told her how he was well and everything was fine and little more than that. He looked at the clock at the top of the screen. His computer time was up. The next pensioner was waiting to look at videos of skateboard tricks and update his Facebook status. Frank pressed send on the email and logged off.

Frank left the library and went into the chemist and bought a fancy new razor, a can of expensive shaving gel, a bar of even more expensive soap, something he'd never realised existed before called dry shampoo, and, purely because he remembered singing the song from the TV advert to his daughter when she was young, he bought a bottle of Matey bubble bath.

Walking past the charity shop on the way home he saw another shirt in the window. If anything it was louder than the previous shirt – the flowers and splashes of random colour shouted BUY ME! at him. He went in and bought it. He also bought a pair of tweezers and a Madonna *Greatest Hits* CD that was in the 'everything £1' basket on the counter.

'Ooh. Is it for your granddaughter?' the woman behind the counter said.

'Yes,' Frank said, annoyed with himself for lying and with the world for making him feel that he needed to.

15

Frank was up before the planes again. If Kelly was going to give him a bath he was going to make sure he was clean first. Frank was going to make himself so clean that it would be like the Queen was coming to give him a bath.

He turned on the taps and tipped some of his children's bubble bath under the running water. The water turned green for a while. He laid out his tools. On the edge of the sink he placed the tweezers he'd bought from the charity shop. He wondered what the previous owner had used them for. Removing splinters and stamp collecting were the only things he could think of, but there were some pretty disgusting people in the world and so Frank had boiled the tweezers in a saucepan for five minutes just in case. On the sink next to the tweezers was Frank's new razor. It had five blades – four more than he'd ever used before – and a lubricating strip. When he switched it on the razor lit up and vibrated in his hand. Frank was wary of running it under the tap because he thought he would be electrocuted. The shaving gel can claimed the gel would 'prepare his beard for shaving and soothe, calm, hydrate, comfort and moisturise' his skin afterwards. It was blue when it came out of the can and white when he put it on his face.

All the smooth shave innovations would be cancelled out by Frank having to shave left-handed. He cut himself on his earlobe and again on the edge of his nostril and missed patches of beard, ending up with a face like Centre Court on the last day of Wimbledon.

Frank unwrapped his bar of expensive soap and put it on the side of the bath. There were two carrier bags hooked over the cold tap of the sink and a roll of brown parcel tape on the windowsill above it.

Frank picked up the tweezers. He moved his face close to the mirror, cleared a gap in the steam of the glass with his hand and, mostly by luck, took hold of one of his nostril hairs. He pulled sharply on the hair and it popped out. Frank's eyes watered and he felt a sneeze on its way. He braced himself and when the sneeze didn't come he felt as disappointed as it was possible to feel about pretty much anything. Getting hold of another nose hair proved more difficult and frustrating, like threading a needle on the deck of a North Sea ferry. Once he had hold of a hair, he pulled more slowly. The hair seemed very long. It was like he was unravelling a jumper. The hair popped free and this time he did sneeze, banging his head on the mirror. He decided a few nostril hairs at his age was not the end of the world.

Frank turned off the taps and looked at the bath and then at his arm. He wondered if there was such a thing as a dry bath. He unhooked one of the carrier bags from the tap and started wrapping his plastered arm in it. Then, keeping the bag in place by holding his arm against his body, he picked up the parcel tape. Obviously he couldn't find where the tape started. Obviously that was going to happen. He took his right arm away from his body to unpick the tape and the carrier bag fell on the floor. Reaching out to catch it he knocked the soap into the bath water. Next week he would swing from a broken clock and let a wooden house fall on top of him.

Eventually, Frank managed to wrap his arm in the two carrier bags and hold them in place with the brown parcel tape, which he then had to tear using his teeth, which, of course, were in a glass, leading to a further delay. But eventually, with his teeth in, he managed to chew through the tape. It was all screwed up and stuck to itself and when he was finished his arm looked like a present wrapped by a drunk dad on Christmas Eve.

He climbed carefully into the bath. The water was now tepid. He wished he'd bought one of those rubber mats the home mobility catalogues were always trying to sell him, as he was terrified of slipping and falling, knocking himself out and drowning. He thought about how long he might lie in the bath undiscovered, but then realised that it wouldn't be that long as Kelly would be here soon. She'd open the front door and call out his name, wondering why he wasn't answering. And then she'd search for him room by room until she saw the steam from the bathroom. Frank didn't want Kelly to be the one to find him dead, his body even more wrinkly than it was already, lying in a bath of Matey.

Frank stood in the bath, he turned the hot tap back on to warm the water up and then he sat down. He looked at his feet sticking out of the water by the taps. His toenails needed cutting. Even if he owned a pair of left-handed scissors he would never have the strength required to cut through his thick toenails. The last time he'd cut them he'd used garden secateurs. It was the closest thing to gardening they'd ever been used for. He let his feet submerge out of sight under the bubbles and he washed himself with his expensive soap.

Frank didn't spend a long time in the bath. He didn't want to fall asleep and go through the same scenario of being found by Kelly – doubly embarrassing by not even being dead. He climbed out of the bath and dried himself. Getting the carrier bags off his arm proved just as difficult as getting them on and he had to tear through the plastic and the parcel tape with his teeth. Once he'd freed his arm, his plaster cast was wet anyway.

He dry-shampooed his hair. Without a brush to brush the dry shampoo properly into his hair he looked like he'd been sandpapering the ceiling.

He went into the bedroom to get dressed. His clothes were laid out on the bed. He needed new underpants. He couldn't remember the last time he'd bought any. Or even if he ever had. Sheila had not only worn the trousers in the relationship, she'd also bought the pants.

Buying underpants would involve a trip further into town. They probably sold them in the charity shop but underwear was on his list of things he wouldn't buy second-hand. Socks were another. He didn't mind wearing dead man's shoes but not dead man's socks or pants.

Another thing Smelly John had said after Frank's accident was, 'I hope you were wearing clean pants. Always wear clean pants, Francis. My mother used to say that all the time. In case you get run over. Were you wearing clean pants, Francis?'

'Yes.'

Which was the simple answer. Frank had been wearing clean pants when he was run over. Or at least right up until the point when he was run over, which was when his clean pants became dirty pants.

Somewhere at the beginning of Frank's hospital trip a member of the NHS had removed Frank's pants. Somebody else had washed them and they were returned to him in the carrier bag with the pint of milk when he left the hospital. Frank went commando in the ambulance home and left the pants in the ambulance with the milk. Two weeks after the accident a padded envelope arrived in the post containing his underpants with a West Sussex Ambulance Service compliments slip. At least they hadn't sent the milk. Yet.

Frank put on the newest-looking pair of underpants he could find. He had thought about putting them in the boiling water with the tweezers to give them a new lease of life but there wasn't time to dry them and he worried that Kelly might notice that his flat smelled of boiled pants.

He put on his best pair of trousers and took the plastic and cardboard stiffeners and pins out of his latest charity shop shirt, making sure he removed all the pins this time. He buttoned the shirt and looked at himself in the mirror. Yes. Awful. Frank had had a lot of conversations with the man looking back at him from the mirror. Sometimes he didn't speak to anybody else for days. Frank would pull faces at him and the man in the mirror would mimic him. It was a good Frank Derrick impression.

He took off his glasses and twisted them to make them a bit straighter. He put them back on. They were still askew. He tilted his head slightly to compensate, as though he was straightening a painting on a lopsided wall. He wished he had his new glasses. They should arrive in two to three weeks, Spencer had said.

Spencer was the optician who'd come round a few days ago to give Frank his free eye test. He wore incredibly thick-lensed glasses in the same way that all barbers have bald-heads. As Spencer followed Frank up the stairs and into the living room Frank tried to remember everything he'd said on the phone when he'd booked his free eye test.

'This shouldn't take too long,' Spencer said.

This is a free eye test, Frank told himself.

'This is a nice flat,' Spencer said.

I am not in a shop.

Spencer set up his equipment.

'Great natural light,' he said.

This is my home.

'Have you lived here long?'

I will not be made to feel obliged to buy anything.

'South-facing garden?'

I will not provide my bank account details.

'My wife would love this wallpaper.'

I will not get sucked into buying any glasses.

'This won't take too long.'

I will have the advertised free eye test and ask for a copy of the prescription and then I will order some glasses from the Internet for less than half the price.

'You have great hair.'

After twenty minutes of reading letters off charts, staring into various bits of machinery and having air puffed at his eyeballs, Frank found himself trying on glasses. A further twenty minutes later Spencer was putting an order into a folder for a pair of glasses that would make Frank look like a Belgian architect and also for a half-price pair of matching sunglasses. If he checked his bank account he would have found that he was now £19.85 overdrawn. A bank computer was already calculating a fine and a fee and typing a letter to him, the letter would put him a further fifteen pounds in the red.

Frank slapped his face with aftershave and it stung. He felt something soft brush his leg. He looked down. Bill had woken up and was standing by his feet waiting to be fed.

'What do you think?' Frank said and he pulled his best-man-in-a-mail-order-catalogue pose. He looked at Bill, hoping to work out what he was thinking. It should have been easier than usual as it was only one word.

Poof.

Frank fed Bill and let him outside and then went back upstairs into the living room to wait for Kelly. On the floor by his armchair he'd placed three photo albums with tartan covers. They were full of family photographs. The albums were arranged at different angles to each other. It had taken him ten minutes to make them look like he'd simply left them there like that without any thought. At five to eleven he pressed play on his CD player, he sat down in his armchair and tried to make himself look as much like a fan of Madonna as it was possible for an eighty-one-year-old poorly shaved idiot in a flowery shirt to be.

At first Frank thought Kelly had a new car when she parked the big white vehicle opposite. In spite of its greater size it was obviously easier to drive than the little blue one. She didn't bump the bollards or crunch the gears. There was no stereo in this car. Kelly wasn't singing along or nodding her head to music. The news could be on, of course. Or the weather, or an advert, or even a song that Kelly didn't like or know the words to.

She was out of the car a few minutes earlier than usual. The clock in the car was probably fast. Or maybe there wasn't a clock in the car either. She'd had her hair done. No geometrically spirit-levelled fringe any more. But not the same as in her Internet photograph either. And she'd put on a few pounds as well. And a few years. She walked differently. If his Belgian architect's glasses had arrived, Frank would have been certain that this wasn't Kelly. Although even without the glasses he knew that this wasn't Kelly.

He watched her cross the road and he started to panic.

The doorbell rang.

He decided he wouldn't answer it.

It rang again. For longer this time. There was a knock as well.

Just wait, Frank thought, she'll go away.

The doorbell rang a third time. She wasn't giving up. She knocked again.

There was a minute's silence, just Frank's heavy breathing as he waited for the doorbell to ring again or for her to leave. And then the phone rang. Frank jumped and squealed like Bill did when he trod on his tail. He made his way across the room and picked up the phone. He was scared to speak straight away.

'Hello?' he said.

'Is that Mr Derrick?'

'Yes.'

'Your care visitor is outside. She says you aren't answering the door.'

'Oh. Er, I was in the bathroom.'

100

'If you could let her in.'

'Oh right, er, yes. There's a key safe.'

'I'm afraid she may not know about that. Could you make it to the door, do you think? Are you on the ground floor?'

'The first.'

'Ah, right. Would you be able to make it down the stairs, do you think?'

'Yes, all right. I'll answer the door now.'

Frank hung up the phone and made his way down the stairs. He could see the shape of the care worker in soft focus through the frosted glass of his front door. It wasn't soft enough. He opened the door.

'Mr Derrick? I've been waiting for five minutes.'

Frank took a step back. He couldn't remember seeing the woman's photograph on the Lemons Care website, which wasn't surprising. She wasn't the face of the company. Michael Aspel would have pulled out of presenting the Miss Care Worker contest in disgust.

'Yes, I'm sorry,' Frank said. 'I was in the—'

'Is the bell broken? I could hear it ringing.' She spoke so firmly it was more like quiet shouting.

'Yes, sorry, I—'

'Well, come on. Let's get on with it, shall we? I've already lost five minutes.'

This was more like it. This was what he'd been expecting in the first place. This was who his dirty protest had been intended for. Robin Williams in a dress. Margaret Thatcher in a bad mood. He wanted to freeze time so that he could go upstairs and make a mess, throw some food on the floor and do a big shit in the toilet and not flush it. He would have to email his daughter and tell her. He'd have nothing to hide now. The woman followed him up the stairs, almost knocking him over and climbing over him. He felt under pressure to speed his walk up and nearly tripped up. They went into the living room.

'Why don't you sit down?' she said. It felt like an order or a threat.

'My name is Janice.' Frank didn't care what her name was.

She walked over to the stereo and switched it off. She picked up the photo albums. 'Let's get these out of harm's way. We don't want to trip over them, do we?' She put the albums on the bookshelf where they didn't belong. 'How have you been managing, Mr Derrick?' She took his file out of her bag. 'Have you been going to the toilet successfully?' She talked down to him as though he was the stupidest child in the world. 'Are you clean? How long has that toe been broken?'

'I—'

'It should be healed by now.'

'I think it—'

Like Kelly's, Janice's questions were all rhetorical but, unlike Kelly, Janice had absolutely no interest in Frank's answers.

'Can you walk?'

'I—'

'You should be walking by now. What's that smell? Are you clean?' If she asked him whether he wanted a bath he was going to jump through the window. He wondered whether he could pick up enough speed to break the glass. She asked more questions. Not leaving Frank enough space to answer before she asked the next question. She pointed at his plaster cast. 'Shouldn't that be off?' She stuck a

102

thermometer in his mouth before he could answer.

'Where's the vacuum cleaner?' She was already out in the hall opening the cupboard and finding the vacuum cleaner herself. She seemed to know where it would be. It was as though she'd been round earlier and cased the joint, or had a particularly sensitive nose for seeking out household cleaning appliances. It was certainly big enough, her nose. Big. Long. Ugly. Like the Witch in the *Wizard of Oz*'s nose. Maybe Frank could click the heels of his slippers together.

'There's no place like home, there's no place like home.'

Janice came back in with the vacuum cleaner, plugged it in and started aggressively hoovering the living-room carpet.

'Up,' she said, instructing Frank to lift his feet, and she hoovered under them. She carried on asking him questions but he couldn't hear what she was saying above the sound of the Hoover. And it wasn't easy to answer with the ther- mometer in his mouth. It was just like his boiling-kettle conversations with Kelly.

It was nothing like his boiling-kettle conversations with Kelly.

Janice finished hoovering and then went into the kitchen to noisily do the washing-up. It sounded like she was playing the drums in a hurry, trying to get to the end of the song before the rest of the band. Frank had had the thermometer in his mouth for a long time now. If he didn't have a temperature before she arrived, he most certainly had one now. Janice came back in and removed the thermometer and looked at the reading.

She looked at Frank. It was the first time she'd stood still for longer than two seconds since she'd arrived.

'You'd be a lot more comfortable with shorter hair, you know,' she said. 'We can get somebody to come round.'

She walked out of the living room and went into Frank's bedroom, where she remade his bed, tucking the sheets and blanket under the mattress with hospital corners so tight that he was going to need to cut his way into bed. She came back into the living room with a glass of water and stood over Frank while he took his tablets.

'Make sure you swallow them. Have you swallowed them?' She took the glass away from him and took it out to the kitchen to wash it up and hurriedly play the drums some more.

When she had left, it felt like a whirlwind had swept through his flat. There was an eerie silence. What had just happened? Had it even happened? Frank felt like he'd been beaten up. Like a victim on a crime reconstruction show. But he didn't need or want a reconstruction and he was definitely going to have nightmares. Just half an hour with Janice had left Frank feeling exhausted, both physically and mentally. She'd set his recovery back at least two Kelly visits. And he hadn't even asked her what he really needed to ask, 'Where is Kelly?'

When Hurricane Janice had died down and volunteers were sweeping up the debris and boarding up broken windows and the National Guard were chasing away looters, Frank rang Lemons Care.

'I'm afraid Kelly has some sort of allergy,' the woman on the phone said. 'She does suffer with them. They can be quite debilitating. All kinds of things can set an attack off. Nuts, wasp stings, a high pollen count, cats, particularly cats. How was Janice?'

16

Graham wasn't in his office in the reception of Greyflick House, so Frank signed himself in to the visitors' book on the counter. Name: Frank Derrick. Visiting: John. Time in: 11 a.m. He walked to the lift. There was a 'lift out of order' sign taped across the door.

He turned and walked a short way along the corridor and went through a fire door where he found Smelly John's empty wheelchair at the bottom of a carpeted flight of stairs. Frank looked up and saw Graham, six steps up and breathing heavily, beads of sweat dripping down his face, as he tentatively made his way down the staircase with Smelly John cradled in his arms like his newly-wed bride whom he was carrying over a series of descending thresholds.

'Francis!' John called out and waved.

Graham carefully moved down a step and stopped to get his breath back and readdress his balance. He bounced Smelly John in his arms to get a better grip, like you might do with a sleeping child or a heavy television you've just bought and are carrying home. Graham seemed a lot more concerned about dropping John than John did about being dropped. John was enjoying the ride. He would probably shout Stairs! when he got to the bottom.

'The lift is broken,' John said to Frank. He gestured to Graham with a nod of his head – 'Hence.' Graham took another step. 'This is the third time he's had to do this this morning.' Graham must surely have been considering dropping John or at least throwing him at his wheelchair. 'I keep forgetting things,' John said.

Graham climbed the last step and placed John in his wheelchair. Between puffs and pants Graham asked Frank if he'd signed in. He said yes and the warden went back to his office to pass out. Frank and John went along the corridor towards the lounge.

'Don't you find it a bit degrading?' Frank said.

'What's that?'

'Having to be carried up and down stairs.'

'I don't,' John said. 'But he does.' Frank held the lounge door open and John wheeled himself in. He parked himself in his usual spot. Frank sat down at the table opposite.

'Mouse Trap or Jenga?' John said.

Frank said he didn't mind and John combined both games by using his Jenga skills to carefully pull the Mouse Trap box from the middle of the pile of board games on the shelf. 'Will your cat be okay?' he said, pausing halfway through removing the lid from the Mouse Trap box. 'With all these mice?'

Frank looked down at the cat box he'd just put on the floor by his foot.

'It's empty,' he said.

Even with his red tartan blanket and his favourite ball of wool inside, Bill hadn't liked getting into the cardboard cat box. He hissed and spat and meowed swear words, showing his teeth and pulling the first easy-to-interpret facial expression that Frank had seen in all the eight years that he'd known him. On the back of Frank's hand there were three scratches. Probably not deep enough to ordinarily scar but, as he had so cleverly pointed out himself, at his age, every cut was a scar.

Of course, Kelly could have been stung by a wasp or eaten a nut; everything seemed to at least run the risk of containing nuts these days. She might just have had a bad attack of hay fever or been in a room plagued with dust mites. A number of things could have made her sneeze, her eyes watering and her throat feeling like she was gargling razor blades and chewing on a stinging nettle. It was the doubt that made Frank climb up on his stool ladder and almost break his other arm trying to reach far enough into the loft to get the cardboard box with the air holes and the lid that folded together to form a handle.

Bill must have guessed something was up when Frank had scooped his breakfast out onto the saucer from a square tin. A square tin! The expensive cat food came in the square tins. Why so posh all of a sudden, Frank? What's going on? Is it someone's birthday? Have we finally won the lottery? And what's this? Rainbow trout in sauce flavour? On a Tuesday morning. Wait a moment, Bill would have thought. Something is definitely a bit fishy. And it wasn't just the rainbow trout. And that box. Bill had been in it two times before. One time somebody cut his balls off and the other time he came home with his head inside a plastic funnel. He certainly wasn't getting in that bloody box again without a fight.

Frank tried to calm Bill down by telling him that he'd

107

come back and get him in a couple of months' time when Kelly's visits were over. He convinced himself that Bill would still be at the dog and cats home then. When people were choosing which cat to adopt they tended towards the more unusually patterned cats and those with characteristics that matched the names written on the signs above their cages. Black cats called Sooty and white cats called Snowy, black cats with white feet called Sox, ginger cats called Ginger. Tortoiseshell cats called Tortoise. Bill was a plain-looking cat. A plain-looking cat called Bill. Who wants a plain cat called Bill? A dog, maybe, but a cat?

Often when people came into the Diamond Dogs and Love Cats Dog and Cats Home looking for a cat they left with a dog. The photographs of homeless dogs hanging on the wall in the reception area of the large building behind the big Sainsbury's were enough to make people change their minds from cat to dog at the last minute. Dogs had an unfair advantage over cats. In the reception photographs they were all doing that thing where they tip their heads at an angle to convey sadness, arching their eyebrows – or at least the illusion of eyebrows, that lumpy bit above their sad take-me-home-with-you eyes. A picture of a sad-eyed dog on an animal-charity brochure made people actually use the stubby free biros for what they were intended for. What did cats have? One face. Frank's Nazi poodle would stand a better chance of adoption than most cats.

Frank told the young woman in the reception of Diamond Dogs and Love Cats how he'd become too old and infirm to look after a pet any more. He exaggerated his frailty in the same way he'd done for Kelly to make her keep opening the key safe every Monday.

'It's probably for the best,' he said, putting his plaster-cast arm on the reception desk. 'I'm eighty-one.' He tilted his head at an angle and arched his eyebrows like one of the sad-faced puppies on the wall.

The woman behind the desk got Frank to fill in a form.

'What's your cat's name?' she said.

'Bill.'

'Bill? That's an interesting name for a cat.'

'There used to be another cat called Ben.'

The woman didn't seem to understand. 'Bill and Ben,' Frank said. The woman still seemed confused. 'The Flower-pot Men. Flobadob ickle Weeed.'

The woman now knew Frank was obviously not well and decided the best way to deal with him was by talking to him like she would a puppy or a kitten.

'Now you leave Bill with us,' she said. She opened the cat box and took Bill out. 'Don't you worry about a thing.' She opened the door of a transparent plastic crate, put Bill inside and closed the door. She wrote 'Bill' on a white card and slotted it into a space on the door of the crate. The woman made a short phone call asking somebody to come and collect the crate and she handed the empty cardboard cat box back to Frank. It was the first time he'd held the box without it shaking violently since he'd taken it out of the loft. All the way to the bus stop Bill had tried to escape, attempting to claw his way through the cardboard. And then on the bus he continued to struggle and fidget inside the box, making it shake and rattle on Frank's lap so much that all the old women giggled and whispered to each other, presumably about Frank's penis.

A man came through a pair of swing doors into the

Diamond Dogs and Love Cats reception. He picked up the plastic crate and walked back through the doors. Frank could see the start of a corridor and he heard dogs barking. When the doors closed the barking increased, presumably because of the arrival of a cat. Frank imagined Bill being taken along the corridor, with pit bulls and Rottweilers on either side, snarling and barking abuse and throwing spunk at him like he was Jodie Foster.

The woman behind the reception desk looked up from her desk and was surprised to see Frank still there. She smiled.

'That's everything,' she said.

Frank took the empty cat box and left. He tried to re-assure himself that at the end of the corridor of angry and dangerous dogs it would be like Greyflick House. Boring sometimes, but not so bad. All the cats would be sitting in different armchairs, drinking tea from green teacups, watching television or singing along with the songs of the 1940s. One of them would be called Smelly Cat – like the one from *Friends* – yes, Frank had seen *Friends* – and Bill would go over and sit with him and they'd play Kerplunk!

If only, before the swing doors had swung closed, he hadn't seen Bill's face through the back of the transparent plastic crate. It was the same blank expression as always, but for the first time Frank understood exactly what it was that Bill was thinking.

Judas.

John shook the dice in his hand for ages and threw it across the Mouse Trap board.

'Another one has bitten the dust,' he said.

'Another what has what the what?' Frank said.

John did a brief Hitler moustache and salute. He pointed at the over-made-up German woman's empty armchair.

'It's the second death this year. The BBC will be doing an undercover investigation soon.' He set up the Mouse Trap board. Frank was already contemplating disappointment for the end of the game when the trap inevitably didn't work properly.

There were half a dozen other residents in the lounge, watching television, reading or dozing off. At least one man looked dead. He looked the least bored. Being dead was the only thing preventing him from pulling up FOR SALE signs, kicking over concrete bollards and changing the sign on the front of the building to Greyfuck House.

'I remember when this was all fields,' Frank said. 'Shall we go out?'

'You've just got here.'

'It doesn't matter. Let's go out. For a change.'

'I've set the board up now.'

'We should definitely go out.'

'What for?'

'I don't know. Fresh air? People?'

'There are people here. I don't particularly like people.'

'Neither do I. The sky, then. There's a lot if it out there. Clouds. Birds. Flowers. Trees.'

'I've got a tree outside my window. I can see a tree any day I want.'

'It's got a bag of dog shit in it.' Frank knew that John wasn't going to give in. 'If I owned this place, there'd be a swimming pool,' he said. He threw the dice.

111

'It does mean there's a vacancy,' John said. Gesturing again at the empty armchair. 'You should apply.'

'I've already got an armchair,' Frank said. He knew John was talking about the empty flat. He was always trying to get him to move into Greyflick House. In spite of all his punk rock bravado, his rebellious ways and his mischief-making, John was lonely. Lonely John. That was his Sioux name.

'Not the chair. The apartment.'

Frank moved his plastic mouse along the board. 'I don't think so,' he said.

'It's a nice apartment. Much better than mine.'

'I've got a flat.'

'Apartment,' John corrected him. 'A ground-floor apartment. No more stairs, Francis.' He shook the dice in his hand for a long time.

'Why don't you take it, then?'

'I like riding the lift.'

'The lift is always broken. Are you going to throw that dice or not? It's irrelevant anyway. I could never afford the rent.'

'Have you got any savings?' John said, and finally released the dice onto the board.

Frank laughed. 'No. I haven't got any savings.'

'Then let the Government pay. Take a little something back, Francis.'

'Is that how you manage?'

'Me?' John said. 'A black man in a wheelchair? They'd pay *me* to live here.' He was suddenly distracted by something on the table. 'Bastard,' he said. He started sorting through the Mouse Trap pieces. 'Bathtub, seesaw. Bastard.'

'What is it?' Frank said.

'He's stolen the diver.'

'What? Who has?'

'And the marble.'

'Who has?'

'Graham.'

'Why would he do that? Are you sure? Perhaps you've just lost them.'

John just kept shaking his head and repeating the word 'Bastard' over and over again. 'The racist bastard.'

The thought of John losing one of his marbles would later make Frank think about why Beth had sent him a leaflet about dementia. He'd presumed it was just something they did in America like Stranger Danger or Thanksgiving. But what if she'd noticed telltale signs when they spoke on the phone. Was it something he'd be aware of himself? She might have even seen something before she moved away. Perhaps it was the reason why she moved. He needed a bigger leaflet.

17

The skies above Frank's flat were quiet. He'd been lying awake in bed for what felt like a long time. He could feel the heat of the early morning sun coming through the bedroom window and he could see light between the threads of his new thick curtains. And yet he hadn't heard a single plane yet. He wondered if the world outside had ended, or changed somehow. When he got out of bed and went downstairs to get his newspaper, would the headlines be about a terrorist attack, an alien invasion, or just another volcanic ash cloud grounding all flights? On page four or five, would he read about a Spanish air traffic controllers' strike or a French baggage handlers' dispute? This month's edition of the village newsletter was due. Maybe it would arrive on Frank's doormat with a story about the United Nations declaring the skies above Fullwind-on-Sea a no-fly zone in retaliation for heavy-handed tactics towards its civilians over the state of their gardens and how it might affect their chances in the Villages in Bloom competition.

'Maybe nobody wants to travel anywhere today, Bill,' Frank said, and then remembered that Bill wasn't there. Even though he thought he could still feel the weight of the cat on his legs. It was the same phantom sensation people sometimes experience after having a limb amputated, or how a nurse had told him he might feel when his plaster cast was eventually removed.

Frank had had a restless night. Before going to bed he'd watched another television crime reconstruction show. In the programme a man in his seventies was filmed on CCTV being punched in the face by a gang of eleven-year-old girls. Then an old lady let a man into her home to phone his sick mother and he stole the old lady's handbag and pushed her down the stairs. There was also a report about a gang of bogus workmen travelling around the country, tricking their way into the homes of pensioners to investigate a gas leak following an explosion nearby. Once inside, they would steal any money and valuables they could find. Next, there was a general round-up of other unsolved crimes and an appeal for witnesses who might have seen a man in the Manchester area who liked to kick the walking sticks away from the elderly. The programme finished with another reconstruction. In this one an elderly man was tied to a chair with a skipping rope, then burned with a cigarette and whipped with the plug from his electric fire until he gave up his debit card pin number. Before the final credits, the show's presenter told everyone not to have nightmares. That night Frank had a nightmare that he was tied to a chair and whipped with an electric plug.

Shaking the ghost of Bill onto the floor, Frank sat up on the edge of the bed, put his glasses on and looked at his watch. It was 6.30 a.m. He'd hoped it was later. Apart from anything else, getting rid of Bill had given him even less to do. There were going to be at least two cat-food tin open-ing-shaped holes in his day. And then there was the time he spent letting Bill in and out, filling and emptying his litter tray and disposing of any dead mice and birds that Bill had brought into the flat. And who was he going to talk to now?

He went downstairs and picked up the newspaper, two red energy bills and the first junk mail of the day. He made a cup of tea and read the day and the date out from the top of the newspaper and announced the weather forecast in the voice of Ron the marbles man. These were all things he normally shared with Bill. Now he was just a lonely old man talking to himself.

After breakfast, Frank took all the cat food out of the cupboard and put it into the cardboard cat box with the tartan blanket and the ball of wool. He got Bill's basket and cat-litter tray and took everything downstairs and out to the garden shed.

When Frank and his wife had first moved into the flat, the shed was going to be their cinema. It was Frank's dream. His retirement plan. He was going to soundproof the shed and lay red carpet and buy matching red cinema seats from a salvage yard. He would install a screen and a surround-sound system and he'd stand at the back of the cinema and show films on a projector. He started buying 16mm films and looking for seats, carpet and a suitable projector. When the cinema was finished he'd sell tickets to the neighbours and all the new friends he and Sheila had made in Fullwind. Sheila would be the usherette, tearing the tickets, showing people to their seats and selling ice creams and soft drinks between reels.

Frank made drawings of how his cinema would look. He browsed the small ads sections of newspapers and looked in specialist film magazines for films and old cinema fixtures and fittings. He made lists of the movies he wanted to show and of the name he was going to give to the cinema – The Roxy, The Regent, Frank's Picture Palace, Frank and Sheila's Movie House, The Garden Odeon, etc. All the time he was planning his cinema Frank filled the shed with garden tools and summer outdoor furniture and things that were too large or too heavy to fit through the square hole into the loft. Soon there was no room in the shed for a single flip-back cinema seat and what with the convenience of DVDs, televisions bigger than cinema screens, home-movie systems, Sheila's death and not making any new friends in Fullwind, Frank never got round to making his dream come true.

He dragged the shed door open, battling against the ivy that had a stranglehold on the door and everything inside the shed. It had grown upwards through the floor and came in through knotholes in the wooden sides of the shed. It snuck in under the roof and prised the glass away to get in through the window. The ivy wrapped itself around garden tools and deckchairs. Threading itself through the rungs of an old rotting stepladder at the back of the shed. It was like *The Day of the Triffids* – a film on the programming schedule for the doomed cinema. Frank feared that if he ventured too far inside the shed, the ivy would take hold of his arms and legs and drag him in to finish him off with its poisonous stinger.

He slotted the cat box, the basket and litter tray in between the cobwebs and the spiders' webs and shut the door.

In Fullwind Food & Wine Frank bought a large yellow sponge, a pack of cheap cloths, some white vinegar and an onion. Back at his flat he got down on his hands and knees – something else that was difficult with one unbendable arm, but nowhere near as hard as getting back up again – and he reached under the bed in Beth's room. Using the knitting needle that Kelly had scratched his itch with, he flicked what was left of the dead mouse until it appeared from under the bed. He picked it up between the tips of his thumb and forefinger and put it in a black rubbish bag.

Frank vacuumed any carpets where he thought there might be cat hair, and with the sticky side of some parcel tape wrapped around his hand, he got back down on his knees to pick up any cat hair that was left behind.

He squeezed the dainty yellow rubber gloves Kelly had left behind after the food clear-out onto his not-so-dainty hands and washed the kitchen floor with a mixture of washing-up liquid, water and white vinegar. He felt as though he was cleaning up a crime scene. Which, in a way, he was. Once he'd finished cleaning he cut an onion in half and left one half in the kitchen and the other in the living room. It was something he'd seen on daytime television. Apparently, it neutralised bad smells. He sat down in his armchair, exhausted and with a strange craving for fish and chips.

That night, sometime between the last plane of the day landing and the first plane of the next day taking off, Frank suddenly woke up. He reached over to the bedside table for his glasses and his watch. It was almost 3 a.m. and he needed to go to the toilet. He tried to put it out of his mind and go back to sleep but the need was too strong. He could just piss the bed. It was almost expected of him. There had to be a few perks other than a bus pass and a free TV licence. Maybe when he was eighty-two . . .

He climbed out of bed and made his way down the hall to the toilet. He shut the toilet door and flicked the light switch. The bulb fizzed for a bit and then popped, leaving him standing in the darkness with his pyjama trousers around his ankles pissing on the floor – or the wall, the ceiling, the window, who knew, maybe even into the toilet; he couldn't see. Unable to do much about it while his bladder was still half full, or half empty – depending on your outlook on life – Frank finished pissing. Every time he heard the sound of liquid hitting porcelain or splashing into the water in the toilet bowl he attempted to steady his aim but it was surprisingly difficult in the dark, half asleep and left-handed.

He pulled up his pyjama trousers. They were wet. He went to the kitchen to get a light bulb so that he could assess the damage. The kitchen drawer was full of free energy-saving light bulbs given to Frank by Age Concern, the Government, the Green Party and three different electricity companies. There were another ten in the cupboard. It was all very lovely for the environment but in a flat where all the light fittings were for old-fashioned bayonet bulbs, the screw-fit bulbs were as useful as a kitchen cupboard full of chocolate teapots.

He thought about taking a bulb out of the table lamp in the living room and using that, but replacing a bulb at three in the morning in the dark with pissy pyjamas and his arm in plaster would probably be impossible. He'd end up falling into the toilet, pulling the tiny curtain away from the window as he tried to stop himself. He'd knock the bottle of bleach from the shelf onto his head and end up with his leg stuck in the U-bend of the toilet while his hair gradually turned blond. He would have to wait until either he lost enough weight to flush himself down the loo or until he was discovered dead, like a West Sussex Elvis.

It would be Kelly who would find him. In a worse condition than if she'd found him in a bath of children's bubbles. His body – or at least part of his body – would have been in water for a lot longer. A situation exacerbated for an extra twenty-four hours by yet another bank holiday.

While everyone else was cleaning their cars, doing DIY, Morris dancing or chasing a cheese down a hill, Frank would be standing in a toilet pickling his leg.

He decided to go back to bed and clean up the mess when it was light. The piss would have dried by the morning. It would be sticky and unpleasant but he'd cleaned up Bill's piss enough times in the past. It would be almost nostalgic.

The next few days flew by with the usual heady mix of cold-calls, daytime television and junk mail. On Thursday, Frank washed the toilet floor and climbed on his stool ladder to answer the question, 'How many one-armed octogenarians does it take to change a light bulb?' It's one. But it's difficult. Boom-tish.

On Friday, he went to Fullwind Food & Wine and bought four tins of cat food. He bought three DVDs and a china mantelpiece dog hiding inside a china mantelpiece fedora hat from the charity shop and went to the library to look at Kelly's Internet photograph. While he was in the library he gave two people Sioux names – Farts in Libraries and Too Old to Be Reading Children's Books. On the way home the handle broke on his bag for life, sending tins of cat food rolling into the road, which was when he remembered he was tired of metaphors and also that he didn't have a cat any more.

18

On Monday people all over the country were enjoying a lie-in. They'd woken up, stretched, groaned, sighed and then realised it was a bank holiday and turned over and gone back to sleep. It was a great feeling. Similar to the sensation they'd felt the night before when the theme tune to *Last of the Summer Wine* or *The Antiques Roadshow* had just started to make them feel nauseous until they remembered there wasn't actually any work or school in the morning.

For Frank it was just another day. Just like any other Monday before his accident. Back when there was no Kelly to mark the day out as different. There wasn't even a party in an old people's home celebrating the end of a war to go to. The war was still on.

Frank was in the kitchen. The woman in the flat downstairs was looking after her grandson for the day. After the success of his previous world record for kicking a ball repeatedly against a wall, somebody had bought him a whistle for his next world record attempt. Frank was picturing what he'd like to do with the boy's whistle when he thought he heard Kelly's voice.

'Mr Derrick?'

It was coming from the bottom of the stairs.

'Are you in?'

Frank stepped out into the hall. He was confused. Was this it? Had he forgotten to tear a date off his calendar? Had he lost a day? Was today tomorrow? He stood in the hall until Kelly appeared on the landing at the top of the stairs. It was mufti day for the home-care industry. Instead of her usual shiny blue uniform she was wearing jeans and a bright orange hooded sweatshirt with the picture of a monkey on the front. She had the hood pulled up over her head. The hood had monkey ears.

'Get your bucket and spade,' she said. 'We're going to the beach.'

'Isn't it a bank holiday today?'

'Yes,' Kelly said. She clapped her hands. 'Exactly. Get your shoes on. We're going to the seaside.'

'But—'

'What do you mean "but"? Come on.' She dragged the word 'on' out to emphasise the urgency.

'Is it jacket weather?' Frank said.

'Who cares? Bring one just in case.'

Frank took his jacket off a coat hook on the landing wall and thought about the twenty minutes it was going to take him to get it on. Kelly held her hand out, Frank gave her the jacket and she helped him put it on – even Houdini must have had an assistant.

'I feel guilty making you lose out on your day off,' Frank said.

'I'll tell you what,' Kelly said. 'If it makes you feel better I won't come tomorrow. I'll have a bank holiday Tuesday. Agreed?'

Frank nodded. He didn't want her not to come tomorrow

but he would deal with that then. He reached for his walking stick hanging on the same hook the jacket had been on.

'Do you need that?' Kelly said. It wasn't really a question. Frank left the stick on the hook.

Frank hoped the neighbours were watching as he climbed into the little blue car. He hoped Hilary was writing all the details down in her incidents book. He hoped she'd seen him follow Kelly down the path without his stick. He wanted Hilary to see Kelly open the passenger door of the car and adjust the seat, moving it back to give him more leg room. He hoped that Hilary had made a note of how Kelly had passed him the end of his seatbelt and told him to mind his fingers as she shut the passenger door and walked around the car to climb in next to him. As Kelly pulled the car away from the grass verge, Frank wanted her to knock some bollards over, turn the stereo up really loud and toot her horn, just in case people hadn't seen them.

Kelly pressed a switch to open Frank's window. 'Let me know if it's too windy,' she said.

He looked out of the window and let the wind blow his long hair across his face. He closed his eyes. Passers-by could have been mistaken for thinking someone was taking their Afghan hound out for the day.

Frank hadn't been in the front seat of a car for a long time. He'd been in the back of taxis and the back of an ambulance and he'd been on the bus to the big Sainsbury's a lot, but the bus driver had never let Frank sit next to him up the front.

As they drove down Sea Lane it occurred to him that he

hadn't been in this direction along the road for ages. When he left his house he always turned left, towards the charity shop, Fullwind Food & Wine or the chemist, to the library or the bus stop. He was like one of those Tibetan monks he'd seen on a documentary who only walked in a clockwise direction. He'd almost forgotten why the road he lived on had been given its name. Sea Lane's Sioux name.

Kelly was almost as bad at driving as she was at parking. The poor condition of the road didn't help and the car bumped in and out of potholes. The road really was in an awful state, Frank thought. It was all the big lorries. The road was never built for the amount of traffic that drove up and down it, and not at the speed they travelled either – everyone ignoring the twenty-mile-per-hour signs and driving at fifty over the white '20's painted on the road surface.

When Frank and Sheila first moved to Fullwind, it was a quiet village with hardly any traffic. There were no pavements and so they walked in the road. Occasionally, one of them would call out 'Car!' and they'd both step close to the verge and wait for the car to pass. The driver would wave and say 'thank you' as they drove slowly by. Now everyone drove as fast as they could, without indicating or caring whether they ran a couple of elderly pedestrians over.

Frank didn't say any of this to Kelly. It would make him sound old. Even though she knew how old he was. It was practically the first thing she saw when she took his file out every Monday – just below his name, Frank Derrick. 'Age: 81'. She typed his birthday into the key safe every week. She knew exactly how old he was. But ever since his thirties or forties Frank had felt uncomfortable about his age. It was the same when he was fifty and he really hated it when he turned sixty. He surely should have grown out of it by his seventieth birthday but he didn't like that either. And then it was just as bad when he was eighty. Frank had a fairly childish attitude to growing old. Don't buy him a numbered birthday card or one with a hilarious joke inside about how he was so old that – blah blah blah – because he won't appreciate it.

So Frank kept his thoughts on the condition of the road to himself. He didn't complain about everyone's lack of driving skills – Kelly's included, Kelly's in particular, especially when she took both hands off the wheel to open a packet of sweets or to adjust her hair – because he wanted her to think he was cool. Not like her other bald old gentlemen, who Frank imagined wouldn't know who Madonna or the Arctic Monkeys were and would have asked, 'The sex what?' when Smelly John talked about the Sex Pistols. Frank didn't want Kelly to think that he was an old fart. He didn't want that to be his Sioux name. As they drove by the red triangular *Elderly People* sign, he hated the idea that it had anything to do with him.

The buildings at the southern end of Sea Lane were as single-floored as those at the north end, but the nearer they drove to the sea, the wider, longer and more elaborate the bungalows became, the larger the gardens and grander the outbuildings. The more like a Monkees song. There was more lawn for the weekend squire to mow, more roses for Mrs Gray to feel proud about. Bigger garages for bigger cars. There were a couple of swimming pools. The closer your house was to the sea the more it was going to be worth, and if you had a sea view, even more so. When Frank and Kelly reached the beach they'd walk past a row of beach

126

huts that had been on the news after someone had painted them in bright colours, plumbed in electricity and running water and advertised them for sale as beach-front studio apartments.

Kelly parked the car on the nearest road to the beach – when they returned to the car later there would be a note under her windscreen wipers politely asking her to kindly not park there, the words 'kindly' and 'politely' both underlined to show they meant neither – and they walked along the alleyway that led to the sea.

The high walls on either side of the alley were built from beach stones and the mortar or cement that held them together was green with what Frank presumed was either moss or something to do with the seawater. Because of the high walls it was quiet in the alleyway, like being in a subway between busy roads and Frank had the urge to shout out to see if his voice would return as an echo. He wanted to at least stamp his feet.

He could smell the sea. He could smell the seaweed and the tar melting in the sunshine on the driftwood and the cuttlefish bones. He thought he could smell vanilla ice cream and the heat from the running engine of the ice cream van – one smell filtered through another to create a new one – but he presumed it must be a memory, because unless they'd built a road since the last time he was here, there was no access to the beach for an ice cream van. He listened out for 'Greensleeves'.

They walked out of the alleyway into a salty coastal wind and Frank wished he had slightly shorter hair as it whipped him about the face. They walked to the low stone wall that ran alongside the path and they saw the sea. The tide was halfway up the sand about fifty yards away. Far out to sea a speedboat bumped up and down in the water. From this far away the water was blue. Up close it would be either green or brown.

They climbed the three stone steps that took them over the wall to the top of the hill of stones. Frank felt unsteady on the uneven ground; Kelly took hold of his arm and they made their way down towards the sand.

'Is the tide coming in or going out?' Kelly said.

'That depends on whether you're an optimist or a pessimist.'

'An optimist.'

'Now,' Frank said, 'is the beach the glass? Or is the sand beneath the water the glass? Or perhaps France is the glass. Are you French?'

'French? No.'

'Hmmm,' Frank said. He suggested they buy a guide from the café for a more accurate tide report. 'If they still sell them,' he said. 'I expect they have a tidal text message service now. Or an app.' Yes, Frank knew what an app was, although it wasn't a word he'd ever used before. This was the very first time. He was trying very hard to be the Fonz. 'Or we could see how soft the sand is and work it out from that.'

'You're very wise, Frank,' Kelly said.

'And a little bit Morecambe.' Frank waggled his glasses up and down like Eric Morecambe and the left arm of the glasses came away in his hand and the rest of the glasses fell onto the stones.

Kelly picked the glasses up.

'I've bought new ones,' Frank said. 'I'm waiting for them to arrive.'

Kelly unwrapped the insulation tape from the glasses. She put her hand in the pocket on the front of her sweatshirt and pulled out a small first-aid kit. It was as though she'd been expecting an accident to happen. She took a roll of fabric sticking plaster and a pair of nail scissors out of the first-aid kit and taped Frank's glasses together. She gave the glasses back to him, he put them on and they walked down towards the sand.

Frank had to tread carefully so as not to fall on the uneven stones. When he used to come here with Sheila he'd walk barefoot across the stones as though the beach was carpeted or his feet were made of shoes.

When they reached the sand, it was still wet. Frank guessed the tide was on its way out. Kelly took off her shoes and without discussing it, they started walking towards the sea.

The nearer they got to the water's edge the softer and wetter the sand became and the footprints they left behind were deeper, until the sand was so soft and wet their footprints didn't look like footprints at all, just momentary smudges, quickly swallowed up again by the sand.

They walked past pools of clear-looking water left behind by the tide and Frank wished he had the strength to lift up one of the slippery seaweed-covered rocks to find a crab underneath so that he could pick it up to frighten Kelly and show her what a tough guy he was.

All over the beach there were little coils of sand, worm castings left behind by burrowing lugworms.

'I always used to think they were actual worms,' Kelly said.

'They're left here by postmen,' Frank said. 'When they run out of red rubber bands.'

They stopped at the water's edge. Frank pointed out to sea. 'There's an old church out there. When the tide was low you used to be able to see the top of the spire.'

They both watched the gentle waves come in, hoping to see the spire.

'I can't see it,' Kelly said.

'Maybe the water is deeper than it used to be,' Frank said. 'Or it's sunk into the sand. I know the shore was further away then than it is now. People say they used to be able to hear the bell, tolling beneath the water. Usually at night.'

Kelly shivered. 'That's quite scary.'

Frank picked up a small flat stone and attempted to skim it across the water, using his right arm. The stone flew sideways and then almost back the way it came, landing on the sand behind him. Kelly suggested they should go to the café before Frank killed a child.

When they were back at the beginning of the hill of stones, Kelly lifted her feet one at a time to brush the sand off the soles of her feet and slip her shoes back on. She had a small tattoo on her left ankle. A flower. Frank decided it was more impressive than anything in the Villages in Bloom competition.

On the way back up the stones Frank said, 'I know it sounds daft but I think I recognise that tin can from about ten years ago. Over by the breakwater.' He pointed at a rusted fizzy orange can.

'Groyne,' Kelly said.

'Oh yes,' Frank said. 'Over by the groyne.'

'You've taught me something, Mr Derrick.'

Frank was only half joking about the drinks can. He genuinely thought he recognised and remembered it. He wondered, if he looked around for longer, whether he would find a stone that looked like his face and another that looked like Sheila's. Still there underneath the groyne where they'd left them on the beach all those years ago.

They walked back up the hill of stones, climbed the three steps over the low wall and walked along the path. They passed the colourfully painted and ludicrously priced beach huts and a lot of people walking their dogs. Frank joked about how strange it was that they all seemed to be carrying the same tiny bags of shopping.

The café was busy with bank holidaymakers and they joined the queue at the counter. While they waited to be served Kelly turned a carousel display of postcards depicting Fullwind-on-Sea from the past and present. Not much had changed. Next to the postcards there was a rack of flip-flops, straw hats and plastic sunglasses.

A couple sitting by a table near the café window stood up and left.

'Quick,' Kelly whispered, 'save that table.' Frank walked over to the table. 'What would you like?' Kelly asked.

'Just a cup of tea please.'

'No ice cream?'

'No thank you.'

'A lolly? Crisps? Cream bun? It is a holiday. You can show me the right way to eat it.'

'Just tea. Thank you, Kelly.' It was the first time he'd said her name out loud. Kelly. It felt uncomfortable. Inappropriate. As though he was a teacher and Kelly was his pupil.

'He's a teacher and she's his pupil,' Frank imagined a

woman on the other side of the café had just whispered to her friend. 'She called him Mr Derrick earlier. I heard the young girl say that he'd taught her something.' Frank felt people were staring at him and Kelly as soon as they'd come in the door. Trying to work out what their relationship was. Grandfather and granddaughter? Father and daughter? He was old enough and she was more than young enough for both to be true. They couldn't be a couple, the café Jimmy Stewarts probably thought. Unless he was rich, of course. He could be her sugar daddy.

Frank didn't have enough sugar to buy a beach hut.

He barely had enough to pay for the cup of tea.

Frank often felt the adverts in between daytime television shows were aimed directly at him. His television was talking to him. Always asking if he had money problems and whether he needed cash in a hurry.

If Kelly was a gold digger she was in for a shock. She was going to need a big spade.

Money had been on Frank's mind from the minute they'd walked into the café and he'd seen the tourist prices on the blackboard behind the counter. He was also worried about what this extended bank holiday care visit would cost. Double time? Time and a half? They'd been out for nearly an hour already. Plus petrol. He should at least pay something towards the petrol. And for lunch. Should he tip her?

Kelly came over and put a cup of tea on the table in front of him, just like on a normal Monday.

'I bought you a Twix,' she said. She put the chocolate biscuit next to the tea. Frank thought about his rickety dentures. He wondered whether they could survive a Twix. A

Kit Kat, yes, a Club biscuit or a Penguin, sure, but a Twix? All that chewy caramel to get through. He feared he would take a bite and pull the chocolate bar away from his mouth bringing his teeth with it. Next week he would let a wooden house fall on top of him.

Frank thanked Kelly and hoped that she would either forget the Twix was there or the sun would soften the caramel so that he could suck his way through it.

He remembered how he used to melt Mars bars in front of the fire for his daughter. It was the one great field of knowledge and set of skills he felt he might have passed on to his daughter – how to eat a chocolate bar, or a candy bar, as she probably called them now.

Frank had shown Beth how to nibble away the biscuit part of a Jaffa cake, before peeling off the chocolate top layer until just the thin orange jelly circle was left to be dissolved on the tongue. He taught his daughter how she should first bite the sides off a Mars bar, then peel away the top layer of chocolate and caramel to leave just the soft nougat to either eat or roll into a ball and then eat. Eating a Twix involved much the same principle as a Mars bar – nibble away the chocolate sides, peel away the caramel and chocolate top layer, then eat the biscuit. All pretty much impossible without a decent set of teeth. Ice cream and the self-proclaimed 'crumbliest, flakiest chocolate' were the only fields of his confectionery expertise left now.

'How much do I owe you?' he said. He meant for the tea and the chocolate, although perhaps Kelly would take out a laptop and give him a run-down of the full day's costs and expenses before presenting him with an invoice.

'My treat,' she said.

133

'Thank you. I really hope I haven't ruined your bank holiday.'

'I wasn't doing anything special. Sean's working anyway.'

'Sean?'

'My boyfriend.'

'Have you been together long?'

'Long enough. We're trying for a baby.'

Don't try too hard, Frank thought and immediately felt bad about it.

Frank sat and watched Kelly looking into her coffee cup as she slowly stirred sugar into it, possibly thinking about Sean and their future son or daughter. Sean was a lucky man, Frank thought. Kelly was very pretty. Her teeth had a slight overbite and she had wide eyes which Frank thought would have been more pronounced when she was younger. She was probably picked on at school and called goofy and bug-eyed up until she grew into her face. Now she was pretty and could laugh in all the ugly stupid bullies' faces.

He had the urge to reach across the table and tweak her nose, pretending to pull it off like he used to do with Beth. Putting his thumb between his index and middle fingers, saying, 'I've got your nose.'

Kelly snapped out of her trance. She looked up from the cup.

'I almost forgot,' she said. She leaned across the table. Her face was close enough for Frank to see the colour of her eyes, which were green. Although if you'd asked him two seconds later what colour they were, he couldn't have told you. There was no doubt something in Ron's leaflet about that. Her face was really very close to Frank's now. As close as when she'd brushed his hair or scratched his itchy arm. But different.

Oh Jesus Christ, Frank thought.

She reached her hand across and gently took Frank's glasses off, taking care to not pull them apart again.

Jesus Christ almighty.

He really hadn't been expecting this. Nope, definitely had not expected this. This was his heart-attack moment. Here it comes. Stroke. Heart attack. Charge up the defibrillator. Call an ambulance. F.A.C.E. Jesus H. Jehovah, he thought. She's going to kiss me.

And Kelly replaced Frank's glasses with a pair of red plastic sunglasses she'd just bought and sat back in her chair and drank her coffee.

On the walk back to the car Frank wondered if he'd taken a deep breath when he'd thought Kelly was going to kiss him. Had he puckered up, like Les Dawson – his dentures moving around inside his mouth as though he'd wound them up before putting them in? Did he close his eyes?

She hadn't said anything after she'd put the plastic sunglasses on him and didn't seem to act any differently towards him afterwards. She didn't appear scared or disgusted by him. She didn't call the police, or send the Old Bat signal up into the sky to call for Janice. She didn't fall off her chair laughing. She just drank her coffee, ate an apple doughnut and talked about babies and about Sean, who Frank was already developing a dislike for. She asked Frank about Sheila and about Beth and somehow got onto the subject of the war. It must have been awful to live through, she thought. The bombs, the air-raid shelters, the rationed food, but Frank shrugged it off as though it wasn't a big deal at all. He told her that he'd been a young boy and his memory of the war was that it was all a big adventure.

When they drove back along Sea Lane Frank put his head out the window again, letting the wind blow in his face as he watched the house prices drop, until Kelly bumped the car up onto the grass verge opposite the cheapest building on the street – the only house on Sea Lane without a name.

Frank climbed out of the car and said goodbye. He wasn't sure what to do next. What was the correct way to end their day out at the seaside? Had it been business or pleasure for Kelly? He was unsure whether he should let her sit in the car watching him until he safely had the key in the door because he was still her patient. Or should he stand in the street like a gentleman, waving until she'd driven away?

He stood outside his flat next to the fallen bollard, which he suddenly felt he was strong enough to pick up, and watched by his neighbours, some of whom hadn't left their windows in the past two hours, letting their lunches go cold and desperate to go to the toilet, but not wanting to miss the little blue car's return. They watched Frank waving to Kelly from behind their curtains and from between the slats of their Venetian blinds. He didn't stop waving until she had driven out of sight. Which didn't take all that long as the red plastic sunglasses he was still wearing didn't have prescription lenses.

19

Kelly Christmas made Frank feel like getting out of bed in the morning. She was like a replacement hip. His half an Aspirin a day. She was his stair lift and his Zimmer frame, Kelly was his grab rail and his large-button telephone. She was his bath hoist. She was his easy-to-grip scissors, his one-touch battery-operated jar opener and his long-handled shoehorn. Kelly was all the vitamin supplements he needed.

On the morning after their trip to the beach, once Frank had come to terms with the fact that as a result of the trip Kelly wouldn't be coming again today as planned on all his calendars, he went to the charity shop and bought a scooter. Not a mobility scooter, with a comfy leather seat, a battery and a shopping basket on the front. Frank's scooter was a child's micro scooter. It had pink tassels hanging from the handlebars and the word POW! in graffiti-style lettering across its metallic silver deck. At speeds over one mile an hour the tiny wheels lit up.

Frank's foot was almost completely better and in two days' time, when the plaster cast was off, he was going to ride the scooter around Fullwind like he was Marlon Brando.

'Hey, Frankie, what are you rebelling against?' people outside the library would ask.

'Whaddayagot?' Frank would reply before pulling a wheelie and scooting off to the shops in a blaze of tiny flickering lights to buy tinned spaghetti.

On Thursday morning, Frank took a taxi to the hospital and sat in an incredibly hot waiting room until somebody came out and called his name.

He was led into a small box-shaped room where a male nurse explained the cast-removal procedure.

'Now, Francis. The saw is going to be quite loud. A bit like a vacuum cleaner.' The nurse looked familiar to Frank. It was probably the green scrubs he was wearing, which Frank had seen so many actors wear on TV. 'The blade cannot hurt you,' the nurse said and demonstrated this with his party trick of rolling up his sleeve and letting the saw blade touch his arm without cutting it off. 'You see. Perfectly harmless.'

The nurse gave Frank a pair of ear-defender headphones to wear. They were pink with pictures of rabbits on and clearly intended only for patients on the children's ward. Frank put the headphones on. The nurse started up the saw and said, '—'.

'Pardon?' Frank said.

The nurse stopped the saw and lifted one side of the headphones.

'This may tickle.'

After he'd cut through and removed the cast he asked Frank if he'd like to take it home with him as a souvenir.

'You can look back at it in the future and remember how your bones got better and look at all the names of your friends who signed it.'

Frank said no thank you, because a) he wasn't five years old and b) nobody had signed it.

'It feels like a great weight has been lifted, doesn't it?' the nurse said. 'After carrying that cast around with you for so long. You probably feel as though your arm may float up to the ceiling as though it's filled with helium.'

And then Frank remembered where he'd seen the nurse before.

'Isn't it such a joyful feeling to be free of the plaster cast, Francis?' He hadn't seen him on TV. 'It is always a wonderful feeling to be freed from those things that hold us back or weigh us down, Francis.' It was the tone of voice that was so familiar, not the hospital clothing. 'In that same way we love that feeling when we take our shoes off at the end of a long day. Why do you think our spirits seem naturally to long for freedom, Francis?' The nurse was one of the two smiling men in suits, who had stood on his doorstep for such a long time. 'Is the story of Christ being raised from the dead not the ultimate story of freedom, Francis? Some people's lives are wrapped in a cast. A cast of addiction or crime or abuse that stops their spirits from being truly free. We can find freedom in Christ, Francis.'

It was about a mile and a half to Greyflick House from the hospital and after his cast was removed Frank went to see Smelly John. He hadn't walked that far for years and a mile and a half sounded like a very long way. He should have dressed up in a Womble costume and collected sponsor money.

He walked around the outside of the hospital building, through an empty car park and some waste ground to an industrial estate and then on to a long straight road with shops on both sides. At the beginning of the road, halfway up the brick wall between a kebab shop and a flat with fire-blackened windows, there was a sign that said 'High Street'. Frank was relieved he hadn't walked on to Low Street.

The majority of the shops on High Street were either closed, closed down, or it was impossible to tell one way or another. Perhaps it was too early for chicken and chips. There were a lot of chicken shops and the pavement and the gutter were littered with chicken bits, French fries and greasy empty boxes. The first twenty minutes of *Saving Private Ryan* filmed with poultry.

Frank walked past a shop with three mannequins dressed in crotchless pants, peephole bras and silk nighties in the window. One of the mannequins had a leg missing and another had a face like the shell of a dropped boiled egg. They were posed awkwardly on a newspaper-covered floor surrounded by what Frank presumed were sex toys. It was the least sexy thing he had ever seen.

There was a pawnbroker, with a neon sign in the window that said CASH 4 STUFF. The second F was broken. Through the metal security grille and the dirt on the window Frank could see computers, watches, cameras and electric guitars. He walked past another chicken shop and a disco, a boarded-up pub that was actually open with three men in their sixties or seventies smoking outside. Another chicken shop, a charity shop that made the one in Fullwind look like Harrods and a tattoo parlour called Fat Pat's Tats. He stopped, turned back and walked inside.

It was the first tattoo parlour he'd ever been into. He'd seen them on television cop shows and in films. And they looked pretty much like this. Loud music was playing quietly. The music sounded exactly like Frank would have expected tattooing music would sound like. He couldn't understand the words, and not because he was old and boring but because the singer was mumbling, probably embarrassed by the lyrics. The tattoo parlour's edgy and dangerous look was spoiled by two hygienic hand-rub dispensers by the door. There was more chance of Frank catching something nasty in the hospital than in Fat Pat's Tats, where the hand-rub dispensers were both full. The one outside the box-shaped room where his cast had been removed was empty and dispensed nothing more than a smoker's wheeze when he tried to pump something out of it.

Frank squeezed some of Fat Pat's Tats hand gel onto his hands and rubbed them together. A large man, whom he presumed was Fat Pat, was tattooing the Bayeux Tapestry onto someone's back. Frank stood at the front of the shop and looked at the pictures on the wall. The tattoo menu.

Perhaps a small butterfly on his ankle or a rose on his buttock to start with. One of those Disney characters up there, or Marilyn Monroe maybe. Popeye the Sailor man or a skull and crossbones with a dagger through its centre. Hmmm. A flaming Satan on his neck, Mum and Dad, Beth, a simple LOVE and HATE across his knuckles, something mythical or mystical, some Japanese lettering or a spider's web across his face, his Sioux name between his shoulder blades, a mermaid. He could have something classic tattooed on his right arm. Kelly would notice it and ask him about it. 'Oh that?' he'd say. 'I've had it for years.' Pretending it had been there all along, hidden under the plaster cast like an unwrapped present – a wolf or a tiger whose back Kelly had unknowingly been scratching every week with a knitting needle. Perhaps he should push the tattoo boat out and get his whole upper body done, so it looked like he was wearing one of his charity shop shirts.

People often say that tattoos are a bad idea because you'll regret them when you're old. But Frank was already old. Eighty-one was the optimum time to get a tattoo.

'Hello, there.' Frank hadn't noticed that the sound of the tattoo needle or pen or whatever it was called had stopped whirring. 'Can I help?' Fat Pat said. Pat had a lot of tattoos. He was almost completely full. Frank wondered whether Fat Pat's tats were all his own work. Or did he get his wife to do his back? And was Fat Pat his punk name or his Sioux name – presuming his name was actually Pat – it did suit him perfectly.

'Something small, I was thinking,' Frank said. 'Subtle. On my arm.' He raised his arm slightly in case Pat didn't know what an arm was.

'What sort of thing?' Fat Pat said. He turned a metal ring in his earlobe. It was one of many shiny metal studs and chains that decorated his face.

Frank looked at the art on the walls again.

'Um. I hadn't really thought about it. I was just passing by. It was an impulse to come in.'

This wasn't true. In his pocket Frank had a hand-drawn map with directions from the hospital to the High Street. Fat Pat's Tats was marked on the map with a cross. On the other side of the map were crude pictures Frank had drawn of flowers and animals and the names Bogart, Stewart and Beth.

142

'Let me take a look at the canvas,' Pat said.

'The canvas?'

'At your arm.'

'My arm? Oh. Yes.'

Frank took his jacket off. He'd forgotten how easy it could be. His arm did feel lighter, the nurse was right there. Maybe not helium-filled but definitely lighter. But it also felt stiff and like somebody else's arm. He thought he could still feel the cast. When it was first removed Frank noticed the skin on his arm was flaky and the smell nearly knocked him off his chair. Where was the religious metaphor in that? The next time someone knocked on his door to discuss the hereafter, Frank was going to ask them.

Before Frank had rolled his sleeve up as far as his elbow Pat said, 'No. Sorry.'

'No?'

'It's not that I can't do it. It's that it will look bad. Your skin is too thin. Too loose.'

'Too loose?'

'May I?' Pat said. He peeled off his black disposable surgical gloves, rolled them into a ball and threw them at a bin and missed. He was not as good as Kelly at slam-dunking rubber gloves. She was the Harlem Globetrotters compared to Fat Pat. He gently took hold of Frank's arm and turned it around. The depiction of Hell and Hades tattooed on the backs of Fat Pat's fat hands at odds with the softness of their touch.

'I'm sorry,' he said. He let go of Frank's arm. 'Maybe a few years ago.'

Frank looked down at the flaky, loose-skinned smelly canvas and wondered if he had enough strength in his arm to pull on the short chain between Pat's nostrils to tear his nose off.

'Sorry,' Pat said again.

Frank put his jacket back on and left the tattoo parlour, washing his hands before he went. If he'd had a tail it would have been between his legs. Still, Fat Pat couldn't be the only tattoo artist in town. Frank would go somewhere else or do his own tattoo.

He walked along the High Street. The chicken shops were opening now. Men in white paper hats were sweeping the pavement outside their shops, moving the rubbish along the High Street one shop doorway at a time, playing pass the filthy parcel all the way to the pile that had built up at the end of the street outside a closed-down electrical shop. Seagulls swooped down and fought over bits of leg, wing and breast. Parked or abandoned dumped cars were whitewashed in seagull droppings.

When Frank was almost at the end of the street, he stopped and took his hand-drawn map out. Greyflick House was in this general direction but there was no detail or scale. He put the map back in his pocket and turned a corner on to a side street. He walked until he was in the middle of a housing estate. Recently it had been on the news when the whole estate had received an antisocial behaviour disorder and been placed under a 7 p.m. curfew. It was at the opposite end of the news to the colourful over-priced beach huts story. The beach huts were the skateboarding dog to the housing estate's suicide bomb.

Frank heard sirens nearby. They were the fourth set of sirens he'd heard since leaving Fat Pat's. In Fullwind the sound of sirens meant that somebody had the window open and the TV up too loud during *Midsomer Murders* or Marion at number eight had had another fall and pulled the panic cord in her bathroom.

At the centre of the housing estate there was a children's playground – two tied-up rusty swings and a graffiti-covered slide. A small group of teenage boys were sitting on bicycles smoking and spitting, spitting and smoking. Multi-tasking. Don't catch their eye, Frank thought. They might also have a cave in Worthing.

The boys were playing music on a phone. Angry music. Swearing, shouty, angry music. 'Granddad!' one of the boys called out.

Frank knew his only grandchild was female and in America and so he kept walking, slightly quicker, not looking back. He heard the sound of an empty drinks can landing on the ground nearby.

'Fucking old twat!'

He put his hand inside his jacket so that they might think he had a gun. He wasn't used to not having his arm in plaster and it felt more natural to hold it at an angle. A dog barked. One of the boys shouted at Frank again. He looked around for CCTV cameras but there were none. He wondered who they would get to play him in the crime show reconstruction. Some old sod in a wig. There were two dogs barking now. Wasn't that one of the red Indians in *Dances with Wolves*? Someone dropped a mattress out of a window of one of the flats. The dull thud as it hit the ground stopped the dogs barking for a moment. Then they were off again. Woof woof. Bow wow wow. More dogs joined in. The mattress sent up a cloud of dust and hopelessness.

'Shut the bloody fuck up!' a woman shouted from a

window of the flats. 'Get in here, you little shit!' another woman from a different window called. It was just like *Oliver!* In a moment barrow boys and flower sellers would high-kick their way through the estate singing. The dogs barked louder. Frank thought of Bill being taken along the corridor of the dog and cats home.

'I *said* shut the fuck up,' one of the cast of *Oliver!* called out again. Two of the teenage boys curve-skidded their bikes to a halt in front of Frank. If this had happened one day later he would have made a quick getaway on his scooter. These punks would never have caught him as he sped off, leaving them behind shielding their eyes from dust and the flashing lights of the scooter's tiny wheels.

'Where are you going?' one of the boys asked. He smelled familiar. It was a sickly sweet smell, like a perfumed bonfire.

'Nowhere,' Frank said.

'Nowhere where?'

'Nowhere nowhere.' He resisted the urge to say 'so good they named it twice'.

'Where's that?'

'What's in the bag?' the other boy said and spat something disgusting out from between his teeth. Frank remembered where he recognised the smell from. It was the smell that came from John's padded envelope.

'Films,' Frank said.

'What films?'

This is like another Mini Mental Examination, Frank thought. Paper-folding next.

In his carrier bag he had some DVDs for Smelly John. John said the only films left on the Greyflick DVD trolley he hadn't already seen had been put there by Graham to wind him up. When he heard the Friends of Greyflick volunteers wheeling the trolley through the dull brick-walled corridors every Friday John knew there was nothing on it for him.

'All they had to offer me last week were both *Zulu* films,' John said. 'And that one about the bouncing bombs. The one with the dog, Francis. The dog with *that* name.'

Frank had put *Jurassic Park*, *Muppet Treasure Island* and *The Goonies* in a carrier bag for Smelly John. He hoped he hadn't missed any hidden racist subplots in any of his film choices.

He told the boys the titles of the films.

'Blu-ray?' one of them said.

'Just normal DVDs.'

'How much money have you got?'

What, in the world? Frank thought. Or on me? Although they both amounted to the same thing. Let me see. Today is Thursday. My pension goes into the bank today. Although this week was a bank holiday so it might be a day late. Council tax came out of the bank this month. That may have put me into the red again which will mean more bank fees. The scooter was £8.00, three tins of spaghetti, bread, milk, a couple of other things, the taxi to the hospital, and a very poor cup of tea from a vending machine in the hospital. I think that's everything.

Frank pulled the change out of his pocket.

The boys looked at the coins in his open palm and laughed and one of them spat on the ground. He wasn't as good as his friend at spitting and he got a bit of gob on his chin. Frank wanted to take a tissue out of his pocket and wipe it off. The boys spun their bikes around and rode off.

*

'I've just been mugged,' Frank told Smelly John when he got to his apartment at Greyflick House. He was out of breath and a bit shaken from the experience. And perhaps a little disappointed that the boys hadn't given him much of an anecdote. They could at least have punched him or actually stolen something.

'What did they take?' John said.

'Nothing. Should I call the police?'

'No. I don't want them coming round here.'

'Why would they come round here?'

'If you call the police, you're here, you're the victim, so they'll come round here and then they'll go through my stuff.'

'Why would they go through your stuff?'

'Seriously, Francis? Seriously? Do I need to answer that?' He wheeled himself over to a chest of drawers, opened the top drawer and took out a padded envelope and passed it to Frank.

'It helps with my spasms,' John said. 'Look.' He held his hand out for ten seconds. 'See.'

'Is it drugs?' Frank said.

'Herbs.'

'Illegal herbs?'

John shrugged.

'Where do you get it from?'

'Mother Nature, Francis. Via Amsterdam.'

'Jesus Christ.'

'Would you like to try some?'

'Oh no,' Frank said. 'No. I don't think so.' But so that John didn't think he was the kind of square who thought the roads were in a terrible state and everyone drove too fast, he said, 'I almost got a tattoo today.'

And then, because the lift was working and it was a Thursday, they went down to the lounge for a glass of sherry and to disrupt the quiz.

20

Frank had just picked up the newspaper from the bottom of the stairs. He read the date out loud: 'Saturday, the first of June.' There would be a new calendar dog today. He made a sportsman's bet with himself that it would be some sort of terrier. He looked at the weather forecast at the top of the newspaper. 'Sunshine, occasional light showers,' he said, in the style of an American weatherman, who sounded remarkably like Ron the marbles guy. Perhaps they were related. An incredible coincidence for such a big country.

While he was looking at the paper the postman pushed the day's begging letters and catalogues through the letter-box. Frank watched the postman's Hitchcock-esque silhouette through the frosted glass of the front door and waited for him to leave. The postman then started to push something else through the door – a padded envelope that was too big to fit through the letterbox. The postman pushed harder. Frank heard the postman swear and then he appeared to try and punch or kick the package into Frank's flat. It stayed where it was. The postman started pushing again. The bubbles of the Jiffy bag popped and cracked like Frank's ankles on the stairs in the morning. The envelope was stuck. The postman carried on pushing. Frank took hold of his side of the envelope and pulled while the post-man pushed from the outside, until the inevitable happened and Frank fell backwards onto the stairs with the crumpled padded envelope in his hands. He stayed there and watched the postman turn and walk away, dropping red rubber bands on the path as he went.

Frank took the post upstairs and sat down at the kitchen table. He looked at the squashed padded envelope. He was thinking that inside he'd find some Dutch dope, a present from Smelly John, and he was unsure about opening it in case the police kicked in his front door the moment that he did. The address was printed onto a label and Smelly John didn't own a typewriter, a computer or a printer. He looked for origins-of-posting clues next to the stamps but the date and place marks were too smudged. He tried to feel the con-tents of the envelope. Something hard. Harder than Smelly John's cannabis or marijuana, or were those the same thing? Frank didn't know. He was no fuddy-duddy but he wasn't Cheech or Chong.

He wondered what could be inside the package. It wasn't quite large enough to contain Frank's milk, returned to him from the hospital after all this time. After shaking the en-velope and then sniffing it, he did the only thing left to do in the situation. Frank opened the envelope. There were two soft-plastic glasses cases inside. Frank had completely for-gotten about the glasses he'd ordered. There'd been so much going on lately. He really needed a secretary.

He opened the first case and took out a pair of sun-glasses. He put them on the table and opened the other case and took out a pair of lightweight, semi-rimless, gunmetal grey glasses. He took his old glasses off – still held together with Kelly's sticking plaster – and he put the new pair on.

They were half the size and weight of his old glasses. So light that he might forget he was wearing them and begin a hunt around the flat to find them. The glasses were made of titanium with scratch-resistant, anti-glare lenses. The only thing they had in common with his old glasses was the left side – what did you call those bits? – arms? The left arm of Frank's new glasses was snapped off. Presumably by the force the postman had used to deliver them. Frank fixed the glasses with the same-coloured insulation tape as his old glasses and started changing his calendars.

He flipped over the previous day's date on the calendar on the desk. Tore off the page, screwed it up and slam-dunked it into the wastepaper basket. It hit the edge but it went in. Frank's basketball chops were somewhere between Fat Pat's and Kelly's.

He said the new date out loud.

He wasn't going to lose any marbles.

Yesterday he'd bought a cassette player from the charity shop. It cost £5.50. He couldn't afford it but he was going to learn Spanish. He just needed some new batteries. He'd asked if they had a saxophone or a drum set too but they didn't. In the afternoon he completed half the easy cross-word in the paper without looking at any of the answers printed at the back of the paper.

He was determined to not lose any of his marbles. He wanted to share them with Kelly. He wanted to tell her about watching the first ever television broadcast and see-ing the first man walk on the Moon. He was going to tell her where he'd been when he heard about Kennedy's assassination and about coal deliveries and how he could remember a time when there was only one gas board, one electricity board and when the post and the telephone all came from the same company. He wanted to tell her about the rag-and-bone man and paraffin heaters and what it was like before decimal currency, explaining how five pence was one shilling and there were twelve pennies in a shilling and twenty shillings in a pound. He wasn't ready to forget any of that yet.

Frank was going to tell Kelly how razors used to have only one blade and no batteries and tell her how long it took to make a phone call when you made a mistake dialling the number on a rotary-dial telephone. He'd seen so many great films that he wanted to tell Kelly about and many others he wanted to warn her against watching. *Vertigo* – good. *Batman and Robin* – bad. He'd tell her how there used to be an interval during films at the cinema and a short supporting film before the main feature. There was only one screen and you could smoke. He was going to get his collection of 16mm movies out of the loft and unroll a strip of film and hold it up to the light to show her a frame-by-frame scene.

Frank was going to turn his back, ruffle his hair, pop a pipe in his mouth and show Kelly his Harold Wilson impression. Then he was going to tell her who Harold Wilson was and how he'd been Prime Minister twice. He'd show her how people amused themselves before video games and the Internet. He'd pretend to pull her nose off and then remove his own thumb and throw it up in the air and catch it in a paper bag. He'd take his old calculator out of the kitchen drawer, put batteries in it and show her how to write the word BOOBS.

Frank had so much to tell her about before he forgot it all. There was a lot to share. His chocolate-eating methods, bayonet light bulbs and, yes, the war. Frank would take her to the library and get the big book off the shelf. Next to the one about Egypt. He'd open it up to page 49, point at the page and say, 'That's me.'

Kelly would look at the black-and-white photograph of a crowd of boys and girls dressed in their best clothes with parcel labels tied to their coats, on the deck of a ship, on the bow, leaning into the wind like Kate Winslet and Leonardo DiCaprio. The children were all smiling or waving at the camera, sticking their thumbs up like they were on their way to the zoo or the fun fair.

'You were an evacuee?' Kelly would say.

'Seavacuee,' he'd say. 'We're on a Dutch ocean liner there. We were on our way to Canada when it was torpedoed.'

'Oh no,' Kelly would say. 'How awful.'

And Frank would tell her his war story. About how they travelled by train to Liverpool and then boarded the ship. Three hundred and something children. He'd tell Kelly he was asleep in a cabin when the sound of bells woke him and he and all the other children had to put lifejackets on and get to the lifeboats. He'd start to remember it as he told the story. He'd remember how, because the ship was listing at an angle, they had to crawl along a corridor in the dark.

'I was still wearing my pyjamas. They gave us blankets to wrap ourselves in. Grey. I remember the blankets were grey.'

'You must have been terrified,' Kelly would say. 'How old were you?'

'Eight.'

'Oh my God.'

154

'But I don't remember feeling scared. Which doesn't make sense to me now. It was a bit like a film, and sometimes I think maybe it was just a film that I'm remembering – *Titanic* or *The Poseidon Adventure* – and it never happened at all. When I try and remember it, it all happens in black and white, making me think perhaps it was a film. But I know there's a passenger list with my name on in the National Archives or somewhere and somebody making a documentary once looked the list up, traced me and wrote asking for an interview about what happened. I said no. I wish I'd said yes. I could have shown you a video of it.'

Frank would tell Kelly how the children had been put into the lifeboats. The crew members had to swing the boats towards the ship and drop the children in one at a time.

'And then all of a sudden we were told to get back off the lifeboat. I don't know why. Perhaps the torpedo damage wasn't as bad as they'd thought. So we got off the lifeboat and went to one of the ship's lounges and then almost straight away we were told to get back in the lifeboats.'

Frank would tell Kelly how they were put back in the lifeboats and lowered into the water. Children were being sick because of the sea's swell. They were unsure of what was happening. And then they were hauled up by ropes onto a tanker.

'The tanker smelled awful. Oil.'

'It must all have been so frightening,' Kelly would say again.

'In a way, I suppose it was but I remember on the tanker they had a big gun and the crew let the boys look through the gun's sights. That was exciting. I suppose they were just trying to distract us. They were probably more scared than we were. We were taken back to Scotland and eventually we went home on a train.'

Kelly would ask how many people died and Frank would say, miraculously just one.

And Kelly would look as though she was about to cry.

'A child?' she'd say.

'A member of the ship's crew.'

And Kelly wouldn't be pleased somebody had died but it would seem less tragic that it was a grown-up.

Frank would tell her how some children would leave the country again on a different ship a few weeks later and that it would sink and that many of the children died.

'That's awful,' Kelly would say and she'd look at the photograph in the book. 'Which one are you again?'

Frank would point to himself in the photograph.

'I sometimes wonder how different my life would have been if I'd made it to Canada.' And he'd put the book back on the shelf next to the one about Egypt with the Sphinx on the front cover.

This was Frank's war story and he wanted to tell it to Kelly before he forgot it. He needed to keep his mind active. He was going to read the newspaper and do the crossword and eat fruit and learn Spanish and play the drums. He'd keep doing all the Ron stuff too – checking the time and saying the date out loud every day.

In the living room, where everything was in sharper focus than it had been for some time because of his new Belgian architect's glasses, he slam-dunked yesterday's date into the bin and turned over a new month on his abandoned dogs calendar. Dog of the month was a mongrel, not a terrier;

he'd lost his bet with himself. Then he noticed he'd accidentally turned over two pages and had skipped a month. He turned back a page. June's dog was a terrier after all. A small handbag dog with a stupid face. And then he paused. He turned the calendar page to July. July's dog was a mongrel called Royston. 'Royston is a loveable scruff,' it said beneath Royston's picture. He was doing that tipping his head at an angle and arching his eyebrows thing. He didn't look like any obvious political leader from the twentieth century. Frank looked at the calendar.

There were thirty-one days in July.

No bank holidays.

And no red crosses.

Frank felt sick.

21

Hello, Beth,

I hope you, Jimmy and Laura are all well.

I am sorry I haven't telephoned but you know how I always get muddled up about what time of day it is there. Is it morning now? There. You see. I'm such an old fool. And then the cost of long-distance calls has rocketed over here. I sometimes feel it would be more economical to jump on a plane than to pick up the telephone. On that subject, I do hope you will be able to come over soon. I do miss you all.

The plaster cast (is that what you call it over there?) has finally come off. The nurse who removed it tried to convert me to God. Can you believe it? I managed to escape with my atheism intact. At least the itch has gone.

My arm has still been giving me quite a lot of pain, though, and I am still quite unsteady on my feet. The accident may have knocked me further sideways than I liked to think. Despite my initial protests the care visits have been invaluable. I think I would have struggled on my own. As much as I love to remain independent perhaps it would be an idea to extend the home visits. Just two or three more weeks or so until I'm back to my usual 93 per cent.

Give my love to Jimmy and, of course, to Laura. She must be a proper grown-up little lady now.

Love

Dad

Frank sat back in the library chair and wondered how emails worked. He imagined his email travelling at thousands or millions or even billions of miles an hour down a phone line to the nearby coast and then under the sea, from the English Channel into the North Atlantic to America and then on through more cable across the country to arrive in his daughter's computer in Los Angeles. He wondered whether the email had arrived yet and when Beth would reply. He could come back later and check. But the library closed at noon on a Saturday. If he went and looked at an atlas and plotted the route his email might take through a long cable from Fullwind-on-Sea to LA, would Beth have replied by the time he came back to the computer? It was unlikely. In spite of all his claims of ignorance about time zones Frank was reasonably sure Los Angeles was eight hours behind Fullwind and Beth wouldn't be sending emails at three in the morning.

The computer pinged.

Hi, Dad,

I'm still always surprised to receive an email from you. I guess I'm as dumb as all those people who expect their dads should still be sending telegrams or Morse code or something.

I'm afraid we've been having a rough time of it lately. Jimmy's contract fell through. He's devastated, to be honest. He'd worked so hard for it. He feels kind of cheated and let down, I guess.

That's good news about the cast (same name here). Did you get anybody to sign it? I hope you kept it. And well done for not joining the Church. You'd find it a lot harder to resist here. Everybody believes in something here, or says they do at least. I am sorry that you are still finding things tough though. Is there any financial support we could get for you from the Government or the council? We're just in such a spot here right now. I feel terrible saying that. What kind of a daughter am I? Let's both think on it for a while and see if we can come up with a solution.

And I promise I will ring, maybe tomorrow.

No, really, I will call you this time. You're not the only one who forgets the time-zone differences.

I hope that this whole situation with Jimmy will somehow sort itself out and we'll be able to come and visit. Maybe after Thanksgiving.

And yes, Laura is certainly one little lady.

All our love

Beth xx

Frank replied.

Hello, Beth,

I wasn't expecting to find you up and about.

Please forget what I said about the home visits. I'll be fine really. I was making a lot of fuss about nothing. It's far

160

more important that you try and get back on your feet again (no joke about broken toes or metatarsals intended there). Let's talk on the telephone very soon. Although these emails back and forth have been almost like a conversation. It would be great to see you when things sort themselves out and I'm sure they will. Maybe after Thanksgiving, as you said.

Give all my love to Jimmy and Laura.

Dad x

Maybe after Thanksgiving. When was Thanksgiving? Wasn't it just the American name for Christmas? He was on the Internet in a library. If only there was some way of finding out.

Thanksgiving. Christmas. Kelly Christmas. The words were like recommendations updating themselves to Frank on an online shopping site – if you like Thanksgiving, you may be interested in Christmas, shoppers who've looked at Christmas have also looked at Kelly Christmas.

Frank found himself on the Lemons Care website.

Kelly was still waiting for the temperature to show up on her thermometer. Still smiling for the camera in her shiny blue uniform.

At the top of the page he clicked on 'What Does it Cost?' Which took him to a page that was much like all the other 'What Does it Cost?' web pages for services aimed at the elderly, in that it did everything to avoid providing an answer. Frank read between the lines:

Lemons Care recognises that everybody is different.

If we tell you how much it costs now . . .

Our visiting care service is arranged around your individual needs and requirements.

. . . then you might decide you can't afford it.

We want to understand your unique circumstances . . .

We want to see what you can realistically afford . . .

. . . and we like to take the time to meet the person we will be caring for and their family before discussing exact costs.

. . . and then try and get you to pay for a bit more.

To ensure we get it right from the start, we like to begin each new Lemons Care relationship . . .

We want to be able to talk you into paying for it . . .

. . . with a visit to you and your family at your home.

. . . in an environment with a closed door and, hopefully, stairs . . .

We can then discuss the exact help that you need.

. . . so that you can't escape.

Please call our 24-hour hotline to talk to one of our care advisors and to arrange a home visit.

Frank left the library and went to the shops. He was walking with a slight limp and his boomer-arm had come back. If there was the slimmest chance that Jimmy's contract hadn't really fallen through and Beth had been playing a wonderful joke on him and had really been in the country all along, having already flown over to surprise him, Frank didn't want to be caught out like someone being videoed playing rugby or bungee jumping out of a helicopter while claiming incapacity benefit. So just in case Beth leapt out from behind a bush with a box of cookies, a model of the Empire State Building and a new dementia leaflet, he faked a limp and held his arm like it was still in plaster.

162

It was a hot day and Frank took his jacket off, pulling his arm carefully out of the sleeve and screwing his face up as though it still hurt. In a way he hoped somebody – Beth and Jimmy and Laura, an incapacity benefit-fraud investigator, Hilary the head of the Neighbourhood Watch or whoever – was watching. Somebody to applaud his skills as an actor.

He checked his bank balance at the cashpoint outside Fullwind Food & Wine. There was £33.90 in his account. He had overdue electricity and gas bills to pay and he was out of tinned spaghetti. By not starving or freezing to death he was living beyond his means. And, more pressingly, his time with Kelly was almost up. And he wasn't quite ready for that yet.

A slight breeze blew his hair. Perhaps it would be the start of a freak cold snap. The coldest summer in history to follow one of the hottest springs. If the temperature dropped below zero for a week, Frank would receive a heating allowance from the Government. Maybe even enough for another home visit. He went into Fullwind Food & Wine and bought £3.98 worth of shopping and a scratch card, hoping it would be snowing when he came back out.

At two o'clock in the morning Frank couldn't sleep. He got out of bed, put his teeth in, drank a glass of water, tried to clear his throat of the last forty years, picked up the phone and called the Lemons Care 24-hour hotline.

'Lemons Care. How may I help you?'

'Hi,' Frank said in an American accent. Not as broadly American as his Ron impression, but like someone from the UK who'd gone to live in America and was gradually taking on the accent – like Catherine Zeta-Jones or Lulu. 'I'm ringing about my father. I hope it's not a bad time to call. It's

163

five after six p.m. over here where I am. In LA in America.'

Frank pretended to be his own imaginary son and told the woman on the phone the kind of things he presumed his actual daughter must have told her to get a list of their prices without them first sending somebody around to assess his needs in person. He said he was thousands of miles away in Los Angeles and couldn't make it over. He talked about his Father's accident and asked what services might be available for such an old guy like that.

The woman asked a few questions and told Frank the various options and levels of care they could offer.

'That sounds ideal,' Frank said, and then, almost as an afterthought – as though money was no object – 'What would be the ballpark cost of that?' He wasn't sure exactly what ballpark cost meant but it was something he'd heard Beth and people in movies say before.

After the woman had told Frank what it was going to cost he thanked her and said he would be in touch. And then he went back to bed to dream of a freezing cold summer, winning the lottery or selling his kidneys.

He was up again before the first Sunday flight to Alicante. He put on Sheila's old scarlet anorak, Kelly's yellow rubber gloves and Beth's pink scuba mask and snorkel and he went out into the garden. Any of Frank's neighbours up early enough to see him in his strange outfit must have thought, '*Somebody* hasn't been following Ron's advice about the importance of eating a healthy diet and keeping physically and mentally active.'

To take his mind off his money problems Frank was going to build his cinema.

Before tackling the ivy that held the contents of the shed

captive he first had to get through the spiders and cobwebs that hung like a net curtain across the doorway. He wasn't afraid of spiders but he didn't want to be picking cobwebs out of his hair for hours or swallow one and getting caught up in that whole time-consuming and inevitably fatal cycle of having to swallow a bird and a cat, dog, cow and so on. So he zipped up the anorak, put the face mask on, pulled the anorak hood over his head, put the snorkel in his mouth, and, feeling hot and claustrophobic, breathing heavily through the snorkel, he attacked the arachnoid curtain with a stick.

This was how the Odeon Empire started. An old man with a dream and a shed. An old man with a dream, a woman's anorak, some rubber gloves, a child's scuba-diving mask and a shed. And a stick.

As the cobwebs cleared he was already planning the programme for the premiere night. It had a theme. He was going to start with a showing of *Ice Cold in Alex* followed by *Some Like it Hot*. Classical music would play quietly between films and Frank would serve ice cream and microwaveable popcorn. He didn't have a microwave oven but he could buy one and, until he found a projector, he'd show the films on DVD. The audience would have to sit on garden chairs until he got some proper seats.

There was, of course, always a risk that once Frank had cleared the cobwebs and started cutting away the ivy he'd discover they were the only things holding the wooden building up and it would collapse on the grass like a clown shed. But that sort of glass-half-empty thinking didn't build Hollywood.

It took him over an hour to cut through the ivy with a

pair of rusty garden shears with handles that kept crossing over each other and pinching his fingers. But eventually he liberated the rotting stepladder and the deck chairs. With three piles of ivy on the grass, Frank was exhausted and took a long lunch break.

In the afternoon he began clearing the rest of the shed, finding things he didn't know he'd lost and things he'd kept without knowing he'd ever owned them or why he would have hung on to them in the first place. He wondered whether somebody else had been using his shed for their attic overflow. Virtually everything he found was rusty or broken or incomplete. The lawn took on the appearance of a post-apocalyptic boot fair.

When Kelly arrived the next day, it looked like it was chucking-out time at the boot fair. The cars, the punters and all the good stuff was gone and all that was left were rusting garden tools, two short lengths of hosepipe, one Wellington boot, three half-rolls of wallpaper, a carrier bag stuffed with carpet remnants, a red tartan shopping basket with a squeaky wheel and the frames of two sun loungers. She stepped over a collapsed damp cardboard box and around three tins of paint the damp box had failed to contain. She walked through the layer of foam stuffing balls – chewed up and spat out by foxes or rats that had once lived in the shed – now covering the lawn like confetti.

Frank wasn't up at the window doing his James Stewart impression and didn't see Kelly arrive. He was in the shed working on his Richard Dreyfus. At the moment he was concentrating on the scene in *Close Encounters of the Third Kind* when Dreyfus appears to be losing his mind as he builds a model of the Devil's Tower from the contents of his garden having failed to do so with mashed potato and shaving cream. Frank had emptied the contents of the shed into the garden. He just needed to get everything up the stairs to build his Devil's Tower.

Kelly sidestepped a bedside table with a buckled top and a carrier bag of television aerials and remote controls. The shed door was open halfway and she could hear sounds of movement coming from inside.

'Frank?' she called out quietly, slightly fearful of what the response might be. 'Are you in there?' She was as close to the shed as she could get without moving anything out of the way. Down at her feet there was a cardboard cat box, a basket and a litter tray and Kelly felt her nose itching and she thought she was going to sneeze.

The sounds of movement coming from inside the shed stopped. The door opened and Frank stepped out.

'Ta Dah!' he said. He was breathing heavily and sweating, wearing the red anorak and the yellow rubber gloves. He was either dragging or being attacked by a decorating table. He coughed and brushed his hair with his hand. Dust, cobwebs and bits of leaf fell from it.

'I hope you've brought your hairbrush,' he said.

He waited for Kelly's laughter or applause but it didn't come.

'You shouldn't be doing this,' she said. 'You've just recovered from a serious accident.' She shook her head with dismay and walked off, climbing over the junk in the garden. She kicked a burst football out of the way and went in the open front door.

Frank dropped the decorating table flat on the grass and a lump of dried wallpaper paste bounced off and hit him on the cheek, making it smell even more of wallpaper paste than it already did.

He wanted to wave a magic wand and put everything back in the shed. He wished he'd just sat at the window impersonating James Stewart. He kicked the same burst football across the garden and went upstairs. Kelly was in the kitchen filling the plastic washing-up bowl with warm water.

'Go and sit down,' she said. He went into the living room and sat in the armchair. Kelly came in and put the bowl of water on the table next to him. She was walking far too briskly for such a small flat.

'Are you going to take the anorak off?' she said. He thought of Janice. He looked at Kelly, with a face like an abandoned puppy. He didn't know. What did she want him to do? Should he take his anorak off? He was waiting for instructions. He didn't want to upset her any further by doing the wrong thing. Her face told him he should take off the anorak. Kelly took it from him and draped it over the back of the sofa. Frank awaited further instructions.

'I know it's a washing-up bowl,' Kelly said. 'But you should probably take the rubber gloves off first.'

'Yes,' Frank said. He felt like he was part of the least erotic striptease act in history. He struggled to find the strength to get the rubber gloves off. The determined energy he'd started emptying the shed with had deserted him. He was suddenly very tired. Kelly took hold of his hand and pulled the first rubber glove until it popped off. It made a thwap sound, the sound of Batman punching the joker. She took the other glove off, rolled them both into a ball, and, in no mood for basketball, she put them on the table next to the washing-up bowl.

'Put your arm in the water,' she said.

Frank lowered his arm into the washing-up bowl. The scratches from the ivy stung. He kept it to himself as Kelly didn't seem to be in a sympathetic mood.

'Now move your arm around.'

He swept his arm across the surface, causing a washing-up bowl tsunami, spilling water onto the table.

'Gently,' Kelly said.

Frank moved his arm back and forth more slowly.

'How does that feel?'

'It hurts a bit. Throbbing.'

'I think you'll live. Keep it in the water for about five minutes. And keep it moving. You should be doing this three times a day. Didn't they tell you that at the hospital?'

'I don't think so.'

'What did they say?'

'I can't remember. They gave me a leaflet but I must have thrown it away. I thought it was another copy of their religious magazine.' He told her about the nurse coming to his door. He wasn't sure that she believed him. She went out to the kitchen and washed Frank's breakfast things. Her washing-up was noisier than usual. More Janicey. The lack of a plastic bowl between the cutlery, the crockery and the metal sink didn't help. It wasn't a deafening noise. Just loud enough to let Frank know she wasn't happy.

After five minutes with his arm in warm water Kelly came in, took the washing-up bowl away and refilled it with cold water. She put the bowl on the table and told Frank to put his arm back in the bowl. She brought a tea towel in from

169

the kitchen, folded it in half and put it on the table to soak up the puddle of spilled water.

'You seem annoyed with me,' he said.

'I'm not annoyed.' She went out into the kitchen and put the kettle on and came straight back in. She stood in front of Frank. Let's say her hands were on her hips.

'You have to look after yourself,' she said. 'Taking a garden shed apart after you've just had a plaster cast removed from a broken arm is not taking care of yourself. And look at the state of your arms. I'll have to clean those. I'm not really supposed to do that.'

Frank looked at his scratched arms.

'It was the ivy,' he said.

Frank hated being told off. He hated it. No one of his age should be told off. There should be a cut-off point for it. It should come with the free bus travel and the TV licence.

'I'm not annoyed with you,' Kelly said. 'I care about you.' She sat down. She dried his arm with the tea towel, took out some cotton wool and a tube of ointment and cleaned the deeper scratches.

'What exactly were you doing out there?' she said. And Frank told her all about his dream, as though he was on *The X Factor*.

He told her how he'd always wanted his own home cinema and he'd planned how it would look and what it might be called and what films he'd show. He told her about soundproofing and the pattern on the red seats he was going to buy, the make and speed of the projector he wanted and how Sheila was going to be the cinema's usherette and tear tickets and show people to their seats with a torch. He went into his bedroom and pulled a box out from under the bed and he found the drawings he'd made of his cinema. He showed them to Kelly.

'Without Sheila, I seemed to lose enthusiasm. Time passed by and the shed got filled up with rubbish.'

They talked for a while longer about films and how much the cinema had changed since Frank was Kelly's age.

'I hardly ever go to the cinema any more,' Kelly said.

'You could come to mine.'

'What's showing?'

'I could put on something you like. What's your favourite film?'

Kelly didn't need time to think about it.

'*Dirty Dancing*.'

'Oh right, the one with . . .' Frank wanted to say Patrick Swayze. He knew that was the right name, but he was wary of making a fool of himself when it was actually Bernard Swayze or Patrick Snazeby.

'Patrick Swayze,' Kelly said.

'. . . ayze,' Frank said, joining her mid-way through the actor's surname. 'Is it good?'

'You haven't seen *Dirty Dancing*?' Kelly said. As though he'd said he'd never seen snow or a rainbow. After talking for ten minutes about how brilliant the film was and all the different times she'd seen it, she looked at her watch. 'Oh my God. I haven't done any of the things I'm supposed to be doing. I'm sorry. I'm going to have to go. Wasting your time, talking all day.' She stood up and started collecting her things together in her bag.

'It's nice to have somebody to talk to,' Frank said. He got up and followed her into the hall.

'You go and sit back down,' she said. 'Rest.'

171

'I just need to shut the shed door.'

'I can do it.'

'It's all right,' Frank said. He followed her down the stairs and out to the front gate. Kelly looked at the scooter that was leaning against the hedge.

'Did that belong to your granddaughter?' she said.

Frank looked at the scooter, its pink handlebar tassels were gently blowing in the breeze.

'It's mine. I just bought it.'

'Mr Derrick,' she said, 'what am I going to do with you?' She walked through the gate and crossed the road to her car, opened the door, and, before climbing inside, she said, 'If I see you on it before your arm is properly healed, I'll run you over again myself.'

She got in the car and started the engine. The stereo came on. She opened the car window.

'By the way,' she said, 'I like your glasses.'

'Thank you,' Frank said.

'They've taken five years off you.'

'I should have got contact lenses. They might have taken off ten years.'

'I see you've broken them already.'

Frank felt the side of his glasses. 'It was the postman.'

'The who?'

'The postman!'

Kelly revved the engine as though she were about to leave, then thought of something else to say.

'We should go to the big supermarket next week,' she said. 'Get something other than tinned spaghetti.'

'The big supermarket? I've never been,' Frank said.

They were both shouting now, to be heard above the

sound of the engine and the music inside Kelly's car, just like they did when the kettle was boiling.

'You've never been to a supermarket?'

'Well, yes. But not the big one. I've been on the bus but I've just never reached its final destination. I'm like Jim Lovell.'

'Who?'

'Jim Lovell. The only man to have flown to the Moon twice without landing on it.'

'Do you know a lot about space travel?'

'I've seen *Apollo 13* three times.'

Kelly revved the engine. 'I'm late,' she shouted. She revved the engine one more time, bumped the car off the grass verge onto the road, and Frank – and surely all the neighbours, because Frank and Kelly really had been shouting quite loudly – watched the little blue car move backwards and then forwards, the gears crunching until Kelly found the one she was searching for and then she tooted the horn and Frank watched her drive away. With his new glasses he could see her right to the end of the road until she turned right and disappeared.

He thought if he looked hard enough he'd still be able to see her once she had turned the corner. Like he had superpowers. Frank Derrick. Superman. Faster than a speeding bullet, more powerful than a locomotive and the only thing preventing him from being able to jump tall buildings in a single bound were all the bungalows.

22

Albert Flowers was behind the campaign to get Fullwind-on-Sea etched onto the Villages in Bloom trophy. His name hadn't been made up for him by Frank because he liked flowers, although the editor of the Fullwind-on-Sea village newsletter did like flowers. He owned a florist, always wore flowery-patterned bow ties and a carnation or a tulip in the buttonhole of his jacket, and he was married to a woman named Rose. But his name was just coincidence, or serendipity.

It was Flowers who had written to Frank about all the fridges in his garden before last year's competition. Fullwind had come fourth then. Albert Flowers wasn't going to let that happen again. As the final of the competition approached he spent most of his day walking around the village inspecting gardens, taking photographs and talking into his Dictaphone, before going home to write polite letters to residents about the length of their grass or the height of their Leylandii.

He was standing on the verge outside Frank's flat. And just by the way the blades of the grass covered the scuffmarks on his shoes he could tell that the grass was too long. He would ask Frank about that in a moment. First there was the matter of all the junk in his front garden.

'It would be helpful if you could get it moved as soon as possible,' Flowers said and he smiled falsely.

Frank looked up and tried to register his acknowledgement via the smallest of facial expressions. Every little bit of him was currently trying to lift a heavy stone bollard and he felt that if he raised an eyebrow too high he'd drop the heavy lump of concrete and break another toe. He had, of course, considered doing just that. If he let the bollard fall onto his foot, breaking a new toe or another metatarsal, Beth would somehow have to find the money for a few more months of home care visits. Frank had also thought about walking out in front of a milk float again, or falling down the stairs on his way to pick up the newspaper. He could tell Beth he was getting the newspaper to read the date on the front page out loud, like Ron had told him to do on the leaflet she'd sent him. It would sort of be Beth's fault then and she'd feel so awful that she'd find the money somehow.

After Kelly had driven away the day before, Frank had thought of little else – how to make her keep driving back. Her visits had made him feel like there was a reason to get up in the morning. His glass wasn't half full but it was definitely less empty. He wasn't just cruising any more. There were more gears after all. He felt like he might run again or punch someone or he might jump up and down on a bouncy castle eating corn on the cob – or build a cinema. He might even get to chew gum or eat a Twix – or, who knew, even a Yorkie or a Toblerone. He wasn't ready to go back to talking to his own reflection, cutting the mould off his sandwiches and weeing by torchlight yet.

The woman on the Lemons Care hotline had told him what it would cost: £300 for another twelve home visits,

£600 for twenty-four home visits, or £1,200 for a full year's worth of visits. There was also a subscription fee of £125.

'Then, of course,' the woman had said, 'there's our Lemons Live-in service. That would be £5,500 for six months. Plus the usual subscription fee and expenses.' Once he'd heard the words 'live-in', Frank couldn't stop thinking that he needed to find £5,625. The amount didn't really matter. Frank didn't have it.

Since ringing Lemons Care, more than ever, Frank's television seemed to be addressing him directly in between programmes. 'Are you in debt?' his television said. 'Do you need cash in a hurry?'

'Yes!' Frank shouted. 'Yes!'

'Have you got money problems?'

'Yes, I have!' he screamed at the TV. When he picked up his newspaper in the morning, leaflets advertising ways to make money would fall out. They offered him cash for his gold, cash for his clothes, cash for his mobile phones and his CDs and so on.

To take his mind off it he decided to use some of the paint he'd found in the shed to paint the three concrete bollards on the grass verge outside his flat. First he needed to replace the bollard that had been lying on its side since Fullwind's mini crime wave. A few weeks ago, even without his arm in plaster, he wouldn't have had the strength or hubris to even attempt it.

He was only Clark Kent then.

Thinking about everything he'd heard at different points throughout his life concerning lifting heavy objects, he placed his feet on either side of the bollard and bent at the knees, making sure to keep his back straight and looking straight ahead like he'd seen the weightlifters do on the Olympics. He wrapped his arms around the bollard and took a deep breath, which was when Albert Flowers turned up.

'Only, the competition is very soon. The judges will be walking through the village.'

Frank looked up at him, still holding on to the bollard. Perhaps he could ask Flowers for a loan. A small payment in return for tidying his garden. A bribe. Blackmail. How much was the Villages in Bloom trophy worth to Albert Flowers? Frank wondered how much the florist himself was worth. He priced his clothes up like the old women in the charity shop did with the dead men's suits. His suit was made to measure. Tweed. His shirt came from Savile Row. His shoes were scuffed but expensive. Frank wanted to mug Albert Flowers.

He let go of the bollard and stood up. 'Do you want to buy any of it?'

'I beg your pardon?' Flowers said.

Frank waved his open palm over the collection of shed shit on his lawn.

'An old bicycle wheel, perhaps? The tyre is flat and the rubber has perished and there is a certain amount of rust to the surface of the chrome, but how about ten pounds? Come on. What will you give for this leftover wallpaper or a piece of carpet? Some garden hose? A Wellington boot? Tell you what, seeing as it's you, take the whole lot for just five thousand, six hundred and twenty-five pounds.'

'Oh. Is it a sale?' Flowers said. 'I don't believe that under the byelaws you would actually be authorised to—'

'It's not a sale. I was joking. Now, I'm a bit busy. Once I pick this up I can clear the garden.'

Flowers looked at the heavy bollard, contemplated offering his help, but decided not to. 'Right. I'll leave you to it,' he said.

Frank said goodbye. He was already taking his place astride the bollard, preparing for his lift. He hugged it and lifted it towards him and stood the bollard upright with less effort than he was expecting. He rocked it from side to side until it was back in its rightful place. The woodlice were settled in beneath the bollard before Frank was back inside his front gate.

After lunch he opened the tins of paint he'd found in the shed. The white paint was completely dried up, so he painted the bollards Sunflower Yellow. It was the same colour as the furniture in Beth's bedroom. Gloss paint. Frank now had the only shiny Sunflower-yellow bollards on Sea Lane. Sunflower. Albert Flowers would be pleased.

23

Indiana Jones and the Search for Coins Under the Cushions of the Sofa and the Armchair was the weakest of the movie franchise, and financially the least successful. Frank had found eight pence under his living-room cushions. After he'd been through the pockets of all his trousers and jackets and shaken all his hollow porcelain figurines and lifted the lids on teapots and peered into vases, he had amassed a grand total of £1.07. If he put some batteries in the calculator in the kitchen drawer he could have worked out that he had enough for two minutes and fifty-six point eight seconds of Kelly's time. Barely long enough for her to get the key out of the safe and make it up the stairs.

Frank looked through the cupboards and drawers for anything that might be made of gold or silver, holding stuff up to the light to see if it was hallmarked. If Frank's flat were to have a name, it wouldn't be El Dorado. He lifted the lids on the pair of matching trinket boxes on the mantelpiece but they contained no trinkets, just two shirt buttons and a coin that was too old to still be legal tender but not yet old enough to be collectable. Frank bit the coin, like they did in the films, to see if it was gold. It told him nothing other than that he needed a stronger denture fixative.

He sat down at the desk in the living room and opened the drawer. He took out Sheila's old purse and popped it open. There was a £5 note inside that would have paid for enough time for a hair brushing if it hadn't been an old fiver and long since withdrawn from circulation but still not old enough to be collectable. Frank put the fiver back in the purse and put the purse back in the drawer; in a way, he was relieved that he wouldn't be able to use his wife's money.

He looked at the balled-up strands of hair that Kelly had removed from the bristles of her brush. They were like a worm cast on the sandy brown wood at the bottom of the desk drawer. He picked up the hair and placed it on his open palm. He stared at it as though it might curl or flip over one way or the other like a cellophane fortune-telling fish, telling him he was jealous, fickle, romantic or daft.

He put the hair back in the desk drawer.

He took a leaflet for 'Instant Spondulicks, payday loans in ten minutes' out of his pocket. There was a picture of a young couple on the leaflet. The man was talking on the phone to Instant Spondulicks. His wife watched him. They were both smiling. The man was actually laughing. The people with money problems seemed even happier about it than the infirm and dying were about stair lifts and funerals. Frank dialled the phone number on the leaflet. A man answered the phone. Frank told him he needed a loan.

'How much?' the man asked.

'What's the most I can borrow?'

'Five hundred pounds.'

'Oh,' Frank said. He was expecting it to be a lot more. 'Could I borrow that please? Five hundred pounds.'

The man took Frank's details and read a long list of terms and conditions out at cattle-auctioneer speed and said he'd call Frank back in ten minutes.

Frank waited by the phone.

Frank had never been very good with money.

When Sheila was alive she'd always paid the bills. Sheila opened and read bank statements and checked till receipts against the contents of shopping bags before leaving the supermarket. Frank didn't open his bills until the print on the front of the envelope was red and he didn't open his bank statements at all. He screwed up till receipts without looking at them. He never looked at the prices of things in shops. He had less idea what the price of a pint of milk or loaf of bread was than a High Court Judge.

Without Sheila around, Frank very quickly dug a hole for himself and filled it up with worthless charity shop bric-a-brac and 16mm films he couldn't watch. And then he jumped into the hole. So when the phone rang and the man from Instant Spondulicks told him his application had been denied, Frank wasn't surprised. He put the phone down and watched the news. It was another pensioners/geriatric ward/dementia/poverty/mugging special. He turned off the TV, did seven press-ups and went out on his scooter.

Frank sped along Sea Lane, flying past Trims His Lawn with Nail Scissors and Washes His Car Too Much. He skidded by Picks up Litter, blowing a chocolate wrapper out of reach of her spiked stick. On the slight downward slope leading to the shops he really picked up speed, his tiny wheel lights flashing, the handlebar tassels blowing in unison with his long silver white hair. Everyone he passed stopped and turned their heads to watch him fly past.

181

'What's the matter? Never seen an eighty-one-year-old on a scooter before?' Frank shouted and laughed.

Not really.

Frank couldn't quite get the hang of how to take both feet off the ground without the scooter toppling over and he didn't even make it up to the one mile an hour needed to turn the wheel lights on. He carried the scooter most of the way to the shops, just like all the other parents did with their children's scooters.

He leaned the scooter against the window of the charity shop and went inside. There were two customers in the shop, both of them waiting to pay at the counter. Frank browsed. He picked up a piggy bank and lightly shook it but it made no sound. He looked for hallmarks on the bottom of a snuffbox and the back of a ladies wristwatch. The other customers paid and left the shop and Frank went over to the counter.

'I was wondering about the card in the window,' he said to a woman sticking small price labels onto packs of Christmas cards. 'Help wanted.'

'June,' the woman called out. 'Gentleman here looking to help out.' She looked at Frank. 'June will be able to help you.' She went back to labelling the Christmas cards.

'Thank you,' Frank said.

He heard high-pitched laughter coming from behind the curtain in the storeroom. There were a lot of different members of staff who worked in the charity shop. He was rarely served by the same person twice. And other than the Chuckle Brothers tribute act who drove the shop's delivery van, he'd never seen any male members of staff. Working here was going to be like travelling to the big Sainsbury's and back, over and over again for eight hours every day.

'I won't be able to work on Monday mornings,' he said to the woman behind the counter.

'June will be able to help you,' she said. 'June,' she called out. 'Gentleman can't work on – when did you say?'

'Mondays.'

'Can't work on Mondays,' she called out.

'Mornings. I can work Monday afternoons.'

'Mornings. Gentleman can't work mornings.'

'Monday mornings. Just Monday mornings.'

Frank waited. Customers came and left. He started to wonder whether June existed. He thought that if he pulled open the curtain between the shop and the storeroom, June's skeleton would be sitting in a rocking chair.

'I'm just looking for a bit of extra income,' Frank said to fill the awkward silence. The woman nodded and carried on pricing Christmas cards.

Frank looked around. He wondered whether there were any coins in the oriental vase inside the glass cabinet at the centre of the shop. When he was working here, he'd open the cabinet and stick his arm inside the vase and find out.

'It is a charity, you realise?' the woman behind the counter said.

Yes, of course it was. A charity shop. Voluntary. What an idiot. He was trying to get a paid job in a charity shop.

'June will be out in a moment,' the woman said. But Frank was already edging towards the door.

'Actually, I should be going. I've just remembered, I . . .' He couldn't think of a single thing he could pretend that he should be doing. 'I'll come back. Thank you.' He walked out of the shop, picked his scooter up and went next door to Fullwind Food & Wine and asked if they had any jobs.

'You'll need to drop off your CV,' the man at the checkout said.

'My CV? Oh, yes, of course,' Frank said. 'I'll bring it in later.' He asked the man for two scratch cards.

'You have to speculate to accumulate,' the man behind the checkout said and looked pleased with himself as though he was the first person to have ever said it. Frank left the shop, picked his scooter up and carried it home. He passed Picks up Litter, Washes His Car Too Much and Trims His Lawn with Nail Scissors. These were people who'd planned their retirements. Frank didn't own a car and his lawn was too long for scissors and covered in foam stuffing and rubbish that was too big to fit on the end of a pointy stick. Here were retired homeowners with fully paid-up mortgages and private pension plans. They probably knew where and how they'd be buried – Simple, Classique, Superb or Royale. They didn't need to write a CV. Who over the age of seventy had ever written a CV?

Frank came from a time when you just had a job. You went to school. You left school. You got a job. He'd had a lot of different jobs in the past but never one that he felt defined by, though. Not a tinker or a tailor or a soldier or a sailor. None of the prune-stone occupations. What would he put on his CV? What would the sarcastic young cashier at Fullwind Food & Wine make of Frank's list of imaginary-sounding jobs for companies that no longer existed? Bus conductor for London Transport. Switchboard operator for the Gas Board. Television repairman for Radio Rentals.

Frank might as well put down that he worked as assistant scrivener on Jupiter.

The sarcastic man and the checkout he worked on would eventually be on that list too. With every new self-service checkout point that opened in the big supermarket they both edged closer to obsolescence. The same applied to the women in the charity shop and the milkman who ran Frank over – he and his battery-powered vehicle were dodos too. And the nurse who sawed his plaster cast in half and told him about God – surely a machine or a computer could do both those things too.

When he was almost home, a young woman whom Frank might have named Walks Five Different Dogs walked towards him. As he stepped aside to let her and her five different dogs pass, she stepped aside the same way. The dogs became instantly disoriented, walking in different directions and wrapping their leads around Frank's legs and around his scooter. The dogs were all barking and the dog walker was apologising, trying to calm the dogs down so she could unravel their leads from Frank's legs. He felt like a maypole. And it was June. The dog of the month was a terrier. There were three Kelly visits left before July – the month of Royston the-flea-bitten-mange-infested mongrel.

On Friday, Frank wrote 'Yard Sale Today 12 Noon' on a piece of paper and stuck it on his gate.

Albert Flowers had given him the idea. Instead of putting everything back in the shed, he'd sell it. He cleared the more obviously unsellable stuff out of the way. He moved the ivy into a pile beside the shed, along with the rotten carpet, the bedside table, the red tartan shopping basket and the sun loungers. He stuffed the perished cardboard boxes into the dustbin and, when nobody was watching, threw the Wellington boot into the overgrown bush that ran along the fence between his garden and the one next door. He leaned the ladder up against the shed. Everything else – the rusty garden tools, the golf balls, the picture of the boat, the TV aerials and remote controls – would be for sale.

Frank stood the decorator's table upright and locked the legs in place, pinching his fingers in the hinges. He'd originally bought the table to wallpaper Beth's bedroom. There were still paste marks along both sides of the table. He hadn't measured the room and had bought too much wallpaper. When he'd finished the room there were three half-rolls left; the pattern was still as good as new from years kept in the darkness of the shed. The only other time Frank could remember having used the table was to put food on for one of Beth's birthday parties.

With the things from the shed on or next to the table, Frank went inside and looked for anything else he might be able to sell. A tea set, some wine glasses, a few books, a table lamp, a carpet sweeper and a bread bin. He sorted through any videos that he'd replaced with DVD copies. In spite of no longer having anything to watch them on, and owning the films on DVD, he still hated the thought of parting with the tapes. He emptied all the free light bulbs out of the kitchen cupboard into a bag and took them out into the garden. He found a pack of unused Christmas cards given to him by a charity and he put them on the table. He filled his charity coffee mugs on the table with charity biros and wrote '10p each' on a piece of paper next to them. If he had

had more time and a jug he would have made lemonade to sell like they always did at the yard sales in films.

At 11.50 a.m., he put on a green kitchen apron because it had a pocket on the front. He thought of Kelly in her monkey shirt. He filled the pocket with change, took his place behind the decorator's table and prepared for the rush.

He soon realised he wouldn't last long behind the counter of Fullwind Food & Wine or the charity shop. Customers are idiots. The general public are annoying. Nobody at his yard sale wanted to pay full price for anything. They all thought they were in a back-street Istanbul bazaar.

'Fifty pence? I'll give you twenty pence.'

'What's your best price? Come on, a pound for the lot.'

And the questions.

'Do you have any clubs?'

'No.'

'Just the golf balls?'

'Yes.'

'It's clubs I'm really after. How much for the balls?'

'Ten pence each.'

'I'll give you fifty p for the whole box.'

'Is it just videotapes? Any DVDs?'

'Just videotapes.'

'I don't have a video recorder any more.'

'Does this lamp work?'

'Yes, I think so.'

'You think so? Can I see?'

'We'd have to go inside and plug it in.'

'Can I take it home and bring it back if it doesn't work?'

'I suppose so.'

'What's this?'

'A bread bin.'

'Do you have any bayonet-fitting light bulbs?'

After three hours the videos were gone and Trims His Lawn with Nail Scissors had bought a garden fork – he was convinced the tea set on sale was one that he himself had given to the charity shop, which it was. But he bought it anyway. Hilary, the head of the Neighbourhood Watch, came in for a look around but didn't buy anything. The man who took the lamp home brought it back because it didn't work.

When Frank took the sign off the gate and shut up shop there was £26.19 in the pocket of the apron. £3 of that was the float he'd started out with. It hadn't been a great success. Not enough people had come. There was probably sport on television or it was too hot to be shopping. He should have made the jug of lemonade. He had eighty-one years' worth of lemons. He just needed a jug.

24

A man around the same age as Frank boarded the big Sainsbury's bus and walked the gauntlet to the back. The doors closed, the bus started moving and Frank watched the man's face silently screaming for help through the back window like a poster for an Edvard Munch retrospective.

Frank was in the car behind the bus. The car radio was entering its fifth minute of shouted advertising. Frank hated adverts. He particularly hated the loud ones. He could find the mute button on his television remote control blind-folded as if he was a marine cleaning his assault rifle. The loud television adverts weren't aimed at him anyway. He wasn't missing out on any great offers or miracle cures by turning the sound down. The adverts hoping to address what was missing in Frank's life – freedom from debt and incontinence and help getting up and down stairs – were more softly spoken. The adverts being shouted from the car radio were for hair gel and mobile phones, pop records and yogurt. Frank didn't mind them today, though. To be honest, he couldn't really hear them because of the song going round and round in his head.

Sitting in the front seat.
Kelly and me.

D.R.I.V.I.N.G.

Frank watched the bus in front pull away and the hula dancer on the dashboard of Kelly's car started dancing again. The Nurse on Call sign next to the dancer was flipped over like a Shop Closed sign, even though, taking Frank on this car journey, she was technically on call. She turned a corner into the low mid-morning sun and Frank screwed his eyes up. Kelly reached over and pulled the sun visor down for him.

'Thanks,' he said.

There was a small rectangular mirror on the back of the sun visor and Frank checked himself out in it. Kelly had arrived today with a small glasses repair kit. She'd put a new screw in the arm of Frank's Belgian architect glasses, using the smallest screwdriver in the world. She'd sprayed lens cleaner onto the lenses and polished them with a small grey piece of material.

As they drove past Greyflick House, Frank looked up to see if Smelly John was at his window. He wanted John to see him in the car with Kelly. But the window was too far away – although Frank could see the carrier bag full of dog shit in the branches of the tree outside like a flag.

Kelly turned another corner and Frank saw the 24-Hour Superstore sign. Past the sign, a bit further on and round to the right, was the Diamond Dogs and Love Cats building. Kelly stopped at the turning for Sainsbury's to let a young family cross. The eldest of two children was carrying a cardboard cat box. Frank wondered whether Bill was inside. He tried to work out what sort of family Bill's new family were, would they be right for him? If it was Bill in the cat box, Frank hoped he was going to a good home. He wanted to jump out of the car, stop the family and ask if he could see inside the box. Then he could quickly assess whether they were aware of their responsibilities as cat owners and that they knew a cat wasn't just for Christmas, even though it was only June. The family crossed the road and Kelly drove along the superstore entrance road, past the petrol station and into the car park. There were two floors to the car park; the lower level was full and Kelly drove up the ramp and parked the car on the upper level.

While she talked to a man offering to hand wash her car, Frank did his best to climb out of the passenger seat unaided and without crying out in pain. He'd woken up in the morning with an ache across the top of his chest and it hadn't gone. At first he thought he was having a heart attack or a stroke. Almost immediately it crossed his mind that either of those things would require convalescence help. Was he actually pleased to have almost died in his sleep? He lifted his arms above the bedspread and said, 'Hello.' That was about all he knew about strokes – something about not being able to lift your arms and slurred speech. He didn't seem to have had a stroke. Sitting up in bed and not toppling over onto the floor, he decided that he hadn't had a heart attack either.

He had probably been overdoing it lately. Just this week he'd lifted and painted heavy stone bollards, he'd emptied a garden shed, carried a scooter to the shops and back and been the maypole for five different breeds of dog. And then he'd held a yard sale. Not forgetting the seven press-ups. He'd never been so busy.

Kelly said no thank you to the man offering to wash her car and Frank followed her across the car park. He wondered whether he was too old to wash cars in a supermarket

191

car park. He tried to memorise the company name and telephone number on the man's waterproof jacket so that he could ring them later and ask if they had any vacancies.

'Six two three, four five five six,' he whispered to himself, trying to remember the car wash company's telephone number. 'Three two five.' But he'd forgotten the number by the time he was inside the large silver lift that took them down to the car park's lower level. 'Something Wash' was all he'd seen of the name on the car washer's jacket.

Kelly put a pound coin into a lock and pulled a shopping trolley free from the trolley train. She pushed it backwards and forwards to check the wheels were okay and then walked with Frank through the doors into Sainsbury's.

Blade Runner.

That's what Frank wanted to say.

It's like *Blade Runner.*

The shop was enormous. It stretched too far for Frank to see where it ended, if it actually ever did. He imagined its length being measured in football pitches and its height in double decker buses. At the centre of the store was a moving walkway leading up to a second floor that sold furniture, electrical goods and toys. The shop was very brightly lit and colourful signs hung everywhere, advertising deals, discounts and special offers. Music played in between the announcements, or the other way around. The adverts and customer service announcements were louder and longer than the music, just like the adverts on Kelly's car radio. Frank didn't mind. He had a new song.

In the big Sainsbury's.

Kelly and me.

S.H.O.P.P.I.N.G.

192

'Clean up in aisle seventy,' one of the announcements said.

Seventy aisles! Frank thought. Sixty-seven more than where he usually shopped. And they were wide aisles, two double decker buses wide, wider than the whole of Fullwind Food & Wine. There was a deli counter and a fish counter. A butcher and a baker and probably a candlestick maker. At the in-store pharmacy a woman was sitting on a stool having her eyebrows plucked by another woman in a white coat.

Frank had plucked his eyebrows this morning. That was something he never thought he'd do. Something he couldn't even remember Sheila or Beth doing. It had made him sneeze more than when he'd pulled the hairs out of his nostrils. The woman in the chair in Sainsbury's didn't sneeze at all. There was obviously more of a skill to it than simply grabbing hold of a hair and hoping for the best.

They walked into the store, past the magazines, cigarettes and flowers and onto the first of three fruit and vegetables aisles.

'Fruit?' Kelly said. 'Apples? Oranges?'

'Ahm . . .'

There was so much to choose from. Frank didn't even know what some of the fruit and vegetables were. They were like props made for a science fiction film set on another planet. He put a bag of oranges in the trolley. Kelly took them straight back out again and replaced them with oranges from the back and bottom of the pile. She showed Frank the label.

'Two days fresher,' she said.

In the tinned beans and peas aisle Frank reached up and took a tin of spaghetti from the shelf.

193

'Tinned spaghetti?' Kelly said. Disappointed that he was making the same food choices as he would in the small shop in Fullwind. 'Do you eat fish and chips on your Spanish holidays too?'

'I've never been to Spain.'

She took the spaghetti out of the trolley and put it back on the shelf. 'At least save yourself some money,' she said, and took a multipack of four tins off the shelf and showed Frank the price. She put them in the trolley and took another four-pack from the shelf.

'I don't like spaghetti *that* much,' Frank said.

'Buy one get one free,' Kelly said.

They walked around the huge store and Kelly showed Frank the special offers and money-saving deals. He didn't normally look at the price of food. He just took it off the shelf and put it in his basket. It was one of the reasons he had no money.

Kelly made him look at the labels on the back of packaging before putting them in the trolley. She showed him the nutritional information, the fat content, the traffic-light rating system and all the artificial ingredients and vitamins he'd never even heard of.

Frank filled his trolley with ready meals from Italy, India, China and wherever couscous came from – Frank didn't know – he didn't know what couscous was. Kelly said he should try it. As the trolley filled he became more confident. He chose a cereal because it reminded him of the jingle from an old TV advert he used to sing to Beth and he picked the larger box because it worked out cheaper. He put three boxes of Oreos in the trolley, even though he didn't particularly like them, but he only had to pay for two of them. He was going to buy jam and tomato ketchup too, and keep it all in the fridge and tell Beth about it when he next spoke to her.

Frank bought a large pizza that was too wide for his fridge. He bought cakes and enough teabags to see him through to the other side of the fall-out from the nuclear war somebody on TV the night before had told him was imminent. He hoped that Fullwind would be nuked on a Monday so that he didn't have to wait out the Nuclear Winter alone.

In the DVD section *Dirty Dancing* was only £2.99. Frank put it in his trolley.

'If you like it,' Kelly said, 'you can watch *Footloose* next.'

A man walked past. He saw Frank and they nodded hello to each other.

'Who was that?' Kelly said.

'Fat Pat.'

'Fat Pat?'

'Yes.'

'Is he a friend?'

'I've only met him once before.'

'Long enough to give him an affectionately horrible name. At least I hope it's affectionate.'

'I've got a friend called Smelly John too.'

'You're joking now.'

'No.'

'Who am I? Smelly Kelly?'

'No. At least, not in a bad way.'

Frank reached up to take a Laurel and Hardy DVD down from the shelf. He felt the stiffness in his arm from his week of activity. He wanted to catch up with Pat, roll his sleeves up and say, 'Look. Tight skin. Now draw me a butterfly, fatso.'

A woman was standing behind a small high table offering samples of cheese. Frank took one and then asked whether he could take a second piece.

'Are you hungry?' Kelly said. 'There's a restaurant.'

'Won't you be late for your next . . .' Client? Customer? Patient? What was he, exactly?

'I can take my lunch hour now,' she said.

They joined the shortest-looking queue at the checkouts. They unpacked the trolley, put the shopping in bags and put the full bags back into the trolley. When Frank looked at the price on the till display he thought he was going to faint. The woman on the checkout asked if he had a loyalty card.

'Er, no.'

'Would you like one?'

'Ahhm.'

'I'll give you a leaflet and you can decide later.'

She gave Frank a leaflet and he folded it up and stuffed it into his pocket. He planned on being unbelievably loyal. They were going to be sick of the sight of him. He paid for the shopping with his debit card. When the card wasn't rejected, he presumed his pension had gone into – and now out of again – his account.

In the supermarket restaurant Frank sat down with the trolley full of carrier bags while Kelly went to the counter. There were none of the doubts in the minds of the customers in this café that there had been in the minds of the customers in the one at the beach. Kelly's uniform told them she was Frank's carer and he was her client, her customer or patient, and she was there to look after him. They probably felt a bit sorry for him. The mugs.

Frank had a cheese sandwich and a fizzy orange and

Kelly asked him about Fat Pat and Smelly John. He explained how John didn't smell, or, at least, if he did, like her, he didn't smell in a bad way. He told her about John's love of board games and for winding people up. When he told her how he'd met Smelly John, she didn't seem to believe him.

'Have you seen *Battleship Potemkin*?' Frank said.

'No. Is it a film?'

'An old silent one. There's a famous scene on some steps. The bit everyone remembers is a pram rolling down the steps out of control. There's a homage to it in *The Untouchables*. Have you seen that?'

'I don't think so. Who's in it?'

'Everyone. Kevin Costner, Sean Connery, Robert De Niro.'

'I probably have. I can never remember films.'

'There's a bit in a Laurel and Hardy film as well. When a piano they're delivering rolls down some steep steps.'

'I don't really like Laurel and Hardy,' Kelly said. 'My dad watched their films all the time. I find it infuriating when everything keeps going wrong and you know it's coming. I want to shout at the screen to stop them making the same mistakes over and over. But how does all this relate to Smelly John?'

'Do you know the steep hill that leads down to the sea up past the hospital?'

'Yes. I think so.'

'That's where I saved his life.'

'You saved his life? How?'

'He was asleep in his wheelchair and it was rolling down the hill, picking up speed. I was passing by and I stopped it.'

197

Kelly didn't say anything. She just looked at him in a way that said she didn't believe him.

'It's true. He'd passed out or something. I stopped his chair, pushed him back up the hill. It wasn't easy. I took him home.'

'Really?'

'To his sheltered-housing flat.'

'Are you sure this isn't actually the Laurel and Hardy film you're describing?'

'It's true. You could come and meet him, if you like. You'd have to go to his place. He doesn't go outside.'

'I thought you met him outside?'

'Any more. He doesn't go outside any more. He has MS. He's in a wheelchair. Did I say? He lives on the first floor of a sheltered housing place where the lift never works, which he seems to actually enjoy. He gets the warden to carry him up and down stairs. He seems to think he's doing it out of revenge.'

'What for?'

'He says the warden's been picking on him. Because he's a racist.'

'Who? Smelly John is a racist?'

'Not John, the warden. The warden is a racist.'

'Has he reported him?'

'I don't think so.'

'He should report it,' Kelly said.

'I don't think so.'

'There's no reason for him to tolerate that. Do you want me to say something?'

'What if it isn't true, though?'

'But your friend thinks the warden is being racist?'

'Yes.'

'Then he should report him.'

'I'm not sure that he is a racist,' Frank said.

'But you aren't sure he *isn't*, though, either?'

'No, but it's more complicated.'

'Why?'

'I'm not sure Smelly John is black.'

'What?' Kelly said, almost spitting her coffee out. 'You aren't sure?'

'Yes. No. Yes. Well, he doesn't look particularly black.'

Kelly was dumbfounded.

'Particularly?'

'Not at all really.'

'Have you asked him?' she said.

'Ask John? If he's black?'

'Yes.'

'I've never said anything before. It might seem strange if I suddenly bring it up now. He might think I'm a racist too, like the warden.'

'Who probably isn't a racist?' Kelly said.

'Yes.'

'Because John's not black?'

'Yes.'

'I don't really know what to say,' Kelly said. 'And how about Fat Pat? What's his secret?'

'He's just fat.'

Kelly drove Frank home and helped him carry his shopping upstairs and then put it away. When she left, Frank looked at the clock. She'd spent over two hours with him. One hour a week was definitely not going to be enough from now on.

25

Frank didn't enjoy *Dirty Dancing*. All the interruptions while he was trying to watch it didn't help. He hadn't even made it to the end of the opening titles when the phone rang. He paused the DVD and answered it.

'Hello. Could I speak to Mr Watson?'

'I'm sorry, I think you have the wrong number.'

The person on the phone read Frank's phone number out to him.

'That is my number,' Frank said. 'But not my name.'

'That is strange. It's the number we have.'

'Can I ask who's calling please?'

'My name is Angela. I'm calling from Lemons Care.'

Mr Watson was the name Frank had given when he pretended he was an American calling Lemons Care about their prices for his imaginary father. He hadn't considered that they might call him back.

'There's nobody by that name here. You must have a wrong number.'

'I am sorry,' Angela said. 'Sorry to have bothered you.'

Frank said goodbye and hung the phone up. He knew that at some point, possibly immediately, Angela would dial his number again, expecting to hear an American voice on the other end of the line. He contemplated answering the phone as Mr Watson and saying he was no longer interested or he couldn't afford it, or that his ill father, Mr Watson Senior, had taken a sudden turn for the worse and had sadly passed away.

He pressed the pause button on the DVD player and started watching the film again, but he was distracted. He kept looking over at the telephone, waiting for it to ring. 'Hello,' he said out loud to nobody, practising his American accent. 'Hi there. This is Mr Watson. How may I help you?' he said. He'd forgotten what American accent Mr Watson had. He was missing the plot of the film thinking about it.

About half an hour later the phone rang again. Frank left the DVD running this time and just muted the sound.

'Hi there,' he said.

'Is that Mrs Sharpes?' a man's voice said.

'No. I think you have the wrong number.'

'Are you the homeowner?'

'No. Who is this?'

'I'm calling from Finance and Debt Finance Finance.'

'No thank you. I'm not interested.'

'Have you been mis-sold insurance?'

'No. Thank you.'

The man carried on talking as though Frank's part in the conversation was irrelevant.

'Is your name Janice?' Frank said.

'Excuse me?'

'Nothing.'

'You have been negligently sold expensive insurance cover.'

'No I haven't.'

'When you applied for your mortgage—'

'I don't have a mortgage.'

Frank looked at the TV, trying to keep up with the story so that he didn't have to start watching the film again from the beginning.

'Could I speak to the homeowner?'

'The homeowner isn't here.'

The man on the phone carried on talking. He mentioned numbers and percentages and started talking in capitals TO STRESS HOW IMPORTANT WHAT HE WAS SAYING WAS AND THEN HE *THREW IN SOME ITALICS ABOUT HOW FRANK HAD TO DO THIS AND HAD TO DO THAT*. When there was a pause Frank tried to fill it.

'I don't know what you're talking about.'

'Are you the homeowner?'

'No.'

'Could I speak to the homeowner?'

'Not here you can't.'

'When will the homeowner be available?'

'I don't know. They don't live here.'

'Could I take your name?'

'No.'

The man started talking about insurance again. It was raining heavily on *Dirty Dancing* and Patrick Swayze seemed animated about something. With the sound off Frank didn't know what he was animated about. Swayze started kicking at a white wooden bollard. He's lucky that's only made of wood, Frank thought. Swayze pulled the bollard out of the ground and smashed a car window with it. Frank expected Albert Flowers would be turning up in the next scene to talk to Swayze about it.

'No. Thank you,' Frank said to the man on the phone. 'I'm really not interested. Goodbye.' He hung up the phone while the man was still talking. The man would make a note of Frank's phone number and one day he'd come round with all the other call-centre employees and door steppers who Frank had hung up on, made funny comments to or slammed the door on. They'd beat Frank with clubs, then sign him up for a no-win, no-fee injury claim.

Frank paused the DVD and went to make a cup of tea. He wasn't sure what was going on in the film but didn't want to start watching it from the beginning again. It had taken ten minutes just to get through the copyright notices and piracy warnings in seven different languages. He'd watch the film from here to the end and hopefully pick up enough information to form an opinion that he could share with Kelly.

He was almost at the end of the film when he heard a squeaking sound. He thought it was the DVD. He tried to ignore it. But the squeaking continued. It wasn't coming from the DVD. The squeaking was behind him. He turned around. At his window there was a man. He had Art Garfunkel hair. That was the first thing Frank noticed. The second thing was that the man was cleaning Frank's window. Frank didn't have a window cleaner. He couldn't afford it. He let his windows get dirty and every once in a while he would lean as far out of them as he could and clean as much of the glass as he could reach. His windows were never completely clean. But neither were they completely dirty. Optimists and pessimists had differing views on Frank's windows.

But he definitely didn't have a window cleaner.

He looked at the curly haired man who nodded hello and carried on wiping the glass. Frank thought about opening the window and knocking him off his ladder like in a sitcom.

'What do you want?' Frank said.

'What?' the man said.

'What do you want?'

Art Garfunkel stopped wiping the window, lifted a clump of curls to cup his hand to his ear and instead of speaking any louder he mouthed the words, 'I can't hear you.'

To avoid yet another boiling-kettle conversation Frank got up from his armchair and went over to the window. It was locked and he didn't know where the key was.

'Just a minute,' Frank said.

The window cleaner cupped his ear again and mouthed, 'What?'

'I have to find a key,' Frank said. He mimed unlocking the window. He went to the bathroom and took a window key from there. He came back and opened the window next to the one the man was cleaning.

'I thought you might want your windows doing,' the man said. 'I do all of them in this street. Nice to get to use my ladder for a change.'

'I don't remember asking,' Frank said.

'There was no answer. At the door,' the man said. He looked past Frank at the TV. 'My wife loves this film.'

Frank turned around. Patrick Swayze had just lifted Jennifer Grey over his head and she was now back down on the ground. Frank had missed the most famous scene in the film.

If he ever watched *Dirty Dancing* again, this moment

right now would be a big part of the film for him – not Patrick Swayze putting Jennifer Grey back down on the ground – Art Garfunkel washing his windows. There were other films that always reminded him of something unconnected to the plot whenever he watched them. It would either be the time or place he saw the film or, more often, something that had happened the first time he'd seen the film that he couldn't help but remember every time he saw it again. An extra dimension to the story the director had no control over.

Years ago Frank had been watching *Blazing Saddles*. During the farting cowboys scene the hospital had rung and told him he should probably get back there as soon as possible. Frank couldn't watch *Blazing Saddles* now. He would be waiting for the phone to ring with news his wife was dying. He could watch far sadder films more obviously related to Sheila dying – *Philadelphia* or *Love Story* – but he never found them as sad as watching cowboys sitting around a campfire breaking wind.

From now on his most vivid memory of *Dirty Dancing* wouldn't be Patrick Swayze lifting Jennifer Grey over his head like a canoe – he hadn't even seen that scene – it would be Art Garfunkel at his living-room window.

'Why are you cleaning my windows?' Frank said.

'They are fairly dirty.'

'I do them myself.' If he'd been sitting in a car at the traffic lights and the man had started washing his windscreen without invitation, at least he would have understood that there was a precedent for it. But not this.

'I rang your bell,' the window cleaner said. 'I don't think it works.'

'It doesn't.'

A few days ago Frank had answered the door to a young man who smiled and lifted a laminate that was hanging on a chain around his neck. Other than now knowing the man's name was Tony, the laminate was meaningless. When did a laminated piece of card become such a trusted form of security? Anyone could take a picture of themselves on their phone and stick it on a piece of card with their name above it. They could print it at home. A laminator machine didn't cost much at all. They had one in the library.

Tony had held his index finger up to suggest that Frank should wait and pay very close attention. Tony then pressed Frank's doorbell.

'Do you see?' Tony had said.

'What?' Frank had said.

Tony had pressed the doorbell again. He'd held it for longer this time. He screwed his face up and shook his head.

'It doesn't sound good, does it?' Tony had said.

And he'd tried to sell Frank a doorbell.

When he'd got rid of Tony, Frank disconnected his doorbell. Nobody he actually wanted to see ever rang it anyway. Smelly John never left Greyflick House, the postman always knocked – both versions of that film were factually inaccurate – and Kelly had the combination to a safe that held her own key. Now he was going to have to put shutters on his windows and anti-climb paint up the walls. They just keep evolving, he thought. Finding a way.

'It's finished,' the window cleaner said. Frank presumed he meant the window but the man pointed with a piece of dirty yellow chamois leather into the living room. Frank turned to see the closing credits of *Dirty Dancing* moving up his television screen. He looked through the open window at the ground below. At his age the fall should kill him but if he aimed for the bush it might cushion his fall just enough to break his legs or an arm. Enough for a few more home visits. If he angled his trajectory right he might be able to take Art Garfunkel with him.

On the back of the *Dirty Dancing* DVD box it said: 'Feature length: 96 minutes approx.' It took Frank 197 minutes approx. to get to the end of it. He hadn't enjoyed *Dirty Dancing*. But he decided he would tell Kelly that he had.

26

Frank brushed the cobwebs from the red tartan shopping basket. He shook a spider off onto the grass and took the basket upstairs where he wiped it with a wet cloth and filled it with anything in his flat that he thought he might be able to sell. He took some ornaments from the mantelpiece – owls and pigs and a small vase. He wrapped a dozen giraffes in newspaper and put them in the basket. He took two tiny silver spoons out of the kitchen drawer and put them in the basket too. He spent half an hour choosing some DVDs he could bear to lose from his collection. It was worse than getting rid of the videotapes. Just looking at the backs of the boxes of films he hadn't watched more than once and probably would never have ever watched again made him want to stop what he was doing immediately and watch them now. He tried selecting ten DVDs at random, without looking at what they were, but he ended up taking them all out of the basket again, terrified that he was getting rid of his most favourite films.

When the basket was full Frank bumped it down the stairs one at a time and pushed it to the bus stop. The wheel squeaked and he was glad when he reached the end of Sea Lane where the traffic was heavier and drowned out the squeak.

When the bus came, the driver lowered the vehicle so that Frank could push the heavy basket onboard. He could feel the old women on the bus shaking their heads, wondering why he needed the bus lowering. He doesn't appear to have a disability. The driver didn't lower the bus for any of our shopping baskets. Perhaps his basket is full. Who takes a full shopping basket *to* the supermarket? Typical lazy man.

Frank pushed his basket towards the back of the bus and the wheels caught against the wheels of one of the old ladies' shopping baskets. It was the clash of the tartans. The green and blue tartan of the old lady's basket against the red tartan of Frank's – the same red tartan as the cover of his photo albums and also of the blanket in Bill's cat basket. Frank didn't know the clan, or if the tartan even belonged to a clan. It was probably just a checked pattern. Frank apologised and untangled the wheels. He sat down and looked out of the back window like a new poster for yet another Edvard Munch retrospective.

The bus stopped at the hospital to let a passenger on and Frank took the opportunity to get off. The driver was annoyed with him for leaving the bus before the supermarket and didn't lower the vehicle to let him off. Frank bumped the basket down onto the pavement and thanked the driver anyway.

He wheeled the basket around the outside of the hospital and through the industrial estate until he was on the shitty High Street. He passed the kebab and chicken shops, wading knee-deep through poultry body parts and discarded kebab salad. There was a new display in the window of the sex shop. The three mannequins had been joined by a fourth. It was dressed in head-to-toe black rubber. Round its waist there was some sort of false solid plastic penis. Frank felt so old.

The pawnbroker's looked closed. The neon CASH 4 STUFF sign was switched off. Frank looked through the filthy window. There was no obvious sign of life inside, other than two flashing signs, one that said CHEQUES and another saying CASHED. Frank wished he'd brought his chequebook with him. If someone would just cash a cheque for him it would make everything a lot simpler. It would bounce, of course.

He tried the shop door, it opened with a loud buzzing noise that didn't stop until he'd dragged his heavy shopping basket inside and shut the door. Once the buzzer had stopped it was very quiet in the shop and the squeaking wheel of Frank's basket sounded incredibly loud as he wheeled it towards the counter.

On every wall there were glass cabinets and shelves containing stereos and DVD players, video-game consoles, computers and electric guitars. There were three drum sets for sale. Typical. You wait ages for a drum set and just when you haven't got any money three turn up at once. Frank walked to the counter. He wondered how much CASH he was going to get for his STUFF. If he got enough, he'd buy one of the drum sets with the leftover money.

The woman behind the counter stopped reading her magazine.

'Yes?'

'Hello. I've got some things to sell.'

'What have you got?'

Frank started taking things out of the shopping basket and putting them on the counter.

'No,' the woman said. Frank put the vase on the counter. 'No,' she said. 'No.' She said it over and over again. Nothing more elaborate than that. Just no. For every object Frank produced from the basket, just 'No.' Frank took out a newspaper parcel and started unwrapping it on the counter. When she saw the first ornamental giraffe the woman was about to say no but seeing there were more giraffes – a collection even – she paused. 'No,' she said after the twelfth giraffe. Frank realised that other than the life-size leopard in the corner his were the only china animals in the shop. He'd come to the wrong shop.

The woman showed a bit more interest in Frank's wristwatch. She held the watch in her hand to feel its weight and looked at the second hand turning for a while. She didn't say yes, but she put the watch to one side on the counter. She did the same with a small silver – in colour at least – box and also one of the tiny spoons. Frank decided this must be the 'maybe' pile. It now consisted of five items. The 'no' pile was everything else.

'I'll tell you what,' the woman said. 'Twenty.'

'Twenty?'

'The whole lot. Stop now. Twenty pounds. Twenty-five. Save you taking everything out of your mum's shopping basket, putting it on the counter and then putting it all back in the basket and wheeling it home again.'

Twenty-five pounds. Frank pictured Kelly leaving for the last time, while he didn't accompany her on the drums. He wanted to walk out of the shop and under a bus. But it wasn't due back from the big Sainsbury's for another half an hour yet.

'I've got a few DVDs,' he said. He started taking the DVDs out of the basket. The woman screwed her nose up and breathed impatiently.

'It's all downloading these days,' she said.

Frank made five small piles of DVDs on the counter.

'Streaming online. Nobody wants DVDs any more. I could take them away from you for ten pounds, I suppose.'

'Each?'

'Altogether. Save you lugging them home again.'

Frank looked at his DVDs. He really wanted to watch all of these films now. He hadn't realised until they were laid out on the counter how much he wanted to see all of these films right now. These films were his favourite films of all time.

'Some of these are classics,' he said.

'Yes. But as I said, it's all downloads these days. Tomorrow it will be something else. Film channels in your glasses or something. Video implants in your brain. These aren't even retro. Retro I might be interested in. These are just old. Out of date. Come back in fifty years and they might be worth something. Twenty pounds. Plus twenty-five for the other stuff. To save you carting it all back home again. Forty-five pounds. Do you have ID?'

'ID?'

'I have to see ID. In case all this stuff is stolen. A utility bill and something with a photo on,' and then she added, '*your* photo,' because he was old and therefore an idiot. She pointed at a sign on the wall that explained it all. 'It's the law. A driving licence or a passport.'

I'm eighty-one, Frank thought. Why would I have a driving licence or a passport?

'I've got my bus pass.' He took his pensioner's bus pass out of his pocket. The bus to the big Sainsbury's was free. This would be the first time he'd actually used his pass.

'Is that you?' the woman said, looking at his photograph.

Frank looked at his photo on the bus pass as though he wasn't sure himself.

'Yes. I was younger.'

The woman's face said, no, you weren't. You were old then. Now you're just older.

'And a utility bill,' she said.

'I could go and get something,' Frank said. He could clearly picture at least two utility bills at home, unopened and unpaid in red-coloured envelopes, somewhere in the pile of newspapers by his armchair in the living room.

'I'll tell you what,' the woman said. 'Call it forty pounds. For the DVDs and the watch and the spoons and so on and I'll ignore the lack of utility bill.'

Frank knew he was being ripped off, but he was used to it and, following some token haggling, and after giving the woman a short lecture on the historical importance of his film collection, he left the shop with £25 and a metal detector.

The man in Fullwind Food & Wine was right.

You have to speculate to accumulate.

On the long walk to Greyflick House, Frank tried to avoid the housing estate by taking an earlier turning off the High Street but just found himself on either a different housing estate or another part of the same one. If anything it was more

213

terrifying here. A small group of men were gathered around a dead tree. There was a pit bull dog hanging by its teeth from a branch and the men were encouraging another dog to jump up to bite the dog hanging from the tree. They threw stones at the dogs and laughed. Frank imagined both dogs would be very lucky if they ended up in a warehouse behind Sainsbury's or on a calendar on his living-room wall. He tried to walk by without attracting their attention.

Whenever people complained that things were so much better in the old days and that crime and poverty were so much worse now, Frank would always disagree. Things were just as bad in the past, he'd say. Hadn't people read Charles Dickens? (Frank hadn't read Charles Dickens but he had seen a lot of cinema adaptations.) But walking through this estate, he changed his mind. It was worse now than it had ever been. Being torpedoed on a Dutch liner in 1940 would be a picnic compared to growing up as a child here.

Walking through the estate quickly and quietly wasn't easy with a red tartan shopping basket with a metal detector sticking out of it and with the basket's wheel squeaking like a siren. The £25 in his inside jacket pocket felt like a flashing beacon. He put his hand over the pocket. It was the same pocket where he carried his imaginary gun.

Frank signed the visitor's book at Greyflick House and took the lift up to the first floor. The lift doors reluctantly scraped open and Frank stepped out. There was a strong smell in the corridor of whatever drugs John smoked. Frank knocked on John's door.

'Come in.' John's words came out as a deep exhale. As

though he'd been holding his breath with those two words, waiting for somebody to knock on the door so that he could release them.

Frank slowly opened the door. He was half expecting to find John flat out beneath silk sheets on a bed full of prostitutes while an ancient Chinaman prepared his next hit of opium. Instead, John was sitting on a metal-framed armchair watching daytime television. He was smoking a spliff, though. Frank had never been in a room with anyone taking drugs before. He sat down on the only other seat in the room, which was John's wheelchair. On the television distant relatives of people who had died without leaving a will were tracked down so that they could be given an unexpected inheritance. John offered the spliff to Frank.

'Oh, no thanks. Thank you, John. I think I'm probably a bit too old to start that.'

A woman on TV was struggling with the mixed emotions of finding out her second cousin had died and being five grand richer.

'Have you been shopping?' John said. He gestured towards the shopping basket.

'The opposite. I was trying to sell a few things.' Frank looked at the television. He wished that one of his cousins was still alive so that they could die and make him five grand richer. 'Go on, then,' he said.

'Go on what?'

'The thing.' He pointed at John's hand.

John held the joint up. 'This?'

Frank nodded.

John passed the spliff to Frank.

'What do I do?'

'Have you ever smoked?'

'Only cigarettes.'

'Pretend it's a cigarette.'

Frank took a tentative drag on the joint.

'Hold it in,' John said.

Frank took another drag. This time he inhaled deeply. If he'd been standing up he would have fallen over. He waited for the dizziness to pass. He felt hot and pulled at his shirt collar to loosen it.

'Why are you selling things?' John said.

'I need money. I sold some of my films. I think I've made a big mistake. Do you ever feel lonely, John?'

'Yes.'

Frank was surprised by the speed at which John had answered the question. He hadn't needed to think about it for a second. John must have been waiting a long time for someone to ask him. Frank gave the spliff back to John. He wondered whether he was now a drug addict.

'You haven't got any spare money, have you?' Frank said.

John answered with a loud short laugh.

'I haven't got a pot to piss in.'

'You should have said. I've just sold one.'

Smelly John suggested all the ways he thought Frank might get rich quick and Frank rejected and dismissed them in the same monosyllabic way the woman had rejected his giraffes and owls in CASH 4 STUFF.

'Nude modelling?'

'No.'

'Rent boy?'

'No.'

'You could sell some organs.'

'No.'

'Do they still buy sperm?'

'Who?'

'I don't know. The blood people.'

'I think they buy blood.'

'The sperm people, then. The bank. The sperm bank.'

'I think mine might be past its sell-by date.'

Both men shuddered at the thought.

John pulled himself up from his chair and made his way via a series of handrails along the wall to a cupboard. He opened the cupboard and started looking through a cardboard box of letters and envelopes. He found a postcard and gave it to Frank. Frank looked at the postcard of John as a young punk – Smelly John – sneering for the camera next to a policeman and a red telephone box.

'You could spike your long hair up, Francis and pose for the tourists. England's oldest punk rocker.'

'I think that's your title.'

On the postcard John's hair was green and in foot-high spikes. He was wearing a silver-studded leather jacket and there was a drinks can ring-pull hanging from his earlobe. Frank looked at the postcard and at John now, comparing the two men. The earring and spiky hair were gone, John's head was now almost as bald as Frank's dad's and he wasn't wearing a studded leather jacket with 'piss off' painted on the back. But he could tell it was the same man. Frank realised he was comparing the colour of John's skin on the postcard to John now. Allowing for ageing and the fading postcard ink there was little change. About two squares on an extensive household paint chart. He stopped short of holding the postcard up to John's face.

As he made his way back to his armchair, John saw the metal detector sticking out of Frank's shopping basket.

'Get up,' he said. He clicked his fingers to signify urgency. Frank stood up from the wheelchair and John took his place.

'Old people are always dropping money, Francis. Comfortable trousers –' he put his trilby on – 'deep armchairs. Come on. Graham has a metal pin in his leg.'

In the lift on the way down John took the metal detector out of the shopping basket.

'Here,' he said, offering the detector to Frank. 'Try it on my Prince Albert.'

'No thanks.'

John switched the detector on. The sound it made as it repeatedly detected the metal floors, walls and ceiling of the lift seemed deafening in such an enclosed space. Frank put his fingers in his ears until John switched the detector off. Both men were laughing. Frank presumed it was because of the drugs and he imagined he would be stopping off on the way home to buy chocolate bars that his false teeth weren't up to but his drug-addled mind told him he could eat.

John carried the metal detector out of the lift on his lap and into the reception area where Graham was talking to the family of one of the residents; he had his back to Frank and John. As Smelly John passed behind him, he flicked the metal detector on and it buzzed and whooped like it had found the *Treasure of the Sierra Madre* inside the leg of the warden, who Frank was really starting to feel sorry for.

They went along the corridor to the lounge. John in his wheelchair with the metal detector pulsing on his lap and Frank pushing his ladies' shopping basket with its wheel squeaking and sticking to the carpet. It would have looked good filmed from behind in slow motion. If it had been the first Sunday of the month, Alice would have been in to play music hall tunes on the Greyflick piano and she could have stopped playing when they burst through the lounge door like cowboys.

27

Putting everything back in the shed was like packing a suitcase at the end of a holiday – somehow it didn't all seem to fit – even though he'd got rid of a lot of ivy, sold a garden fork, and put a lot of stuff in the dustbin. Also, he now had all the things he'd brought down from the flat for the yard sale to fit in the shed as well.

While he was putting everything back in the shed, Albert Flowers turned up again to ask Frank about putting everything back in the shed. He also enquired about the colour of the bollards.

'Sunflower Yellow,' Frank said.

'White is the more traditional colour.'

'I didn't have any white.'

'There is quite a bit of paint on the grass.'

'It wasn't quite as non-drip as it said it was on the tin.'

'Perhaps you could cut the grass.'

'I don't have a lawnmower.'

'I could give you the name of a very good gardener.'

'I'm short of finances at the moment.'

'He's very reasonable.'

'I'm very short of finances.'

And it went on like that for a while.

'Well, if you could tidy the garden up a bit, that would be helpful.'

'I'm doing it now. I was doing it when you stopped me to ask me about it.'

And so on.

When Flowers had gone and Frank had finished repacking the shed, he put six new batteries in the metal detector. It beeped and a display he didn't understand lit up at the top of the handle. He thought about what he might find buried beneath the ground. The earliest remains ever found in Fullwind-on-Sea were from the Bronze Age – when there was more Fullwind and less sea. Perhaps he'd find some bronze. There had been a Roman bathhouse fairly nearby. Romans were always leaving gold coins around. Surely some loose-trousered Roman OAPs had dropped a few quid before taking a bath.

Frank didn't know how powerful the metal detector was. It looked more like an expensive toy than it had when he'd seen it hanging on the wall of CASH 4 STUFF. It had worked fine on the armchairs at Greyflick House and on Graham's gammy leg but would it pick up anything that had been buried under Frank's garden a thousand years ago? He couldn't help feeling some excitement about what might lie under the soil or the subsoil of his garden. Even if it was just a few coins dropped by the builders when they were building the flat in the 1950s.

Frank wondered what had led to the metal detector being taken into the pawnbroker's. Had its owner dug up such a great fortune as a result of the detector that they'd decided to not be greedy and give it to the shop to let someone else have a go? Or had the metal detector been such a failure at detecting metal that the only way it was ever going to find any treasure for its owner was if they sold it?

Starting over by the shed he made his first sweep of the ground. The metal detector beeped steadily to signal nothing was there yet. He moved the metal detector across the grass.

He could hardly claim to be bored any more.

If he ran through the village kicking bollards over and changing the names on road signs, it would just be mindless vandalism. He couldn't remember a time when he'd been so busy. He hadn't had time to open his junk mail for ages. Anybody passing by who looked through the gaps in the hedge at the front of his garden would have presumed that Frank had finally found himself a hobby. Just as Hilary had found a way to pass whatever time she had left by spying on her neighbours and Trims His Lawn with Scissors, Washes His Car Too Much and Picks up Litter had all found something to fill the end of their lives with. Even Albert Flowers with the Villages in Bloom competition – which surely Frank was going to lose for Fullwind by the end of today – and all the women in the charity shop. Frank appeared to have a hobby at last. He'd never been so busy and yet so retired.

The metal detector made a whooping sound. He moved it back over the ground till it whooped again. He moved the detector back and forth in shorter and shorter sweeps until he'd found the source of the noise. He lay the detector on the ground and started digging, first with a sharp kitchen knife and then with a soup spoon. About an inch down he found a hairgrip.

After an hour of detecting metal Frank's arm was killing him. It was getting dark. The garden was covered in holes and divots. He'd found two hairgrips, a battery, a bulldog clip, a front-door key that didn't fit his front door, a broken drill bit, the tiny screw from the left arm of his old glasses, five pence in very small change and a round silver-coloured name tag engraved with the name *BILL*.

Feeling he might be on a roll, Frank went indoors and wrote his CV. He gave himself a posthumous promotion from bus conductor to bus driver and 'thesaurusised' switchboard operator to telecommunications facilitator. Under the title HOBBIES AND INTERESTS he wrote, Impressions (Michael Caine, James Stewart, Tommy Cooper, and the Prime Minister). He might stand a better chance of being given a job if he made himself sound like he'd be fun to work with.

The next morning he typed the CV out on one of the library's computers, adding Sea Evacuation Survivor to his list of experience to pique any potential employers' interest enough to at least ask him about it, leading to a story of adventure and heroism – complete with impressions of Churchill and Hitler – that would end in him getting the job.

He printed five copies of the CV, gave one to the librarian and left the library – immediately regretting not mentioning his DVD alphabetising skills.

In Fullwind Food & Wine Frank bought a small amount of shopping. He looked at the prices and at the nutritional information on the packaging but hadn't paid enough attention to Kelly to really understand what any of it meant. At the counter he bought two scratch cards and a lottery ticket, using numbers from film titles – *3 Days of the Condor*, *The Magnificent 7*, *10*, *12 Angry Men*, *Catch 22* and *Summer of '42*.

'Speculating,' he said to the man on the checkout and gave him a copy of his CV.

In the charity shop he planned a robbery.

He pictured himself being lowered by his accomplice – he was going to need an accomplice – through a gap in the polystyrene ceiling tiles to open the glass cabinet at the centre of the shop and steal the oriental vase. In the morning the old ladies would open the shop and not notice the cabinet was empty for hours or even days. And then they'd wonder whether the vase had ever even been there in the first place, presuming they were losing their marbles and consulting their American Ron leaflets.

Nobody would be expecting a robbery in a charity shop.

Frank could walk up to the counter with his hand in the gun pocket of his jacket and quietly demand the cash from the till. The old ladies would give a description of Frank to the police. He just looked like an old man, they'd say. They all look the same to us. Although, they'd pause and say, there was something vaguely familiar about him. And after the police had left, like Donald Sutherland at the end of *Invasion of the Body Snatchers*, they'd point open-mouthed at the My Little Pony on the toy shelf.

Frank browsed for a while before putting a brooch in his pocket and leaving the shop. If there was a line, it was stretched out across the threshold of the charity shop and he'd just crossed it.

28

The bus trip to CASH 4 STUFF was even more stressful than usual. Frank struggled to get both his tartan shopping basket and his kid's scooter onto the bus and then to the seats at the back without taking somebody's eye out with the scooter or dropping it on somebody. He felt like a Buckaroo! mule.

The woman in CASH 4 STUFF wasn't interested in the stolen brooch and it was only after Frank had demonstrated the scooter's lights by scooting back and forth across the shop that she offered him a fiver for it.

'Is that it?' the woman said.

Frank reached down into the shopping basket and started taking out his 16mm film collection. He felt sick again. When he was up on the stool ladder with the top of his head inside the loft space, he'd thought of Morgan Freeman in *The Shawshank Redemption*, opening his penknife, appearing to consider hanging himself before carving his name and the words 'was here' into the wood below the ceiling. How would anybody ever know Frank had been here? He didn't even own a penknife.

Frank had reached up into the loft and slowly dragged the heavy box towards him and removed the film boxes a few at a time. Climbing up and down the steps to place them in the hall below. He'd sat down on the carpet and looked at the film boxes, some were flat, square and cardboard, and others were round silver tins. Was he ever realistically going to get to watch any of these films or show them to anyone? He didn't even have a projector.

He piled the films on the counter of CASH 4 STUFF. The woman turned away and started typing something into a computer.

'What would somebody who bought them watch them on?' the woman said.

'A sixteen-millimetre projector.'

'Do you have one of those?'

Frank looked around the shop, sure that they would have at least one film projector for sale. There were piles of DVD players and four or five different video game systems for watching films on but no projectors.

'I don't myself. No,' he said.

'Hmmm,' the woman said and carried on looking at the computer.

'They're collector's items,' Frank said. 'Retro,' he added, remembering what the woman had said about his DVDs.

The woman turned back from the computer. She started opening one of the film tins.

'Careful,' Frank said, and then, slightly less hysterically, 'they can unravel.'

The woman opened the tin. 'Just checking there are actually films inside and not just empty tins,' she said, and closed the tin.

'I've brought a gas bill,' Frank said. He showed the woman his bus pass again and a red gas bill.

'They're going to cut you off, you know,' she said. 'Is this why you're selling everything?'

Frank said yes, because he was ashamed of what the truth might say about him.

One afternoon during a game of Battleships in the lounge of Greyflick House, Smelly John had pointed out which residents he thought had dementia and what their symptoms were. Frank had felt bad about laughing about something that had taken his wife away from him, and he hated to think that he would have sat there laughing after giving Sheila the name Can't Remember What A Cup Is or Thinks Her Husband Is Trying To Poison Her, but he joined in with John anyway, giving everybody in the lounge Native American names. Gets Famous People's Names Wrong, Walks at an Angle, Sees Things That Aren't There, No Interest in Personal Hygiene, Misery Guts, Goes Walkabout in the Night, Easily Distracted, and then there was one man who Smelly John said liked to undress in public and had lost his sexual inhibitions, thinking all the young female relatives and visiting health workers and nurses found him attractive. Was that Frank's dementia too? Thinking he was Peter Stringfellow?

He left CASH 4 STUFF with an empty shopping basket and with £75 and a stolen brooch in his pocket. He went to see Smelly John where he made a nonsensical joke about Schrödinger's shopping basket and while John was in the toilet he stole half his dope.

29

Kelly's eleventh visit was perfect. She arrived ten minutes early with a lemon meringue pie and Frank immediately gave her the day off. She sat next to him on the sofa and together they ate pie and watched *Singin' in the Rain*.

For 'approx. 103 mins' the phone didn't ring. Nobody tried to sell Frank insurance or a doorbell. No one knocked on the door to talk about the afterlife, no roofers called to give him quotes he hadn't asked for. There were no unexpected cockney Art Garfunkels at the window ruining the bit where Gene Kelly sings in the rain. Whenever Frank watched the film from now on, this would be what he would think of. Sitting with Kelly eating lemon meringue pie. This would be his Director's Cut.

'I used to be able to do that,' Frank said during the scene where Donald O'Connor runs up a wall, does a somersault in the air and lands on his feet.

Kelly smiled. 'Really?' she said.

'Did you know,' Frank said, 'Donald O'Connor spent three days in hospital after filming this bit?'

'Wow,' Kelly said.

'He said it was like being run over by a milk float.'

'A milk float? Can you imagine such a thing?'

'I know. Hollywood, eh.'

They paused the film while Kelly made them both tea and then Frank continued with his DVD commentary.

'Gene Kelly filmed this in one take,' he said during the film's title song-and-dance routine. 'There was a water shortage in town on the day. The script was written to go with the songs, you know. It was the original jukebox musical. I'm not entirely sure what a jukebox musical is, but I remember hearing someone say it on the television.'

'How do you know all of this?' Kelly said.

'I have a lot of free time –' Frank lifted his foot and grimaced in a show of pain, 'since the football injury.'

Near the end of the film when Gene Kelly tells the theatre audience that it's Debbie Reynolds' character who is the real star and she starts crying, Frank said, 'She had to rub onions in her eyes, you know.'

After the film Kelly washed the cups and plates and put the triangle of leftover lemon meringue pie in the fridge next to the unopened Oreos, strawberry jam and tomato sauce.

Just before she left, Kelly said, 'Take care of yourself. Because I won't be here to take care of you soon.'

30

There were dark clouds over Fullwind on Tuesday morning and it looked as though it might rain. Frank hoped it would. He was going to walk to the shops as Gene Kelly, jumping in puddles and hugging lamp posts. He would stand under the leaking gutter outside the charity shop and sing his heart out until Maureen – Fullwind's police community support officer – stopped him and told him to go home.

He had the feeling he might be on a roll again. Two of the numbers on his lottery ticket had come up and when he was getting ready to go to the shop to collect his winnings, he'd found a pound coin in the torn lining of his blue jacket.

With a black collapsible umbrella in his pocket Frank set off for the shops. Disappointingly, there was no rain, just the dark clouds and a wind strong enough to have blown his umbrella inside out and snapped the material from the spokes if he had tried to open it. On certain days, Fullwind was very much the West Sussex village's Native American name. If Gene Kelly had been singin' in the Fullwind rain, he would have spent half the film chasing his trilby along Church Road.

Frank went into Fullwind Food & Wine. He gave his lottery ticket to the man behind the counter who fed it into a machine. The machine did its thing, clicking and whirring, checking the numbers and working out Frank's prize.

Frank and Smelly John had often talked about what they would do if they won the lottery. John was going to Spend! Spend! Spend! He was going to buy a speedboat and a helicopter. He was going to live on an island in the Caribbean and surround himself with dolly birds and drink champagne out of a shoe.

'We have a winner,' the man behind the counter said. He opened the till and gave Frank his lottery spoils. *Catch 22* and *The Magnificent 7* had won him £2.40. It was such a small amount that it felt worse than not winning at all. He was almost embarrassed to accept it and couldn't even be bothered to work out how many extra Kelly minutes it would buy him. He left the shop and immediately broke his promise to Smelly John to spend his lottery cash on a Beverley Hills mansion with an enormous art deco cinema in the garden by going next door to the charity shop and blowing it all on a small china owl.

On the way home, Frank almost bumped into a phone box while he was looking at the pavement for dropped coins. He checked inside the phone box for any money left behind, something he hadn't done since he was a small boy. Frank wondered whether he would ever see Kelly again after next week, his twelfth day of Kelly Christmas (or eleventh if he didn't include his terrifying hour with Janice). He started singing to himself. 'On the first day of Christmas . . .' And then he couldn't get the song out of his head and he spent the whole day trying to remember how many swans-a-swimming there were, what it was there were nine of, and what those nine things were doing, and also how handy five gold rings would have been to him right now.

Frank had to pull the shopping basket with some force to free it from the ivy that, in just a few days, had already begun to reclaim the contents of his garden shed.

He oiled the wheel of the basket. The squeak was at least quieter now, although at this time of the morning it sounded like thunder on helium. He pushed the basket slowly. It didn't reduce the volume of the wheel's noise but at least the squeaks were less frequent. He tried to keep to the grass verges that ran along both sides of the road to further muffle the squeak but every now and then the verge would end and he'd push the basket out into the road and the volume would rise. He would tense his jaw and try to use the flow of blood to block his ears, as if not being able to hear the wheel would somehow make his progress quieter for everyone else.

He was dressed in his darkest clothing and his softest shoes. He'd considered putting boot polish on his face but remembered how Smelly John had teased him about wearing clean underwear in case he was ever run over. He decided that being run over and taken to hospital with boot polish on his face would be seen as worse than wearing dirty pants. Particularly by Smelly John.

Not that he was likely to be run over at three o'clock in the morning on Sea Lane. There was no traffic. There was no street lighting either. When the security light outside his front door switched itself off, Frank was plunged into darkness. The sky was as black as a children's crayon picture of sky. Black paper with the stars stuck on. He switched on the red torch that would have been Sheila's usherette light. Nothing happened. He shook the torch and a dim yellow beamless light reluctantly came on. Frank thought he could smell popcorn.

About ten yards along the road he stopped to get his bearings. He shone the torch on the gate in front of him – '3 Chimneys,' the sign on the gate said. He tried to remember whether the bungalow actually had three chimneys. Why would a bungalow need so many chimneys? He didn't want to point the torch at the bungalow's roof to find out in case he woke somebody in the bedroom below.

There was a sudden noise close by. Frank froze. He switched off the torch. The noise stopped. He held his breath. He heard the noise again. It was coming from a bit further along the road. A rustling sound. He slowly moved the switch along the torch back to the on position. The dull light came on and the rustling stopped again. Frank froze again. There was a whistle up his nostril. If he sniffed to clear it, he might wake up the whole of Fullwind. The rustling began again. Frank slowly raised his arm and aimed the torch in its direction.

A fox stared back at Frank. It was a look Frank had seen before. The same blank stare of judgement and disappointment that was on Bill's face as he went through the swing doors at the dogs and cats home. The same look the actors on the front of the DVD boxes had given him when he'd placed them on the counter of CASH 4 STUFF.

'It's not stealing,' Frank wanted to say to the fox. 'Taking things from plastic charity bags left outside people's houses is not stealing. The charity name printed on the bags is probably fake, anyway. There is no such charity. Everybody knows the charity bags are a scam. Everybody. And even if, on this one particular occasion, the charity turns out to be genuine, any bags that haven't been used as rubbish bags – like the one you're scavenging your dinner from now – will have to be collected in a few hours' time by a man in a van. He's going to have to drive them to a warehouse where the contents of the bags will be sorted into piles. Clothing and shoes, linen and textiles, curtains, bedding, DVDs and CDs, books, toys, jewellery, watches, gold and silver, etc.

'Everything will then have to be sorted again. This time by quality and resaleable value. The wheat will be sorted from the chaff. The DVDs from the video cassettes. Some of it will be recycled or sent straight to landfill. Everything else will be loaded back into vans and taken to charity shops. Old ladies are going to have to spend hours on the Internet and looking in mail order catalogues to decide what the items would cost if they were new. Based on that information, they'll write out price labels and stick them on everything and then wait for people to come into the shops and buy the items. After the cost of the manufacture and printing of the bags, the van driver's wages and fuel, the sticky labels and various other expenses are all taken away, any proceeds left will be used to help the charity's intended beneficiaries. In this case, the elderly. Me.'

So there, Basil Brush. Frank was merely cutting out the middleman. At the very worst it was like filling in lottery numbers with one of the charity pens that had come through his door, or drinking Nescafé from his Fairtrade mug.

The fox shook his head, sighed, tutted, turned and trotted off down the road with a chicken bone in his mouth. Frank watched him disappear almost immediately into the darkness in search of more scraps of food – some chips to go with the chicken, or some dessert, maybe an espresso, or just a place where he could eat in peace without old men, who should be in bed, shining cinema torches in his face.

Frank had seen a lot of films where, following a great crime caper, the hero or heroine throws hundreds of dollar bills or pound notes up into the air and then lets them rain down again like confetti. If Frank had thrown the spoils of his charity bag robbery up in the air, when it came back down again, the large bottle of perfume would have hurt. And the carriage clock would have killed him.

Police investigating his unexplained death would have said, 'At least we know the exact time of death was three thirty-five a.m. And just what is that delightful smell?'

Frank laid out his spoils on the living-room carpet. The people of Fullwind were clearly suffering from compassion fatigue. There were better things in his shed. He looked at the broken carriage clock and wondered what the actual time was. He wondered what the time was in Los Angeles. This could be the ideal time to ring Beth.

He took his address book out of the desk drawer and dialled her number.

'Hello?'

'Beth? How are you?'

'What time is it?'

Their conversations always seemed to begin like this, establishing the time.

'Oh, I don't know. Quite late,' Frank said. 'Or quite early. It depends, I suppose.'

Beth sensed something wasn't right in Frank's voice.

'Is everything okay, Dad?'

'Oh, yes. Everything is fine. How is everyone? Laura and Jimmy?'

'They're both fine, Dad.'

It seemed so quiet in his living room at this time of day, his lone voice like the squeaking wheel of the shopping basket on the deserted road outside, and he felt like he was shouting into the phone. He picked up the remote control and switched the television on to filter out the silence. *The Antiques Roadshow* was just finishing. The volume was incredibly loud at this time of night.

'Oh no!' Beth said. 'That music!' She laughed. 'Is that show still on? I feel like I've got school in the morning now.'

Frank laughed and muted the TV, blindfolded US Marine-style.

'It was always *Last of the Summer Wine* for me,' Frank said. 'As soon as I heard the music all I could think of was another new week at work.'

'At least you don't have to worry about that any more.'

'The joys of retirement.'

'What have you been doing? Anything fun?'

'Oh, this and that. I went to the supermarket.'

'Ooh,' Beth said, immediately regretting her mock-sarcasm.

'Not the normal one,' Frank said. 'The big one. Two floors. It would probably seem tiny to you over there. Like a corner shop.'

'I think we're pretty even supermarket size wise these days.'

'I went to the beach too.'

'Swimming?'

'No. Not this time. I haven't been there for years.'

'Has it changed?'

'Not much. Still the same sand and stones and a big expanse of salty water. The café has been painted. You wouldn't believe the price of the beach huts.'

'I'm glad to hear you're taking your retirement seriously at last. You watch way too much TV. You need to get out more. Do you remember when we used to fly kites on the beach?'

'Of course. I've still got the scar.' Frank looked at his hand. He turned his fingers over. He did the same with the other hand. He couldn't find the scar from the time Beth had let go of the kite and Frank had tried to catch it and had cut his finger on the string.

'I wonder if the kite ever came back down,' Beth said.

'I expect it's still up there. Somewhere. Do you still swim?'

'Not much, to be honest. I did when I was teaching Laura. She swims like a fish now. Like Mum. The way she used to swim out to sea for miles. I never liked it. When I asked you where Mum was going, you'd say France. You'd say she was going to buy French bread and I'd ask how she'd keep it dry. I can't remember what you said.'

'She holds it above her head.'

If it hadn't been for the window cleaner preventing him from seeing that part of *Dirty Dancing*, an image of Patrick Swayze holding Jennifer Grey above his head like a baguette would have flashed through Frank's mind.

'What are you up to today?' Beth said.

'The usual.'

'In a minute, darling,' Beth called out to somebody. 'I better go, Dad. I'll ring soon.'

'Say hello to Laura from me. And Jimmy.'

'Sure. Love you.'

Frank put the phone down. A second episode of *The Antiques Roadshow* was on. A man was looking at the expert, open-mouthed. And then he probably said, 'As much as that?' And then lied to the expert that he would never sell it because it had been in the family for years.

Frank looked on the carpet at the things he'd stolen from his neighbours' charity bags. It wasn't impressive. He should have walked the other way along Sea Lane, towards the sea and the bigger houses.

He put a DVD on and fell asleep in his armchair. When he woke he went to the shops. He stole a small plate and a ring from the charity shop and tried the lock on the cabinet at the centre of the shop that contained the supposedly valuable oriental vase. He went next door to Fullwind Food & Wine and when the man behind the counter's reflection in the big round security mirror was looking the other way, he put two batteries and a bag of sweets in his pocket and left the shop.

Frank filled the rest of the day with another garden sweep for treasure, finding five pence and a drawing pin. When it was dark and Sea Lane was free of traffic, he put new batteries in the usherette torch, put it in the pocket of his anorak and set off again with his shopping basket. This time he walked in the opposite direction along Sea Lane, towards El Dorado and Xanadu.

When his basket was full he continued walking until he was at the beach. He was so tired now he was practically sleepwalking. He sat down on a bench. The tide was almost completely out. The edge of the water was further away than when he'd been here with Kelly. He sat and watched the sunrise over the horizon. He looked for Beth's kite. He checked his hands again for string cuts. He was hungry. He fancied an ice cream. Some bacon and eggs. The beach café wouldn't be open for another three hours yet.

He had the urge to cry but couldn't. He felt as though he should be crying. He tried to force himself by thinking of the sadder times in his life. He pictured Sheila in her hospital bed, not knowing who he was any more but still convinced he was trying to murder her. He thought about the two or three times the hospital had miraculously saved her life but how she always left the hospital slightly less well than when she'd been taken in. He looked at the sea and remembered Sheila swimming out of sight. He thought of dangling Beth's feet into the water for the very first time and how she'd struggled, trying to wriggle her legs back up, as though she could fold them back inside her body like the ladder of his kitchen stool. And, soon after that, how they could never get her to come out of the water because she loved it so much. He thought of the cowboys sitting round a campfire farting. He thought about Debbie Reynolds rubbing onions into her eyes in *Singin' in the Rain*. Frank sat on the bench for ages, trying to make himself cry like a method actor, without shedding a single tear. When the first aeroplane of the day flew overhead he went home.

31

Frank overslept. With the exception of when he was in hospital it was the first time he'd been in bed later than 11 a.m. for as long as he could remember. Since records began, as they always said on the television.

Shoplifting and stealing from his neighbours had worn him out. He'd slept through the sound of twenty or thirty different aeroplanes, a heavy thunderstorm and who knows how many cold-callers.

He knew it was late but he wasn't sure exactly how late. He reached over to get his watch and remembered that he'd sold it 4 CASH. Unless he retraced his steps backwards until he reached something that told him what the previous day had been, he wouldn't really know what day this new day was. It was liberating.

Frank lay in bed and remembered what was on last night's television. Snooker and a gardening show, a war film and a camcorder calamities clips show, *The Antiques Roadshow*.

'Shit!'

Frank got out of his bed like it was on fire. He cricked his neck. He almost twisted his ankle. He was too old for such sudden movement. He had pins and needles. He stamped his foot until they went. He opened the curtains, almost pulling them off the rail. A white plastic curtain hook shot across the room.

'Shit!'

It was light outside. There was traffic on Sea Lane. The free bus to the big Sainsbury's went by. If the windows were open and the wind was blowing in the right direction, Frank would have heard the old women cackling and wolf-whistling at the postman as the bus overtook his red bicycle.

'No!'

It was Monday and Frank had missed Kelly.

It was the last time he was ever going to see her and he'd slept through it. Yes, she had her own key in a safe screwed to the wall, but Frank had put the chain on the front door before going to bed. Kelly wouldn't have been able to open the door. She would have called his name out through the gap between the door and the frame. 'Frank? Hello?' And then she would have rung the doorbell, not realising that Frank had disconnected it. She would have called him on the phone next. Surely he would have heard the phone ringing? But he had been in a very deep sleep. Stealing was exhausting. He might have slept through it.

He went into the living room. It was a mess. The tartan shopping basket was in the middle of the room surrounded by Fullwind's charity donations. DVDs spared from the CASH 4 STUFF cull were scattered all over the carpet. He looked at the clock above the fireplace. Twenty-five past eleven. It was eleven twenty-nine on the clock in the kitchen and a row of eights were flashing on and off on the DVD player.

Frank had gone to bed in his clothes. He hadn't even

really gone to bed. He'd just gone for a lie-down and must have drifted off into a deep sleep. He couldn't remember if he'd dreamed. Maybe this was a dream. He was Judy Garland and he wasn't in Kansas any more. He put his ruby slippers on and went downstairs. The newspaper was on the doormat. The paperboy always only pushed it half-way through the letterbox. Frank presumed Kelly must have pushed the newspaper the rest of the way through the letterbox, so that she could look through and see if he was collapsed unconscious at the bottom of the stairs, and to call out his name through the gap. 'Mr Derrick?'

Frank walked down the garden path. For a second he wondered what all the holes were in his lawn. He put his hand in his pocket and felt the five pence in small change, the hairgrips, Bill's name tag and the brooch he'd stolen from the charity shop. Somewhere buried deep in the fluff and loose cotton in his pocket was the tiny screw from his glasses.

He stood on the verge outside the front gate and looked both ways along the road for Kelly's blue car. The grass was wet, but with no knowledge of the thunderstorm he pre-sumed it was just particularly heavy dewfall. Seeing no trace of Kelly's car, Frank started walking along the road in the direction of the shops. He took his glasses off and rubbed his eyes. He wasn't completely awake yet. He felt as though he should be running. He wondered if he still knew how. If he gradually broke into a trot and worked his way up through the gears, his legs might collapse under him before he was properly running.

Washes His Car Too Much was washing his car. He said hello. Frank didn't answer but forced a smile. He had a vague recollection that on his second night of charity-bag theft he'd keyed the side of his car. He felt in his pocket for the car-scratching weapon – a hair grip or a coin, the brooch or Bill's name tag . . . keys, he had no keys; he'd left his keys in the flat. Frank had locked himself out. What if he couldn't remember his birthday to open the key safe?

He was about ten yards along the road when he saw a car coming towards him. It was the same blue as Kelly's car. He wanted to wave but he wasn't sure it was her. He didn't want to end up with the Sioux name Waves At Strangers. When it was closer he could see there were two people in the car. Kelly was driving and there was a man in the passenger seat, in Frank's seat. Kelly suddenly pulled the car across the road towards Frank. He thought she was going to run him over. Either deliberately or by accident – she wasn't a great driver. If she ran him over, would that disqualify her from being his home care visitor while he recovered?

He stepped back further onto the verge, almost leaning against the fence in front of 3 Chimneys. He looked back at the bungalow to see that it did indeed have three chimneys and again he thought why would a bungalow need three chimneys? Maybe they built the house to match the name on the gate. If he wasn't so tired, he would have worked out that there were probably three fireplaces.

Kelly pulled the car onto the edge of the grass and opened the window. Frank walked over and bent to look in.

'The chain was on,' Kelly said. 'So I knew you must be in. I rang. You weren't answering the phone. Is everything all right?'

'I overslept,' Frank said. He knew from Kelly's concerned expression that he looked awful. The same man she'd met

243

for the first time three months earlier following his dirty protest. He was sweating and out of breath. There were bags under his eyes. His hair was all over the place. He hadn't shaved for a few days and nose hair was escaping from his nostrils. He needed to put *Denis Healey Impression* back on his CV.

The man in the passenger seat was Frank's Dorian Gray portrait. He was young – around the same age as Kelly, perhaps a bit older – he had a short, tidy haircut, like an Army officer or a policeman's, his even layer of stubble looked airbrushed on, probably by fairies.

'Oh sorry,' Kelly said. 'This is Sean.' And then to Sean, 'This is Mr Derrick.'

'Frank,' Frank said. 'Mr Derek was Basil Brush's straight man.' Neither Kelly nor Sean knew what Frank was talking about. His speech was strange too. He hadn't had time to put his teeth in. Kelly's training would be telling her that he might have had a stroke. She'd be checking his face and body for other signs. 'Basil Brush,' Frank said. 'He always had a human sidekick. Mr Roy, Mr Rodney and Mr Derek. Mine is a different spelling. Like the oil rig.'

'Shall we go inside and talk about it?' Kelly said to Frank. She spoke calmly, talking a suicidal man off a window ledge. Frank wondered who was included when she said '*we* go inside'.

She turned to Sean and they talked. Frank tried to read their lips. And then he couldn't see their lips at all while Kelly leaned across and kissed Sean. She opened the door and climbed out of the car.

'Sean is going to drive back to work,' she said to Frank as

244

she was halfway out of the car. 'I'll take the bus there later and pick the car up.'

Sean climbed over onto the driver's seat.

'Nice to meet you, Mr Derrick,' he said, and to Kelly, 'See you later.' She pushed the car door shut. Sean did a reverse U-turn and drove off.

When he was gone Kelly turned to Frank. 'Have you got moles?'

'What?'

'Let's go inside.' They walked back towards Frank's flat. 'Somebody's been digging up your garden,' Kelly said. 'Seeing that and then not being able to open the door, I was a bit worried. I didn't want to call the police or the Fire Brigade, just in case you were only asleep or in the bathroom. I'd just dropped Sean off close by for a job he's on, so I went back to get him to unscrew the chain. I knew he had his tools with him. It probably wasn't my brightest idea. I don't think dismantling front doors is in the Lemons guidebook.'

'I overslept,' Frank said again.

They walked through the gate into the garden. Frank hadn't realised quite how many holes he'd dug. He didn't know how best to describe to Kelly what had happened. The truth wasn't good enough. Moles did seem like a suitable patsy but instead he said that he'd been gardening and it wasn't something he was very good at. He showed Kelly his fingers.

'Definitely not green,' he said. They walked to the front door. 'I forgot my keys.'

Kelly took the keys out of the safe and opened the door. Frank went in. He picked up the newspaper and the post.

Kelly followed him upstairs. He thought about the mess on the living-room floor – the stolen charity bags and the shopping basket – he thought of how he was going to explain it. He couldn't blame the moles. Could he blame the moles?

At the top of the stairs he caught a glimpse of himself in the mirror and wondered when he'd put up that portrait of an old tramp.

It was all supposed to be so different.

He'd planned on getting up early this morning. Or not going to bed at all, to leave him sufficient time to make himself look pretty for Kelly's last visit. He was going to run a deep bath and fill it with bubbles while singing the song from the advert. He was going to shave with his many-bladed razor and splash his face with aftershave until it stung.

He was going to put on his loudest shirt, pluck his ears, nose and eyebrows until he sneezed and head-butted the mirror. When his makeover was over he'd have a bowl of the cereal he'd bought because it reminded him of the TV jingle. He'd sing it to himself between mouthfuls. Then he'd read the newspaper and watch some breakfast television while he tidied the living room before taking his position at the window. He'd turn around, ruffle his hair and pretend he was Jimmy Stewart until she arrived.

But he'd slept through all of that.

When he looked in the mirror at the top of the stairs he almost didn't recognise the children's doodle looking back at him. His face was a dirty stain on the glass. 'What does your boyfriend do?' he said to Kelly.

'He's a roofer.'

Of course he was.

*

Kelly asked about the mess in the living room and Frank said he'd been having a clear-out and was going to give everything to charity. He'd had to run after the man delivering the plastic bags to ask for more bags to put it all in. When Kelly asked about the missing ornaments from the mantelpiece Frank told her he'd put them away in the spare room. It was the first time he'd referred to Beth's room as the spare room.

Kelly started tidying, putting the stolen goods back into charity bags. She was now an accessory.

She picked up a handbag.

'I think this was once an alligator,' she said. She screwed her nose up because the bag smelled and held it at arm's length between her fingertips before dropping it in a plastic charity bag. 'Oh Frank. I'm sorry. I didn't mean to be rude. Was it Sheila's?'

'Yes,' Frank said. And added, 'I think it's actually crocodile.' Just in case saying yes wasn't a big enough lie.

When three charity bags were full Kelly picked them up, two in one hand and one in the other, just like the milkman who'd run Frank over and brought her here in the first place.

'I'll put these outside now,' she said.

'I can do it later.'

But Kelly was already out in the hall and carrying the bags downstairs. Getting stuff done. That was Kelly. He was going to miss her. He went over to the window and watched her put the bags on the verge outside the gate. While she was there she straightened the dustbins. She picked up a bit of paper blown in from the road and put it into one of the bins.

If she had looked in the recycling bin she would have

seen it was almost full. Frank kept forgetting or not bother-
ing to put the bin out on the verge on the right day for the
bin men. Not getting stuff done. That was Frank. He forgot
to empty his bins, he didn't pay his bills, the grass needed
cutting, the garden was a mess, and the cinema wasn't built.

All those roofers who came to his door. They were right.
There *were* loose tiles on his roof. They did need fixing.
The debt management cold-callers hadn't dialled the wrong
number. His debt did need managing. If Frank ever bought
batteries for the tape machine to play his Spanish language
cassette on he wouldn't get much further than '*Hola, mi
nombre es* Frank Derrick'. The drum set would never have
been played.

If the milkman hadn't run Frank over, the food in his
fridge would have continued to pass further past its sell-by
date and the upended bollard would have stayed unpainted
and on its side until the grass grew over it. Frank would
have sat watching television, wearing his clothes over his
pyjamas, filling his house with DVDs and worthless charity
shop bric-a-brac, left on the shelf and gathering dust. That
was Frank. On the shelf and gathering dust. Not getting
stuff done.

He watched Kelly put the charity bags out and straighten
the bins. She pulled the ends off a few overgrowing plants
and put them in the dustbin. And then she was talking to
somebody. Albert Flowers. He said something to her and
she turned and looked at the garden and then turned back.
He was obviously asking about the holes in the lawn. Frank
watched them talking. He tried to read their lips. Kelly
appeared to say either moles or perhaps holes. Frank hoped
Kelly wouldn't end up kissing Albert Flowers like she'd

done with Sean. She nodded and looked up at the flat. Frank pulled quickly away from the window. When he looked back they were gone.

'Frank!' Kelly called out from halfway up the stairs. 'Albert is here to see you.'

Frank heard more than just Kelly's footsteps on the stairs.

Kelly had invited him in.

Like a vampire.

He looked around the room for two things he could hold together to form the shape of a cross. If only he hadn't sold those spoons. There may have been just enough silver in them to stab Albert Flowers through the heart and kill him.

Kelly and Albert Flowers came into the living room. Frank knew Flowers was immediately unimpressed by everything about the room. The rusty tartan shopping basket and the empty charity bags on the floor. The DVDs scattered about the carpet and the near-empty mantelpiece. Flowers made a mental note of the flashing numbers on the DVD player, thinking what a silly old idiot Frank must be if he was unable to program a simple digital display clock. Frank imagined Flowers lecturing him on the upcoming Living Rooms in Bloom competition.

Behind Flowers' thinly veiled disgust there was joy. Joy at getting to see inside somebody else's home and then discovering that it was nowhere near as good as his own. He looked at the most recent bunch of flowers Kelly had brought Frank. They were drooping over the edge of the vase of stinky water. Dead flowers. Frank wished they weren't the only dead flowers in the room.

'I'll leave you both to it, then,' Kelly said.

She went off to do the washing-up and tidy the flat while Albert Flowers banged on about the holes in the garden and the foam stuffing on the lawn. He asked again about the colour of the bollards and the grass growing underneath and over them. He said he would be happy to organise for his gardener to cut the grass on the verge and also repaint the bollards.

'He is very reasonable.'

'I'm fine, thank you.'

'Hmmm,' Flowers said. 'Can I suggest, merely as a temporary solution, that it would be enormously helpful if you could at least keep the gate closed. Just until after the competition, of course.'

Kelly was in the bathroom folding towels and changing the water in Frank's dentures glass. She went into the toilet and changed the toilet roll, folding the end over into a point like a chambermaid in a posh hotel. She was singing to herself. Frank wanted to tell Albert Flowers to shut up so that he could hear her sing.

'If perhaps there was something that we could put up temporarily in front of the gate. Just to block the view,' Flowers said.

'What? Yes. Right,' Frank said. He looked at the clock. Kelly would have to go soon. This wasn't working out right at all. First oversleeping, then Sean, and now this idiot. This wasn't how he'd imagined Kelly's final visit to be. This wasn't in the script.

Kelly walked past the doorway and into the kitchen, still singing.

'So I'll speak to my gardener about the verge? And the bollards?' Flowers said.

'The verge?' Frank said.

'And the bollards.'

'Right. Yes.' Frank had never been more distracted.

'Would you like a cup of tea?' Kelly called out from the kitchen. She didn't address him by name but she was clearly talking to Albert Flowers.

Flowers looked at his watch. It was an expensive-looking watch. The kind of watch the woman in CASH 4 STUFF would have put straight onto the yes pile. Frank wanted to hack it off his wrist, taking his hand and his wedding ring with it. He'd probably make enough money from their sale for another twelve months with Kelly.

'I do have some time to kill,' Flowers said. Kill, Frank thought. And then Flowers called out to Kelly, 'Thank you. A cup of tea would be lovely.' He smiled at Frank and Frank wanted to punch his teeth out of his mouth, sell the gold fillings and turn the rest into new dentures for himself. He wanted to hang, draw and quarter Albert Flowers on the living-room carpet. Bury him under the Sunflower-yellow bollards.

Kelly made tea and the three of them sat in the living room. She small-talked with Albert Flowers all the way to the end of her visiting time. Frank hardly said a thing. He didn't want to extend the length of the conversation by contributing to it. Why was she talking to Flowers? Beth had paid a lot of money for her time. And she could hardly afford it. Jimmy's contract had fallen through. Beth wouldn't want to see Jimmy's hard-earned money squandered on small-talk with Albert Flowers. He owned a florist. He had an expensive jacket and shoes. And a fancy watch. He could afford his own home visits. Why didn't he just go away? Go away, Albert Flowers, go away.

It was twenty minutes before he finally did leave. He held his hand out for Frank to shake. Frank took his hand. He wanted to squeeze. When Beth was young, Frank would go and wake her in the morning. He'd say to her, 'Make a fist.' And Beth would lie in bed and try to make a fist but she wouldn't be awake enough yet to make a proper fist. That was the power of Frank's fist now, at all times of the day. He had the strength of a just-woken-up tiny female child. If he squeezed Albert Flowers' hand with all his might, it probably wouldn't be hard enough for Flowers to even notice somebody was holding it.

Frank walked with Flowers out into the hall.

'Say thank you to your nurse,' Flowers said. He looked up the hall. 'This is a nice flat. Stairs in Fullwind. Whatever next.' Frank wanted to push him down those stairs. 'We will need to move the charity bags too,' Flowers said.

'Somebody is collecting them,' Frank said.

'Yes, of course. You do know some of these charities are not charities at all?' He lowered his voice to show his racism wasn't entirely casual, 'Eastern Europeans. Right. Goodbye.' And at last, he finally left.

Frank went into the living room. Kelly was putting her anorak on and closing her bag.

'You're free,' she said. She unfolded a wad of paper. 'I just need to sign you off.' She handed the sheets of paper to Frank and gave him a pen. Frank looked at the pen. It was the same blue as Kelly's car. It had the same Lemons Care logo along its side. The tip of the pen had been chewed slightly.

'I don't want you to go,' Frank said. He felt a lump in his throat.

'What?'

'Don't go. I don't want you to go.'

Kelly looked at her watch.

'But—' she said.

'I'm not well enough.'

'You're fine, Frank. You're in better shape than most men half your age.'

'Not yet. I'm not well enough. Not yet.'

A moment passed. Frank felt the tears he couldn't manage to cry on the beach, coming in like the tide.

'You said you cared about me,' he said.

'I do. Of course I do.' Kelly repacked her bag to reaffirm she was leaving.

'Don't you care about me?'

'Frank. I'm a carer. That's my job. I *care*. For you, yes. And for all my other gentlemen . . .'

'I don't want to know about them.'

'Oh Frank.'

And even at this awful time, when he was in the middle of some sort of huge breakdown, Frank found himself wanting to turn his back, ruffle his hair, put a beret on, wiggle his shoulders and say, 'Mmmm Betty.'

'I have to go,' Kelly said.

'Why?'

Kelly looked at her watch.

'I'm late.'

'What am I going to do?' Frank said.

'Frank. You're being silly.'

'What am I going to do?'

253

'What do you mean?'

'Without you?'

'Without me?'

'Yes.'

Kelly sighed. 'What did you do before?'

'Before?' Frank shook his head. 'Nothing.'

'Oh, that's not true. What about your films? You love your films.'

Frank looked over at his depleted DVD collection. He tried to remember which films he'd given to CASH 4 STUFF. He thought of his beloved collection of 16mm films, all gone, probably on their way to a collector in Japan who'd paid thousands of pounds for them.

As though Kelly was reading his mind she said, 'Your cinema. What about your cinema?'

'It's a shed,' he said. 'A shed full of rubbish.'

Kelly sat down. She sat on the arm of the sofa, to show that although she wasn't going quite yet, she wasn't staying either. She didn't speak, leaving space for Frank to say what was on his mind. Letting him be the one in control of the situation. Kelly the pensioner whisperer.

'I'd just planned for today to be different,' he said. 'With fewer people involved. And now –' he looked at his bare wrist as though he was hoping to check the time. He sighed. 'I imagine I won't ever see you again.'

'Oh, I wouldn't bet on it,' Kelly said. 'It's a small world. And an even smaller village. Now, you're going to be all right, aren't you, Frank?' It was another one of her rhetorical questions. An instruction. 'And I don't want you to sit in here all day,' she said. 'Okay?'

Frank nodded.

'There's a great big world out there.'

'You just said it was small,' Frank said.

'I did, didn't I. Hmm. Well, big or small, the world is your oyster, Mr Derrick, remember?'

Frank managed half a smile.

'Like the ice cream,' he said.

'And there's something I would never have learned if I hadn't met you,' Kelly said. 'I'll never eat an ice cream the same way again.'

They didn't speak for what seemed like a long time and then Kelly gestured towards the DVD player. 'Did you like it? I forgot to ask,' she said.

Frank looked at the *Dirty Dancing* DVD case lying open and empty next to the DVD player. He found that he couldn't remember a single frame of it.

'It was good,' he said.

'Now, I really should be going,' Kelly said. She stood up. 'Don't worry about this.' She put the wad of unsigned forms and time sheets in her bag, 'I'll deal with them. You can keep the pen. Don't say I never give you anything. Now, I really have to go. I need to pick up the car. Sean will wonder where I am.'

Frank went over to the DVDs.

'You can borrow this,' he said. He held a DVD of *Top Hat* out to Kelly. 'It's Fred Astaire and Ginger Rogers.'

'I won't be coming back,' Kelly said. She wasn't going to be tricked into coming back that easily.

'Post it,' Frank said.

'I'm not sure I should really . . .'

'Keep it. I've seen it hundreds of times. I've got two copies.'

Kelly thanked him. She took the DVD and put it in her bag.

'Well. Goodbye, Frank,' she said. 'Try not to get run over by any milkmen.'

And she left.

Frank stood at the window watching her walk down the path. She opened the gate. If she turns and looks up, Frank thought. She went through the gate and closed it behind her. She didn't turn or look up. It wasn't a film.

He watched her walk along Sea Lane. All the other Jimmy Stewarts would be watching too. Hilary would be making an entry in her incidents book: 'No car'.

Frank watched Kelly for as far as his Belgian architect's glasses, the angle of the window and the bend in the road would allow. From his first-floor window he could see more of her and for longer than all the other nosy neighbours in their bungalows with their hanging baskets, chimneys and Sioux names above their front doors. Frank was glad he lived one floor higher than all of them. He watched Kelly follow the curve of the road and then she was gone. He looked down at the charity bags on the grass verge. He needed to bring them back inside before someone walking by recognised the shape of one of the bulges in the bags as something that had come from their home.

32

Lemons Care rang four times over the course of the next few days. They wanted to talk to Mr Watson. Frank told them they had the wrong number. Then he said that Mr Watson wasn't in. On the third phone call Frank summoned the spirit of Ron the marbles man to tell them that sadly his father had passed away. The woman on the phone was very sympathetic and kind but still rang back a day later to ask to speak to Mr Watson. Frank told them they had the wrong number. He put the phone down. He knew that they would eventually ring again. Lemons Care were now just somebody else with his phone number in their system.

Frank watched television, he ate badly and infrequently, and got out of bed long after the flight attendants had cleared away the breakfast trays and collected the empty plastic coffee cups. Something he himself had stopped doing.

On the first Monday that followed Kelly's final visit you might have expected that Frank had forgotten that she wasn't coming and had got out of bed early and washed, shaved and dressed himself in a loud shirt to sit at the window and wait for her to arrive. Frank hadn't forgotten that Kelly wasn't coming. He would have preferred it if he could have.

The tartan shopping basket was still in the living room and the charity bags full of his neighbours' stolen donations were in the hall. He might never have left the house ever again if it wasn't for an advert in the free local paper for *HUGE! GIANT! BOARD GAMES IN THE PARK! Buckaroo! A mule as big as a mule! KerPlunk with football-sized marbles! Jenga as high as a house! Mouse Trap and many, many more!*

It was just the motivation he needed. He would go and see Smelly John and surprise him by taking him out to the park to play giant Kerplunk! and Connect 4. The park was a mile from Greyflick House. They'd take the bus. The driver would have to lower the vehicle for John's wheelchair and nobody on the bus could complain. It would be the first time the bus had seen more than one male passenger. The old ladies were going to think the Chippendales or the cast of *The Full Monty* had just got on.

Frank and Smelly John would ring the bell to stop the bus at the park. The driver would lower the vehicle again to let them off. He wouldn't tut and moan in the way he usually did when Frank wanted to get off the bus before its final destination. Not for a black man in a wheelchair.

Frank and Smelly John would go to the park and they'd trap a giant mouse. They'd connect four and pile huge Jenga blocks up higher than most of the buildings on Sea Lane, before watching them all fall down again as Smelly John shouted out 'Jenga!' louder than he'd ever shouted it before.

Frank got dressed and put the charity bags into the tartan shopping basket. He thought of the time Kelly had surprised him with a trip to the beach. He pictured the look on

258

John's face when he turned up unannounced and showed him the advert for the life-sized board games. It would be John's first trip outside since Frank had stopped him from rolling down the hill into the sea.

Frank walked to the library and parked the shopping basket outside. He went in and borrowed the book with the picture of himself standing on the deck of the Dutch liner. It was the first book he'd taken out of the library for ages. He was going to tell Smelly John exactly what he did in the war.

In the charity shop Frank took the plastic bags out of the basket and donated the contents to the shop. As he tipped them out onto the floor at the back of the shop, a woman said she thought she recognised some of the things and she wondered whether they'd already been sold before by the shop. Frank asked the woman if they would like the shopping basket as well. She said no.

On the way out of the charity shop Frank saw a Sex Pistols CD for sale. He bought the CD and put it in the front zip pocket of the shopping basket with the library book. He left the shop and walked to the bus stop.

He sat on the bus behind a woman who was a lot younger than all the other old dears. She had a small child with her. The child was standing on the seat and staring at Frank. He didn't know where to look. Children always stared at him on public transport and in queues in shops. He always felt embarrassed and awkward and worried that he was blushing or sweating in the way a man who had an awful disgusting secret to hide might.

He turned and looked out of the window, hoping the child would have stopped staring by the time he turned back. The child continued to stare. Every time Frank looked back, there the child was, staring. He seemed particularly fascinated by Frank's long white hair. When Frank walked to the front of the bus to get off, the staring child said, 'Father Christmas.'

It was what Father Christmas did in June. He shaved his beard off and went out after dark stealing toys from sacks.

The reception of Greyflick House was empty. Frank signed himself in and took the lift up to the first floor. There was no answer when he knocked on Smelly John's door. He tried the handle. The door was unlocked as usual. Nobody locked their doors at Greyflick House. There were no thieves here. Frank felt John's dope in his pocket.

He opened the door and went inside. The empty wheelchair was by the window as though Smelly John, too, had been impersonating James Stewart. His impression would have been superior to Frank's because John had props. Frank could do the voice but Smelly John had a wheelchair. Frank had a better view though. All John had to spy on through his rear window was the top of a tree and a carrier bag full of dog shit.

Frank stood by the window and waited for John to come out of the toilet. He wondered if there was time to return the drugs before he came out but he was too fearful of being caught. He'd wait until later.

After about five minutes he called out John's name. There was no answer. He knocked on the toilet door. There was still no answer. Frank slowly opened the door. The seat of the toilet was raised and there were foam-padded arms on either side of it. There were grab rails along both sidewalls of the room and an emergency cord which Frank immedi-

260

ately had the urge to pull and pretend that he'd thought it was the light switch. There was no sign of Smelly John.

He took the lift back down to the ground floor. When the lift doors opened, Walks at an Angle, Sees Things That Aren't There and Gets Famous People's Names Wrong had just come in through the main entrance. They were dressed up for a wedding or a funeral. Even No Interest in Personal Hygiene had combed his hair and put a tie on.

Frank presumed another resident had died. Three deaths in a year. John would get his undercover television documentary. Frank was about to go into the lounge to find John when Graham the warden came in.

'Hello,' Frank said. 'I was looking for John.' He realised that he didn't know John's surname. He knew his punk name and could come up with a number of suitable Sioux names for him, but he didn't know his surname.

'Are you a relative?' Graham said.

Frank had seen enough films to know what that meant.

Smelly John was dead.

Frank couldn't speak. He shook his head.

'I don't suppose it matters,' Graham said. 'I'm afraid he passed away, just over a week ago.'

Frank still couldn't find the right words.

'He had MS,' Graham said.

'But I just saw him,' Frank said. 'I didn't think it was fatal.'

'Sometimes it isn't the falling so much as it is the hitting the ground.' It was something the vicar had said at the funeral service and Graham was passing the piece of wisdom on.

'How? How did he die?'

'I'm not exactly certain. He picked up an infection. I think he had difficulty swallowing. He had pneumonia and then organ failure. Although they do tend to die slightly younger, I'm afraid.'

'*They?*' Frank said. 'What do you mean *they?*' He wanted to tell John he was right. He wanted to ring Kelly and tell her too. Graham was a racist.

'People with MS,' Graham said.

'Oh.'

'Did you want to come through? We're having a small drink in the lounge.'

Frank gave the answer that his character would have given in a film, 'No. No, thank you. I should be going.' Even though he really did want a drink. And not a small one. Frank wanted a big drink. He wanted to get really drunk.

'He was quite a character,' Graham said. 'He'll be missed.' He held his hand out and Frank shook it. Graham asked Frank if he could sign himself out. He said goodbye and followed the residents to the lounge.

As Frank was signing the visitors book, he saw on the shelf of Graham's office what looked like a small green plastic figure in the pose of a man who was about to dive from a seesaw into a tub causing a cage to shake and fall, trapping a mouse.

Frank didn't know where to go or what to do. His whole world was collapsing – Jenga! Kerplunk! Bucka-fucking-roo! He didn't want to go home, not yet, so he walked in the opposite direction. Perhaps he should still go to the park and play some oversized games in Smelly John's memory. Shout their names out at the top of his voice.

262

Without intending to, he walked through the housing estate and towards two young boys who were play-fighting so violently that it was only their laughter that distinguished it from real fighting. How would they have fared on a torpedoed ship at night in the middle of the Atlantic? Frank wondered. Maybe some of his more stereotypical contemporaries were right and what the youngsters of today needed was a war.

The boys stopped fighting each other and turned their attention to Frank. He put his hand in his pocket – the same pocket where he carried his imaginary gun and his money and, today, John's dope. The boys could probably smell it.

Frank wanted to scoop the boys up, one under each arm, and take them as far away as possible from this dreadful place. Before it was too late for them. He thought he should at least stop and talk to them. Tell them something useful or insightful. He must have something worth sharing from his many years' experience. Perhaps he should come back with two ice creams and some chocolate bars. He didn't imagine the ice cream man ever stopped here either. It would probably even be a no-go zone for the Child Catcher.

If he did speak to them, would they listen? There was a chance that, like Kelly, they might think he was a wise man. They might not be like everyone else their age who thought old people were all incontinent dribbling halfwits, to be ridiculed and laughed at, spoken down to and stolen from, the only victims left for television comedians to bully. The boys might stop to listen to this wise old man. They'd end up thanking him for changing their lives for the better and he'd ruffle their hair before they waved him safely on his journey.

If his wisdom fantasy failed, Frank would throw Smelly John's dope as far as he could and make his escape while the boys chased after it like dogs after a stick. As he walked through the centre of the boys, they spat on the ground and laughed at him. He thought they had a point.

At the edge of the housing estate Frank saw two men. They both carried babies on their chests in slings. It was an unexpectedly touching sight in amongst all the filth and fury and spit and dog mess – these two otherwise tough men in touch with their feminine sides, looking after their young and giving the mothers a well-earned rest. Perhaps there was hope and a future for the boys after all. As he walked by, Frank saw the men weren't carrying babies in the slings but small angry dogs.

Frank walked onto the High Street. He waded through giblets and lettuce and went in through the door of CASH 4 STUFF. It was only when he lifted the shopping basket up the steps into the shop that he realised that, other than a library book and a Sex Pistols CD, the shopping basket was completely empty and he had nothing left to sell.

'Do you want to buy a shopping basket?' he said to the woman behind the counter.

'No.'

33

Frank's latest retirement plan wasn't one he would have found advertised or written about in the Sunday supplements. Not least because he hadn't paid his paper bill and the only thing the paperboys put through his letterbox now were handwritten notes from the newsagent reminding Frank that his bill was overdue.

He'd taken the phone off the hook and then unplugged it from the wall after the receiver had started sending out an alarm signal and a woman's voice, repeatedly saying, 'Please hang up.' It had taken him twenty minutes to discover the source of the alarm signal. He'd unplugged various things and climbed up on the stool ladder to take the smoke alarm apart. It had been his most productive ten minutes in as many days.

He was eating. But he wasn't washing up afterwards, tipping another tin of spaghetti into the saucepan on top of the dried tomato sauce left from the previous day's spaghetti. He was cutting so much blue from the edges of the bread to make toast that he was losing the small slices of bread in the toaster, leaving behind bits of stale bread that would burn the next time he used the toaster. In his one other recent moment of activity he'd tipped the toaster upside down to clear it and showered the kitchen with toast crumbs. Two days later the crumbs were still there – on the kitchen floor, in the grooves of the draining board and in Frank's long white hair.

A week after finding out about Smelly John's death, Frank started watching his DVD collection in alphabetical order. When he reached *Blazing Saddles* his tears during the farting scene continued all the way to the opening credits of *Blue Murder at St Trinians*.

Some of his DVDs seemed to be trying to tell him something in the same way all the television adverts had done when he was thinking about money. *Home Alone*, for instance, and *The Goodbye Girl. Brief Encounter* and *The Day the Earth Stood Still*. He didn't really notice.

He ignored Liza Minelli's advice in *Cabaret* about the uselessness of sitting alone in his room and also the simple motivational message in the titles of all four of his *Carry On* films. He abandoned *The Dam Busters* halfway through out of respect for Smelly John and, although he attempted impersonating James Stewart while watching *Harvey*, he just couldn't get the voice right. It was the same for his Michael Caine during *The Italian Job*. Towards the end of *Jaws*, shortly after the shark had swallowed Robert Shaw, Frank decided to go for a swim.

It was a long walk to the beach. He could have taken the bus as it made its return journey from the big supermarket but he didn't think he could face all the mad old women.

He walked through the alleyway that led to the sea. The high stone walls blocked out the sound of the outside world, or at least changed it so that it was like holding a shell to his ear or a cardboard tube. If he could have just stopped there he would have been happy. What a great place to die. 'He passed away peacefully in an alley,' people would say. About halfway along the alleyway Frank stamped his feet and listened to the short, metallic echo.

He came out of the alleyway and walked to the low wall and looked at the sea. The tide was all the way in. There was no sand visible. Just stones and then water. He climbed the steps over the wall and stood at the top of the hill of stones. He watched a dog playing a game of chicken with the tide until his owner called out to him and threw a tennis ball for the dog to chase instead.

Frank walked down towards the sea. He stopped by the groyne about fifteen feet from the water's edge and undressed, putting his clothes in a pile on the stones by the rusty orange drinks can. He took his glasses off, placed them on top of the pile of clothes and walked into the sea.

The feel of the seaweed under his feet took his mind off how cold the water was. Frank hated seaweed. He wished he'd kept his shoes on. When he'd been to the big Sainsbury's with Kelly, she'd shown him crispy seaweed. She'd told him it was delicious but he'd refused to believe that was possible. The seaweed under his feet was not crispy. It was soft and greasy. It felt alive, like it might drag him under the water and take him prisoner like the ivy had done to the ladder in his garden shed. When the water was deep enough to tread, Frank lifted his feet and took his first stroke.

Already he knew that his arms were going to ache later, even if he stopped now, got dressed and went home. He took a second stroke and a third and he was swimming. A wave filled his mouth with water and took him back about

267

six strokes towards the shore. He coughed and spat salty water out.

He wondered how far he could swim. As far as the first orange plastic buoy? Out to the church that had been swallowed by the water a hundred years ago when the sea moved closer inland, annexing the dry land? He wondered whether he could swim as far as Sheila used to do. When her memory had started to fade, Frank had worried that Sheila might forget where she'd started swimming from and would think she was French and carry on swimming away from the shore, until she was picked up by a fishing boat with no idea who she was, like Jason Bourne. Or that she might forget not just who she was but what she was, and, thinking that she was a stone or a crab or a piece of seaweed, would stop swimming and sink to the bottom.

Frank stopped to tread water and get his breath back. He turned to see how far sideways the current had taken him. He could see the roofs of the brightly coloured beach huts and the word CAFE painted in large white letters on the roof of the café like the top of a police car. He didn't know why it was written so big on the roof or who it was written for.

He started swimming again. He could see a ship in the distance. If he swam for long enough, the current might pull him massively off course until he was in the same place where the Dutch liner had been torpedoed. If he turned back and swam to the shore then, he might be able to start a new life somewhere new. Ireland or Scandinavia. He could just keep on going until he found his way to Canada, where the Dutch ship was heading for, to see how different his life might have been if he'd grown up as a Canadian.

He carried on swimming. He was like a finger on a map in the library or an email on its way to Beth. What time was it in LA now? Had anybody ever swam that far? Would the time difference mean he would get there before he left? He could just keep going until he ran out of water, like Tom Hanks running in *Forrest Gump*.

Frank was tired now. He began to doubt whether he'd left himself with enough energy to swim back. He'd seen Ethan Hawke do that in *Gattaca* a couple of days ago as part of his DVD marathon. Was there anything to swim back for? Once he made it back up the stones, over the wall and along the alleyway, what was there waiting for him? He was Morgan Freeman at the end of *Shawshank Redemption*, he was James Stewart on a bridge in the snow in *It's a Wonderful Life*, and Phil Daniels riding his scooter up and down Beachy Head in *Quadrophenia*. Frank was Harrison Ford about to take a 'leap of faith' into mid-air as Indiana Jones or over into a waterfall in *The Fugitive*. He was Patrick Swayze coming back for a final dirty dance with Jennifer Grey. He was Frank Derrick swimming back to Fullwind.

Although he hadn't really swum that far at all – Sheila would have laughed at such a paltry distance – it had seemed like a very long way to swim back. When he reached the shore he was too tired to notice the slimy seaweed beneath his feet again. He didn't hear the air bladders in the seaweed – Albert Flowers could have told him this particular seaweed was called sargassum – popping like bubble wrap as he stepped on them. As he walked the last few feet, the waves hit the back of his legs and he struggled to stay upright. He collapsed exhausted on the stones and sat shivering and panting, his false teeth almost chattering free from his gums.

After five minutes he stood and walked back along the beach to his pile of clothes, he put his glasses on and got dressed. He would have attempted Sheila's beach towel trick, but he hadn't brought a towel. Or clean underpants. Smelly John would be turning – probably with laughter – in his grave at the thought of that. It made Frank smile, picturing Smelly John laughing, slapping the arms of his wheelchair and upsetting all the other residents in the lounge of Greyflick House.

Frank wondered what the time was. He suddenly felt busy. As though there were a lot of things he needed to be getting on with. Places to go, people to meet. He had no idea what, who or where any of them were, but he had a definite feeling of purpose.

He pulled his trousers on over his wet swimming trunks. He put the rest of his clothes on and stood up. He put his hand in his trouser pocket and felt the five pence in small change, the hairgrips and the stolen brooch. He took them all out of his pocket and walked closer to the sea. He threw the coins at the water, hoping to skim them, but they disappeared under the water. He waited for the next wave to come in, looked for a calm stretch of water, and then he threw the brooch. It bounced six or seven times across the surface of the water *Dam Busters* style.

He clipped his long wet hair back with the hairgrips and looked at Bill's name tag. He turned it over in his hand, held it for a moment next to the scar from Beth's kite string, and then put the name tag back in his pocket. He picked his shoes and socks up, and, carrying them at his side, he walked barefoot up the stones, as though they were carpeted, or his feet were made of shoes.

The bus to the big Sainsbury's was empty at this time of day. Frank made a mental note of that for future reference. He took the bus all the way to its final destination. The driver opened the doors and Frank walked past the supermarket entrance to the warehouse building behind.

He wondered whether he would still be there. It had been such a long time. When the woman came through the swing doors and put the plastic crate onto the counter, Frank wondered whether the only friend he had left in the world would forgive him, or even recognise him. And how would Frank know if he did? Would he be able to read anything from his cut-out from a magazine poker face?

But as the woman opened the door of the plastic crate and he looked at Bill, for only the second time ever, he found that he could:

I've bloody missed you, you silly old fool.

Epilogue

Frank was sitting at the window of his living room. He'd just named a man walking by 'Man Walking By'. In the living room there was a new calendar and a new set of stray dogs. Frank didn't know the breed of this month's dog and it didn't look like anyone from the Second World War that he could mimic. The dog's name was Ollie. Frank presumed that Stan had been run over.

There were now twenty-five giraffes on the mantelpiece. Probably more than there were left in the wild and definitely enough to be described as a collection, if he ever got round to advertising them on the Internet.

Frank had seen Kelly once since her final visit.

It was about three months ago. He was in the big Sainsbury's when he saw her with Sean. They were holding hands, looking at baby clothes and toys. They both seemed very happy. Everything Frank had learned from watching Sherlock Holmes films told him that Kelly was probably pregnant.

'Mr Derrick,' she said when she saw him, and then she corrected herself. 'Frank. You remember Frank?' she said to Sean. Sean said hello. 'You came back,' Kelly said to Frank.

'They don't sell couscous in Fullwind,' Frank said.

Kelly looked at the couscous in his shopping trolley and smiled. He knew she would also have seen the six tins of spaghetti.

'Buy one get one free,' he said.

She smiled again. Her super-straight fringe had gone and she looked more like her photo on the Lemons Care website. They talked for a short while. She asked Frank if he'd built his cinema.

'Not yet. But I did find an old "Exit" sign on the Internet. At least people will know how to leave.'

'You just need to find one that shows them how to get in now,' Kelly said.

They chatted for a minute or so more and then said goodbye and went their separate ways into the vast superstore, bumping into each other again in the biscuits aisle and once more at the checkouts.

'We must stop meeting like this,' Frank said as he paid for his shopping before saying goodbye one more time.

He never did find out whether Smelly John was black, or white or neither. It didn't make any difference to Frank. In spite of all the times he'd teased Beth with predictions of what he would one day become, he was no more a racist than Graham the Greyflick warden was.

The doorbell rang. Frank had recently reconnected it when he saw a second-hand bell for sale in the charity shop. He walked over to the stereo and turned the volume of the Sex Pistols CD down and made his way downstairs. He picked up the day's post. There was even more junk mail today than usual. Somehow the stair-lift companies and charities all knew it was his birthday and they took the opportunity to personalise their begging letters.

There was a card from Beth. Inside the card she'd written how sorry she was that she couldn't be there for his birthday and that she hoped to be able to make it over for Thanksgiving or after 'The Holidays'. She was properly American now, Frank thought.

The latest edition of the village newsletter was already talking up this year's Villages in Bloom competition. Fullwind had come fifth last year. Frank repainting each of the bollards outside his flat a different colour – Eating-apple green, Moroccan pink and Duck-egg blue, like the ludicrously priced huts on the beach – it probably hadn't helped. He picked up the newspaper. He didn't read the date out aloud as it was his birthday and he knew the date.

Frank looked at the silhouetted shape through the glass of the front door. A roofer, perhaps, or somebody who wanted to talk about Jesus or guttering? Frank looked down at Bill.

'I'm eighty-two,' he said. He took the chain off the door. 'Come and have a go if you think you're hard enough.'

Acknowledgements

Extra Ordinary thanks to Nicola Barr at Greene and Heaton, Natasha Harding and everyone at Pan Macmillan, to Holly and Jakki, to my mum and my sister. Thank you to Neil Witherow and Marc Ollington for reading the early versions and not telling me to go back to my day job (watching telly). Thanks to Jonathan and Justine at the Bookseller Crow in Crystal Palace, to Tim Connery, Les Carter and Chris T-T.

AUTHOR Q&A

J. B. Morrison

1. *Do you know anyone who has been run over by a milk float?*
Not so far. If I see a milk float I do keep a safer distance than I might have done before. I know what potentially – and yet hilariously – dangerous vehicles they can be now.

2. *Why did you decide to make your protagonist 81 years old?*
I was spending a lot of time with my mother, who was 81 at the time. Like Frank, she lived on her own in a first-floor flat in a small Sussex village. People were always telling her to get her roof fixed even though there was nothing noticeably wrong with it. She was getting a lot of junk mail too and annoying telephone cold calls. I wanted to write about that in some way.

3. *Did you base Frank's character on anyone you know?*
Not really. I'm sure I will have unconsciously put bits of my mum in there, and also some of me. Mostly, though, Frank is a figment of my imagination.

4. Can you see yourself becoming like Frank as you grow older?

It's fairly likely, if I'm not already like him. It was another reason I started writing the book. Realising how it wouldn't really be all that long until I'd be a pensioner and I wondered about what kind of pensioner I'd be? Would I still be playing loud rock music and growing my hair long?

5. What music do you think you will be listening to when you are 81?

I imagine I'll be listening to a lot of the same music that I listen to now. Which is also the same music I listened to when I was eighteen. It was one of my first thoughts before writing the book. How, just because Frank was eighty-one, he wouldn't have to change the music he liked. Or that he wouldn't be able or allowed to discover new music. In the sheltered housing complex in the book many of the residents would have been young enough to have been Beatles or Rolling Stones fans as teenagers. Some of the residents are actually younger than the Rolling Stones. A good real life example of this is that my mum's favourite singers are Bob Marley and R Kelly.

6. Who is the inspiration for Kelly Christmas?

She's entirely fictional, although because Kelly is the same age as my daughter, that hopefully helped me not make her completely unbelievable.

7. What would you say the themes of the book are?

Friendship and loneliness. A fear of mortality. I don't think of it as a book about an old man but a book about a man who just happens to be old. The forty-year-old Frank Derrick

277

wouldn't have been a lot different to the Frank Derrick aged 81.

8. Do you have a favourite moment in the book?

Maybe when Frank goes swimming towards the end of the story, and the whole beach trip with Kelly chapter. I also like the epilogue. I've always loved epilogues in films where they tie up any loose ends and let the viewer know what happened to everyone in the story. 'Jeff never did go back to college, Jimmy died in the Vietnam War saving his best friend' etc. And then there's all the Bill stuff of course. I enjoyed writing about Bill the most, even though he doesn't really do anything.

9. What do you hope readers will take away from your novel?

If they're entertained and amused and moved by it that would be nice. Perhaps they'll telephone their parents or grandparents just to ask them how they are.

10. Do you have any favourite books or authors?

A lot of American and North American authors. Chuck Palahniuk, Kurt Vonnegut, Dave Eggers, Douglas Coupland, Cormac McCarthy and Brady Udall.

11. How did you become an author?

It was an accident. I had a fairly long career in pop music and wrote an autobiographical account of that. Having the book published was such a genuine thrill that I wanted to write more. I've been very lucky being able to somehow follow one pretty dream occupation with another.

12.   What do you enjoy most about being an author?

When I really get into a writing flow and I can't get things down quick enough. With my way of writing it doesn't happen too often. It will usually be in a long section of dialogue when the conversation between two characters just takes over and it's like they're actually having a real conversation and I'm just writing down what they say. I also love it when I think of something that in a moment makes the whole story suddenly make sense.

13.   Describe a typical day in your life.

I'm terrible at the whole getting up at five a.m., taking the dog for a walk, dropping the kids off at school, grinding my own coffee beans and then writing a thousand words before lunch thing. I haven't got a dog and my daughter is twenty-seven, so that doesn't help of course. I really have no discipline or routine other than getting up whenever I wake up, watching BBC Breakfast news roll over and over again and then going on Twitter. As an example, while I'm supposed to be writing this I'm on Twitter pretending I'm at the Q Awards. I do go swimming on Tuesday mornings. In the water I tend to come up with my best writing ideas, which is a bit inconvenient.

The Little Old Lady
Who Broke All the Rules

ISBN: 978-1-4472-5061-6

**An incredibly quirky, humorous and warm-hearted
story about growing old disgracefully – and breaking
all the rules along the way!**

79-year-old Martha Andersson dreams of escaping her care
home and robbing a bank.

She has no intention of spending the rest of her days in
an armchair and is determined to fund her way to a much
more exciting lifestyle. Along with her four oldest friends
– otherwise known as the League of Pensioners – Martha
decides to rebel against all of the regulations imposed upon
them. Together, they cause uproar: protesting against early
bedtimes and plasticky meals.

As the elderly friends become more daring, they hatch a
cunning plan to break out of the dreary care home and land
themselves in a far more attractive Stockholm establishment.
With the aid of their Zimmer frames, they resolve to stand
up for old-aged pensioners everywhere. And that's when the
adventure really takes off . . .

Perfect for fans of *The 100-Year-Old Man Who
Climbed Out of the Window and Disappeared*
and *The Best Exotic Marigold Hotel.*